OLD NOG S[...]

But I didn't get a chance t[...] [...]an-to-man
advice on personal hygiene. Though I saw nothing that
looked like hands or arms, the blackness that was Nog
got ahold of me anyhow and dragged me back into the
street, to the huntress. She leaned down, hoisted me like I
was a doll, and flipped me down across the shoulders of
her mount. She let out an earsplitting shriek of triumph,
hauled back on her reins. Her unicorn reared, pounded
the air with huge hooves; then we were off at a gallop,
Nog the Inescapable floating alongside.

It was a long ride, out of the city completely, into the
region of wealthy estates south of town. I don't like it
out there. Every time I go I get into big trouble. This time
didn't look like it would be any exception. . . .

**Praise for the
Garrett, P.I., Novels**

"Garrett, private detective, returns after too long an
absence. . . . Cook makes this blending of fantasy with
hard-boiled-detective story seem easy, which it isn't,
and manages to balance the requirements of both genres
superbly."
—*Chronicle*

"Eminently satisfying." *Booklist*

"A wild science fiction mystery that never slows down for
a moment." —*Midwest Book Review*

The Garrett, P.I., Series
by Glen Cook

Glen Cook

PETTY PEWTER GODS

A GARRETT, P.I., NOVEL

A ROC BOOK

ROC
Published by New American Library, a division of
Penguin Group (USA) Inc., 375 Hudson Street,
New York, New York 10014, USA
Penguin Group (Canada), 90 Eglinton Avenue East, Suite 700, Toronto,
Ontario M4P 2Y3, Canada (a division of Pearson Penguin Canada Inc.)
Penguin Books Ltd., 80 Strand, London WC2R 0RL, England
Penguin Ireland, 25 St. Stephen's Green, Dublin 2,
Ireland (a division of Penguin Books Ltd.)
Penguin Group (Australia), 250 Camberwell Road, Camberwell, Victoria 3124,
Australia (a division of Pearson Australia Group Pty. Ltd.)
Penguin Books India Pvt. Ltd., 11 Community Centre, Panchsheel Park,
New Delhi - 110 017, India
Penguin Group (NZ), 67 Apollo Drive, Rosedale, North Shore 0632,
New Zealand (a division of Pearson New Zealand Ltd.)
Penguin Books (South Africa) (Pty.) Ltd., 24 Sturdee Avenue,
Rosebank, Johannesburg 2196, South Africa

Penguin Books Ltd., Registered Offices:
80 Strand, London WC2R 0RL, England

First published by Roc, an imprint of New American Library,
a division of Penguin Group (USA) Inc.

First Printing, November 1995
10 9 8 7 6 5 4 3

PETTY
PEWTER
GODS

1

I greeted the morning the only way that makes sense. I groaned. I groaned some more as I pried me off the sheet. Several thousand maniacs were raising hell out in the street. I muttered dreadful threats, dropped my feet into the abyss beside my bed. My threats didn't scare up any peace.

Pain blazed from my right temple to my left, ricocheted, clattered around inside my skull. I must have had a great time. I told me, "You got to quit drinking that cheap beer."

The guy jacking his jaw was yakking way too loud. I clapped a hand over his mouth. He shut up. I used my other hand to open a curtain a peek. I had some morning-mad notion that by looking I could grab a clue about all that racket.

A club of sunshine whacked me right between the eyes. Like to laid me out. Gah! An ill omen for sure. These bright days are never kind. Everybody I ran into would be just like the weather: warm and sunny. Argh! I was in the mood for low overcast and light drizzle, maybe with a frigid south wind.

I peeled layers of fried skin off my eyeballs, took another look. Where there is life there is hope.

"Well." Across Macunado, standing out like she might be the source of the brightness, was a trim piece of work who would have no trouble making the short list for girl of my dreams. She looked right at me, like she knew I was watching. My toes curled. Wow!

I didn't notice the human rights guys and their ugly banners shoving dwarves and elves aside as they chased a gang of centaur refugees, flinging bricks and stones. I didn't chuckle when some fool bounced a rock off a fourteen-foot troll's beak and took up a brief career as a human club. Just another day of political dialogue in my hometown.

I was focused. Maybe I was in love. Again.

She had all the right stuff in all the right places in absolutely perfect proportion. She was a small thing, not a rat's whisker over five feet, and of the redheaded tribe. I would have bet the deed that she had green eyes. I drooled. I wondered what madness was loose upon the earth, that all those lunatics down there weren't dropping their sticks and stones and surrounding her, panting gales of garlicky breath.

"Whoa, Garrett," I muttered, after the curtain slipped from numb fingers and broke the crackling magic connecting my eyes with hers. "Where have we heard all this before?" Female is my weakness. Pretty redhead will do me in every time.

Oh, but what a delicious failing!

I wrestled with my clothes for a minute before daring another look. She was gone. Where she had stood, a drunken one-armed war veteran was trying to assault an even drunker centaur. The centaur was getting the best of it because he had more legs to keep him off the ground.

That troll must have been in a bad mood anyway. He bellowed his intention of clearing the street of anyone who didn't have green skin. He had a good work ethic, too.

Down the way Mrs. Cardonlos and her broom vigorously defended the stoop of her rooming house from fugitives. How would she blame this on me? I was confident that she could find a way. Too bad she couldn't saddle that broom and fly away.

Some dreams arrive stillborn. There wasn't a sign of that redhead anywhere.

But nightmares always come true.

Instead of young and gorgeous I spied old and homely and not even female.

Old Dean, my resident cook, housekeeper, and professional nag, was home from his journey north to make sure one of his numerous ugly duckling nieces didn't weasel out of her wedding plans. He was standing at the foot of the front steps. He stared up at the house with pinch-lip disapproval.

I shambled toward the stairs. Somebody had to let him in.

Dean's knock set the Goddamn Parrot to squawking obscenities.

Garrett! Oh, boy. That was my sidekick, the Dead Man, only recently awakened for the first time in months. He had a lot of vinegar stored up. *Kindly set aside your sensual maunderings and still that horrible thumping.*

It was, for sure, going to be one of those days.

2

T. G. Parrot—whose given name is Mr. Big—started whooping as I worked the latch. "Help! Oh, please, Mister, don't hurt me no more." He sounded like a terrified child. He thought it was great fun trying to get me lynched.

Mr. Big was a practical joke that had been played upon me by my alleged friend Morley Dotes, who must have spent years teaching that bird bad manners and worse language.

Dean wrinkled his nose as he pushed inside. "Is that *thing* still here? And what *is* that dreadful odor?"

By "thing" he meant the bird. I pretended to misunderstand. "He was too heavy for me to move by myself." The Dead Man goes somewhat over four hundred pounds. "Maybe he's getting ripe. You better work on his room first thing." Dean hates the Dead Man's room. He doesn't like being in the presence of a corpse, possibly because that rubs his nose in his own mortality.

Your sense of humor has putrefied.

Dean, of course, didn't receive the Dead Man's mind message. Wouldn't have been fun for His Nibs if he caused a reaction that the old man understood.

I didn't pay him any mind. That always irks him. I was preoccupied, anyway. Still looking outside, I noticed that the redhead was back, watching from across the street. Our gazes met. That energy crackled. Down the block my favorite neighbor, the widow Cardonlos, spotted my open doorway. She pointed, jabbered, probably telling one of her tenants that I was the linchpin of all the evils plaguing our street.

Her mind would not stretch any farther.

Other than making herself a boil on the bottom of my happiness, she did not much matter in my life.

Dean expelled one of his mighty, put-upon sighs. He dropped his duffel, stood there shaking his head. He wasn't three steps inside, but he had to assure me that his absence had been a domestic disaster. As had been inevitable.

I looked for the girl again. Redheads are trouble. Always. But that kind of trouble looked real appetizing.

Gone again, damn it. A mob of street rowdies had come between us, pursuing the ethnic debate with club and brickbat. Enterprising folk of several tribes tagged along, hawking sausages and sweetmeats and souvenirs to the participants. Never is there an event so wild, so dire or disgusting but what some entrepreneur can create collectible memorabilia.

Story of my life. Find my true love and lose her in a matter of minutes, while being tormented by a hangover and a carping housekeeper.

What were you gawking at?

"Huh?" You don't usually get much expression out of the Dead Man's mind messages. This time he seemed puzzled. "A girl." He ought to be able to figure that just because I was drooling.

More puzzled. *I see nothing but chaos.*

Neither did I, now. "That's the way it is these days. You didn't spend all your time napping, you'd know we're getting into the hell times." Damn! Me and my mouth. Now he would insist I spend another day bringing him up to date. A lot had been happening.

The Goddamn Parrot was squawking with a vengeance now. He had discovered that I had not put out birdseed before I'd hit the sack. Hell, I'd barely remembered to lock the door. I'd only just survived a near terminal case of redheaditis complicated by psychopathic killer transvestites and I had wanted to unwind.

Dean got to the kitchen before I could head him off. His howl stilled hearts for miles. Mr. Big squawked in fear. The Dead Man offered some mind racket meant as commiseration. Fetishist household order is not a priority with him, either.

Dean had started through the kitchen doorway. He froze there. He posed, the most put-upon old boy who ever lived. "*Mister* Garrett. Will you please come here and explain?"

"Well, I did kind of get behind on the dishes." I headed for the stairs. He wanted to give me a few choice pieces of advice, but the words all tried to come out at once. He began shaking in frustration when he could not get them untangled. I made my escape.

Sort of. I headed for his room upstairs, which I had not gotten straightened up after having stashed a fugitive girl there while he was away. He would get really excited if he saw the mess she had left.

I could feel the Dead Man's thoughts riding with me, amused, looking forward to the explosion. To him the world is one grand, enduring passion play, going on without end. He is settled comfortably in the wings enjoying it at little risk because he has been safely dead for four hundred years already.

Somebody clever and really fast stuck a knife into him way back then. That or some ordinary dumbbell caught him taking one of his naps. Did Loghyr take those long naps when they were alive? I'd never seen a living Loghyr. I knew nobody who had, save the Dead Man himself. He hadn't been born dead. Hell, I've only ever run into one other dead Loghyr.

A rare breed, they. And major pains in the social fundament, generally, which probably has something to do with why they are so rare.

One is compelled to support your earlier remark concerning the quality of the beer you imbibe. Those cheap barley squeezings have poisoned your mind with premature bitterness and cynicism.

"That's on account of my environment and evil companions. How come you're following me around the house?"

I hurled things around in Dean's room as fast as I could, but I knew I was fighting another losing battle.

Maybe the stress of the kitchen mess would burst his heart before he decided to put his stuff away.

It was unusual for the Dead Man to extend himself beyond the walls of his room, though he could reach a long way when he wanted. He claims he limits himself out of respect for others' privacy. I have never believed a thought of that. Laziness has got to be involved somewhere.

I am sure that even were he alive he would not move an ounce or an inch out of his room for years at a time. My guess is he died because it would have been too much trouble to get out of the way of the assassin.

Not only bitter and cynical, but uncharitable.

"You didn't answer the question."

The deterioration has progressed faster than I anticipated. The city is at the brink. I have wakened to imminent chaos.

"Yeah. We're beating up on each other instead of the Venageti."

After so many of your mayfly generations. Loghyr live for ages, apparently. And they do take their sweet time dying. *Peace. Can you stand the strain?*

Us humans are a hobby with him, by his estimation created exclusively for his amusement. He likes to study bugs, too.

I had gotten distracted from my mission. A sound like that of a strangling crow startled me. Dean stood in the doorway, duffel at his feet, mouth open. The noises came from behind his teeth but maybe started out in a dimension where people didn't let undisciplined young ladies invade your quarters in your absence.

"I had to hide . . ."

"Another of your bimbos. I understand completely." He articulated each word in isolation. "No doubt you had another already installed in your own bedroom."

"Hey! It wasn't that way at all."

"It never is, Mr. Garrett."

"What the hell does that mean?" Downstairs, the Goddamn Parrot went crazy. And the Dead Man insisted, *Come to my room, Garrett. You must tell me more. So much more. I sense so many wonderful possibilities. Glory*

Mooncalled is here in TunFaire? Oh, the marvel of it! The wonder! The insane potential!

"Glory Mooncalled here? Where did you get that idea?" Mooncalled was a legend. He started as a mercenary general during the recent generations-long disturbance between Karenta and Venageta. He fought for the Venageti at first, but their arrogance offended him so he came over to our side. Where he was treated about the same despite his being the only skilled field commander in the theater. So somewhere along the way he got together with the sentient natives of the Cantard and the whole crazy bunch declared the war zone an independent republic. That led to some intriguing triangular headbutting.

In the end, though, Karenta triumphed, our generals and sorcerers having been marginally less incompetent than those of Venageta while outnumbering anything Mooncalled could muster.

The tribes were on the run. And every refugee seemed determined to immigrate to TunFaire—at the very time when returning soldiers were coming home to find most jobs already taken by nonhumans and most businesses now owned or operated by dwarves or elves. Thus the permanent floating riots in our streets.

Is it not self-evident? He must *be here.*

Actually, I had begun to suspect that weeks ago. So had the secret police.

The Goddamn Parrot grew louder and more vile of beak. Dean became more articulate with every word, nagging in double time. And the Dead Man grew increasingly insistent.

My hangover didn't bother me nearly as much as those three did.

It was time to go somewhere where I could be alone with my misery.

3

They didn't turn loose willingly. In fact, as I descended to the street, Dean wished me bon voyage in words I had not realized he knew. The Goddamn Parrot fluttered past him and chased me up the street. That flashy little garbage beak did tone it down because the Dead Man shut him up. I mean, if they hang me on the testimony of a bird, who's going to keep a roof over his head?

He would have no trouble finding somebody to take him in, but he wouldn't find anyone as undemanding. Most folks would expect him to stay awake and devote his multiple-brained genius to their enrichment.

Oh, yes, the Loghyr is a genius. His intellect dwarfs that of anyone else I have ever met. He just don't want to use it.

I was barely a block from the house, contemplating selling the Dead Man into slavery, when I glimpsed red hair. Since I was glancing over my shoulder at the time, it seemed possible the girl with the goodies was following me.

This did not excite me as much as you might think. Like the Dead Man, I am not big on work. Still . . . that was one tender morsel.

She wasn't much of a sneak. Her good looks weren't a handicap, though. You'd think every guy on the street would drop whatever throat he was throttling or would close the lid on his display tray so he could look without becoming vulnerable to shoplifters, or whatever, but hardly anyone noticed the girl. The few who did were nonhumans who shuddered as in a sudden draft and looked befuddled.

Of course you wouldn't expect a normal dwarf to get excited about a sweet slip like that, but . . . It was weird. And I don't like weird. Weird comes at me like I am a lightning rod for the bizarre.

I left the house considering a visit to Morley Dotes' Joy House, to see how he was doing at turning that vegetarian thug's harbor into an upscale hangout called The Palms. But there was no way I was going to drag this redheaded sweetmeat across Morley's bow. He had dark elf good looks and charm to waste and was not a bit shy about taking unfair advantage of them.

I bustled down Macunado till I reached the mouth of Barley Close, a tight, dark alley no longer used to make back door deliveries because all the mom-and-pop businesses had been scared away. Buildings leaned together overhead. The alley was dark and dirty and stank of rotting vegetation despite recent heavy rains that should have sluiced it out. I stepped over the outstretched legs of a drunken ratman and tried to stay near the centerline of the Close, where the footing was least treacherous. I disturbed a family of rats making a holiday feast of a dead dog. They showed their teeth and dared me to try stealing their dinner. I gave the biggest rat a quick toe in the slats. My new honey might be scared of rats.

I drifted deep into the gloom, past sleepers of various tribes and sexes, careful to disturb no one. I'm a Golden Rule kind of guy. I don't like it when people bother me in my home.

I paused at a cross alley eighty feet in. The sunlight blazing in from the street dry-roasted my eyeballs.

I waited. I waited a little more. Then I waited some. Then, after I had done some waiting and was about to say oh well and give it up, a woman did come to the mouth of the Close. She was the right size, but her age was off by four generations. She was a slow, raggedy street granny propped up by a crooked cane. She peered out from under a yellow straw hat with devilish concentration, like she was sure some evil was afoot inside the Close. A woman her age could not have survived the streets without becoming constitutionally paranoid.

I like to think I'm a nice guy. I did nothing to frighten her. I just waited till she decided not to enter the alley.

To my utter astonishment the Goddamn Parrot never said a word. The Dead Man really had the muzzle on him.

Looked like my ploy had failed. A girl amateur had outwitted me.

I would keep that to myself. My friends ride me hard enough as it is. I did not need to pass out ammunition.

I eased back into the street. My luck turned no worse. No traveling brawl tried to suck me in. I went to a watering trough, used some green fluid to swab the muck off my shoes. I didn't mind making the liquid thicker. Provision of public horse troughs encourages the public to harbor horses. And horses are nature's favorite weapon when it comes time to tormenting guys named Garrett.

I had cleaned my left shoe and was trying to get the right off without getting anything on my hand when I spotted the redhead through a sudden parting in the crowd. Our eyes met. I gave her my biggest, most charming grin and a look at my raised right eyebrow. That combination gets them every time.

She took off.

I took off after her. Now I was in my element. This is what I live for. I would have called for foxhounds and a horn, but they would have brought horses along.

The Goddamn Parrot made some kind of interrogatory noise. I didn't catch it and he didn't repeat himself.

4

Again I noticed that curious phenomenon: guys didn't pay the girl any mind. Maybe my eyes were going. Maybe my run of bad luck was giving me a case of wishful thinking. Maybe those other guys were so happily married they never looked at pretty girls. Maybe the sun came up in the west this morning.

I ducked a swooping shoat and tried to catch up a little since I could not track the girl by the stir she was causing. The street was crowded like today was a holiday, but everybody was growling and snapping at everybody else. We needed some miserable weather to cool everybody down. A really hot spell might be like a torch to tinder.

I spied a familiar face headed my way, ugly as the dawn itself. Saucerhead Tharpe towered above the crowd. Nobody gave him any grief. He was a bonebreaker by trade, which meant prosperous times for him. He spotted me and hoisted a ham-sized hand. "Yo! Garrett, my man. How they hanging?" It is always good to have Saucerhead on your side, but he isn't overly blessed with brains or a flair for language.

"Low. You notice a cute little redhead about a hundred feet up? She's so short I can't keep track."

His grin broadened, exposing the remnants of truly ugly teeth. "You on a case?" Cunning fellow, he had an idea he could get me to hire him to help.

"I don't think so. She was watching my house, so I decided to follow her around."

"Just like that?"

"Yeah."

His grin turned into a horror show. "Dean come home? Or did the Dead Man wake up?" He winked at the Goddamn Parrot.

He was smarter than a rock, anyway. "Both."

Saucerhead chuckled. It was the kind of chuckle I get too often. My friends figure I was put here to amuse them with my travails.

"Look, Saucerhead, this gal is going to lose me if I don't ..."

"Speaking of ones that got away, I seen Tinnie Tate yesterday."

Tinnie is one ex that my cronies won't let go away. "Great. Come by the house later. Tell me all about it."

"I seen Winger, too. She ..."

"That's your problem."

Our mutual acquaintance Winger, though female, is as big as me and goofier than Saucerhead. And she has the moral sense of a rabid hyena. And, despite that, she is hard not to like.

"Hey, Garrett, come on, man."

I was drifting away.

"She had a good idea. Honest, Garrett."

Winger is chock-full of good ideas that get me up to my crotch in crocodiles. "Then you go in on it with her." There was a small thinning of the crowd uphill. I caught a glimpse of my quarry. She seemed to be looking back, puzzled, maybe even exasperated.

"I would, Garrett," Saucerhead shouted. "Only we need somebody with real brains to get into it with us."

"That leaves me out, don't it?" Didn't it? Would a guy with real brains keep following somebody when it was evident that that somebody had decided that she wanted to be followed and was getting impatient with my delays?

Seemed like a good idea at the time. We have all said that.

I considered waving so she would know I was coming, but decided to keep up pretenses.

Saucerhead followed for a way, babbling something about my manners. I showed him my worst. I didn't answer. I trotted after my new honey. The crowds were thinning. I kept her in sight. Her passage caused no more stir than if she were the crone I had seen looking into Barley Close.

We were just past where Macunado becomes the Way of the Harlequin when she glanced back, then turned into Heartlight Lane, where some of TunFaire's least competent astrologers and diviners keep shop.

5

"Hey, buddy," I called to a stout-looking old dwarf lugging an old-timey homemade club. That tool was as long as him, crafted from the trunk and roots of some black sapling that had wood harder than rock. "How much you want for that thing?"

The price went up instantly. You know dwarves. You show interest in a broken clothespin ... "Not for sale, Tall One. This is the world-renowned club Toetickler, weapon of the chieftains of the Kuble Dwarves for ten generations. It was given to the first High Gromach by the demiurge Gootch ..."

"Right. And it's still got dirt on its roots, Stubby."

The dwarf swung that club down hard enough to crack a cobblestone.

"Three marks," I barked before he gave me more details of the club's provenance or maybe demonstrated its efficiency by tickling my favorite toes.

"Not one groat under ten, Lofty." Even national treasures are for sale if you are a dwarf. Nothing is holy except wealth itself.

"Thanks for talking, Lowball. It was just an idea." I started moving.

"Whoa there, Highpockets. At least make me an offer."

"My memory must be playing tricks again. I thought I did make an offer, Shorty."

"I mean a serious offer. Not a bad joke."

"Three and ten, then."

He whined. I started moving.

"Wait, Tall One. Four. All right? Four is outright

theft for such a storied weapon, but I *have* to get some cash together before you people run us out of town. I tell you, I'm not looking forward to rooting around in the old home mines again."

Sounded like there might be a tad of truth in that.

"Three ten and a parrot? Think what you could do with his feathers."

The dwarf considered Mr. Big. "Four." Nobody wanted the Goddamn Parrot.

"Done," I sighed. I turned out my pockets. We made the exchange. The dwarf walked away whistling. There would be tall tales told at the dwarf hold tonight, of another fool taken.

But I had me a tool. And with fate seldom able to gaze on me favorably for long, I would not have long to wait to field-test Toetickler's touch.

Heartlight Lane was not crowded, which surprised me. Given the political climate, more folks ought to be checking into their futures. I saw a lonely runecaster tossing the bones, trying to forecast her next meal, and an entrail reader much more interested in plucking his chicken carcass. Palm readers and phrenologists swapped fortunes. Aquamancers, geomancers, pyromancers, and necromancers all napped in their stalls.

Maybe customers were staying away in droves because they did not need experts to tell them that bad times were coming.

I got some interesting discount and rebate offers. The most attractive came from a dark-haired, fiery-eyed tarot reader. I promised, "I'll be right back. Save a dance for me."

"No, you won't. Not if you don't stop here. Now."

I thought she was telling me, "That's what you all say." I kept on keeping on. The Goddamn Parrot started muttering to himself. Maybe the Dead Man's compulsion was wearing off.

"I warned you, Handsome."

How did she manage to see her cards?

I had not seen the redhead since before my negotiations with the runt arms merchant. I didn't see her now, but something flashed around a turn of brick up ahead.

The guy who laid out Heartlight Lane was either a snake stalker or a butterfly hunter. It zigs and zags and comes close to looping for no reason more discernible than the fact that that is the way it has got to go to get between the buildings. A few quick turns and the lane became deserted except for a big brown coach, its door just closing.

Empty streets are not a good sign. That means folks have smelled trouble and want no part of it.

Maybe somebody just wanted to talk to me. But then why not just come to the house?

Because I don't always answer the door? Especially when somebody might want me to go to work? Maybe. Then there is the fact that the Dead Man can read minds.

I took a couple of cautious steps, glanced back. That tarot girl sure was a temptation. On the other hand, red hair is marvelous against a white pillowcase. On the third hand . . .

I got no chance to check my other fifteen fingers. From out of the woodwork, or cracks in the walls, or under the cobblestones, or a hole in the air came the three ugliest guys I have ever seen. They had it bad. I think they wanted to look human but their mothers had messed them up with their hankering after lovers who spelled ugly with more than one G. All three made me look runty, too, and I am a solid six feet two, two hundred ten pounds of potato-hard muscle and blue eyes to die for.

"Hi, guys. You think we're gonna get some rain?" I pointed upward.

None of them actually looked. Which left me with a nasty suspicion that they were smarter than me. I would have looked. And *they* hadn't followed some wench-o'-the-wisp up here where some humongous brunos could bushwhack them, either.

They said nothing and I didn't wait for introductions and didn't wait for a sales pitch. I feinted left, dodged

right, swung my new club low and hard and took the
pins right out from under one behemoth. Maybe the
dwarf did me a favor after all. I went after another guy's
head like I wanted to knock it all the way to the river
on one hop. Big as he was, he went ass over appetite
and I started to think, hey, things aren't going so bad after all.

The first guy got up. He started toward me. Meantime, the guy I hadn't hit planted himself resolutely in
the way in case I decided to go back the way that I had
come. My first victim came at me. He wasn't even
limping. And his other buddy was back up, too, no
worse for wear, either.

You could not hurt these guys? Oh my oh my.

"Argh!" said the Goddamn Parrot.

"You said a beakful, you piebald buzzard."

I wound up for a truly mighty swing, turned slowly,
trying to pick a victim. I picked wrong. I could not have
chosen right.

I took the guy I hadn't hit. The plan was to whack
him good, then display my skill as a sprinter. The plan
didn't survive first contact with the enemy. When I
swung he grabbed my club in midair, took it away, and
flipped it aside with such force that it cracked when it
hit a nearby building.

"Oh my oh my."

"Argh!" the Goddamn Parrot observed again.

I went for the fast feet option, but a hairy hand attached to an arm that would have embarrassed a troll
snagged my right forearm. I flailed and flopped and discovered ingenious ways to use the language. I got me
some much needed exercise, but I did not go anywhere.
And big ugly didn't work up a sweat keeping me from
going.

Another one grabbed my other arm. His touch was
almost gentle, but his fingers were stone. I knew he
could powder my bones if he wanted. Which did not
slow my effort to get away. I didn't give up till the third
one grabbed my ankles and lifted.

The Goddamn Parrot walked down my back muttering to himself. Mumble and mutter was all he seemed capable of anymore.

The whole crew lockstepped to the coach. I lifted my head long enough to see a matched set of four huge horses, the same shade of brown. On the driver's seat was a coachman all in black, looking down at me but invisible within the depths of a vast black cowl. He needed a big sickle to make the look complete.

The coach was fancy enough, but no coat of arms proclaimed its owner's status. That didn't do wonders for my confidence. Here in TunFaire even the villains like to show off.

With nary a word, the ugly brothers chucked me inside. My skull tried to bust through the far door. That door didn't give an inch. My headbone didn't give much, either. Like a moth with his wings singed, I fluttered down into that old lake of darkness.

6

When you are in my racket—confidential investigations, lost stuff found, work that doesn't force me to take a real job—you expect to get knocked around sometimes. You don't get to like it, but you do catch on to the stages and etiquettes involved. Especially if you are the kind of dope who trails a girl you know wants to be followed, right into the perfect spot for an ambush. That kind of guy gets more than his share of lumps and deserves every one of them. I bet guys like Morley never get bopped on the noggin and tossed into mystery coaches.

Your first move after you start to stagger back toward the light—assuming you are clever enough not to do a lot of whimpering—is to pretend that you are not recovering. That way maybe you will learn something. Or maybe you can take them by surprise, whip up on them, and get away. Or maybe they will all be out to dinner and some genius will have forgotten to take the keys out of the door of your cell.

Or maybe you will just lie there puking your socks up because of a rocking concussion rolling your hangover.

"O what foul beasts these mortals be! Jorken! Fetch a mop!" The voice was stentorian, as though the speaker was some ham passion player who never ever stepped offstage.

A woman's voice added, "Bring an extra bucket. They leak at the other end as well."

Oh no. I already had a bath this week.

"Why me? How come, all of a sudden, I get stuck with scutwork?"

"Because you're the messenger," said a wind from the abyss, cold as a winter's grave. That had to be my buddy the faceless coachman.

I was confused. My natural state, some would say. But this was bizarre.

Maybe it was time to get up and meet the situation head-on. I gathered my corded muscles and heaved. Two fingers and a toe twitched. So I exercised my skill with colorful dialogue. "Rowrfabble! Gile stynbobly!" I was on a roll, but I didn't recognize the language I was speaking.

I cooled down fast when a load of icy water hit me.

"Freachious moumenpink!" Driven by a savage rage, I managed a full half pushup. "Snrubbing scuts!" Hey! Was that a real word?

Another bucket of water hit me hard enough to knock me off my hands and roll me over. A ragmop came out of the mist. It started swabbing. Somebody attached to the mop muttered while he worked. That was a dwarfish custom. But this beanpole was so tall he could only have been adopted.

There was something weird about the mopman. Beside the fact that he carried on several sides of a conversation all by himself. He had little pigeon wings growing out of his head where his ears ought to be. Also, you could sort of see through him whenever he moved in front of a bright light.

A really intense light blazed up. I managed to get into a sitting position but could not look up. That light was worse than sunshine on the brightest-ever morning after a two-kegger.

"Mr. Garrett."

I didn't lie about it. I didn't admit anything, either. I didn't react at all. I was busy trying not to make more work for that princely fellow with the mop. I succeeded. And I managed to get one hand clamped over my eyes. Somewhere way in the back of my head a little voice told me I should take this as a lesson in chemistry. Don't play with stuff that might blow up in your face. Like strange redheads.

I know. I know. All redheads are strange. But there is strange and strange.

A different woman said, "Ease up on the glow. You're blinding him." She had a voice of a type you never hear except from the women who haunt your fantasies. It was the voice of the lover you have been waiting for all these years.

Something was going on here.

The light faded till I could stand to open my eyes. It continued to wane till there was no more than you would find in your average torchlit dungeon, which was my first guess as to my whereabouts. But I didn't recognize any voices. I thought I pretty well knew everybody who had a dungeon in the family inventory.

Well, it's a big city.

Hell. No. Not a dungeon. This was some kind of big cellar with a high ceiling and only a couple of really dirty windows practically lost in rusty steel bars, way, way up at the back. The cellar was mostly empty except for pillars supporting the structure overhead. The floor was old stone, a dark slate-gray. Hard as a rock, hard on a sleeper's back.

I took inventory. I didn't have any bits missing or any open wounds. My headache had not abated, though. My main injury was a knot on my conk from my attempt to dive through that coach door.

And I still had a hangover.

Maybe they turned down the lights too far. Now I could see my captors. All eight of them. I would rather not have.

There was a long drink of water who maybe used to be a pigeon, your basic roof rat, leaning on his mop. There were the three characters I had met already, all looking bigger and uglier than ever. Those guys could get work as gargoyles at any of the major cathedrals. Then there were three females. None was my redhead. The closest to her was a brunette with a paler skin and eyes that were smouldering pits of promise and curves that had been drawn by a dreaming celestial geometrician. Her lips made me want to bounce up and run over there. Presumably she owned the sexy voice.

Next to her was a gal with the biggest hair I have ever seen. What looked like snakes seemed to peek out. Her skin was a sort of pale pus-green color. Her lips were gorgeously tasty but dark green. When she smiled she showed you sharp vampire teeth. Not to mention that she sported two extra arms, the better to whatever you with. I decided I would put off asking her out.

She stared at me with a heat—or a hunger—that set those old frozen-toed mice to rambling along my spine.

The third woman was a giant of a blonde, maybe ten feet tall and at least that many years past her prime. She had put on weight where women generally do not need much, and overall she projected a sort of middle-class goodwifely dowdiness—with a suggestion of all the hidden bitterness that so often goes with that.

A guy I took to be her old man sprawled on some sort of stone throne that was so chipped and crumbly it looked like it could collapse under his weight. He was a couple of feet taller than the blonde. He wasn't wearing much but a stripely leather loincloth that looked like it had been ripped off a saber-toothed tiger on the fly and nobody bothered to cure it. He was built like a muscle freak who had gone to seed. He could have lugged minotaurs on those shoulders in his prime.

His eyes were a blazing blue, almost as gorgeous as mine. His hair was white and there was a lot of it, flying out all around his head in tangles and spikes. His beard was white, too, and had not been trimmed in decades. Despite his lovely eyes he seemed to be bored or almost asleep.

Everybody stared at me like they expected me to do something clever. I did not have my cane nor my tap shoes, so I couldn't go into my dance routine. Those words that escaped my mouth still had no discernible meaning, so I could not sing. I reached deep into my trick bag for the last thing left.

I tried to stand up.

I made it! But to stay standing up I had to hang on

to one of the ugly guys. This particular one lacked a forehead and had a mouth like a lamprey. I bet all the girls wanted to tongue-kiss him. His eyes were fish eyes, too, yellow and shadowy and covered by that milky membrane.

That popped up and down a couple of times, but otherwise he ignored me. I managed to croak, "Who *are* you people? *What* are you?"

Two of these characters could pass for giants and one for human, but the rest were not like anything I had ever seen on the streets of TunFaire. You spend any time at all out there, you will see members of virtually every sentient species, from pixies the size of your thumb to giants twenty feet tall. You will even see some horrors like the ratmen, who were created by sorcery run amok.

Maybe that was what we had here, fugitives from some cellar way up at the pinnacle of the Hill, where our magician masters live. Trouble was, for the last four generations most of them people had spent their lives in the Cantard, managing the war. None of them would have messed up this much.

Some things you could be sure of just by experience.

I sagged. My ugly buddy did not help. I hung on like a drowning man, gradually pulling myself back into our world. I had had practice climbing lampposts on nights when the weather had turned incredibly alcoholic. "I know you people can talk."

Speaking of talk, where was my curse, the feathered prince of gab, the Goddamn Parrot? He sure wasn't in this basement—unless he was dead. Even the Dead Man could not stop his beak from rattling here.

The big guy, who was pretty obviously the head weirdo, nodded to the guy who had feathers for ears. But Beanpole Man just looked at me and shrugged like he did not have a notion.

I muttered. "I have been kidnapped by morons."

Yeah. Right. And what did that say about the blinding intellect of the guy who got kidnapped?

Gravity would not leave me alone. I sagged yet again.

Maybe I should let go, fall back down, go to sleep, and eventually wake up again somewhere else, where all the nightmares had not yet wormed their ways into every human mind.

Et tu, Cthulhu? The world is full of crackpots, and who can you trust?

7

The greenish woman moved toward me. "Please accept our apologies, Mr. Garrett. We needed to see you quickly. Daiged, Rhogiro, and Ringo," she said, aiming a wicked nail with each name by way of making introductions, "had to work fast. They aren't used to being gentle."

"No kidding."

I looked around for the Goddamn Parrot. Still no sign of him. Maybe he had had sense enough to get away. Maybe I was in real luck and he mouthed off and got his neck wrung.

Somehow some of the woman's arms had disappeared. Her hair had become more managable. Her color had improved, her teeth had lost their sharpness, and her neckline now plunged to navel level.

I had fallen in with shapeshifters.

Now that I noticed it, the giants were several feet shorter, the ugly boys were less repulsive, and the long pale guy had ears. The sexy gal had changed, too, though she had been fine the way she was. She had shortened up and gone blonde. She giggled. Her appeal had not faded a bit.

Why would she want to turn into a bimbo?

Soon they all looked normal, within the very extended range considered normal in TunFaire. They could have gotten by outside—except that they tended to be a little ethereal in a strong light.

Did somebody feed me magic mushrooms while I was asleep?

I said, "That's a better look for you." The woman

was too close. I watched her hair. Fleas and lice are bad enough.

She flashed an inviting smile, licked her lips with a tongue that split at the end. She told me, "I appreciate your thoughts. They're flattering. But you don't want to get too close to me." She gestured at the blonde, who stared at me like she wanted me for dinner. In a less stressful moment I would have leaped onto her plate. I failed to correct the snake woman's misconception about her effect on me.

"You got any chairs around here?" I had a concussion for sure. I was keeping my balance about as good as a ratman on weed.

"I'm sorry. We jumped into this rather precipitously."

I lowered myself back down to the floor so I would not have so far to fall when the time came. "Tell me something useful. Who are you? What are you? What do you want? Give me some of the good stuff before I fade away again here." My head really hurt.

"We are the last of the Godoroth. Through no wish of ours, nor any fault, we have become entangled in a struggle with the Shayir."

"The sun of knowledge shines on me," I muttered.

"I'm afraid not." I didn't have a clue.

"Only one group can survive. This place is the cellar of our last mortal follower. We will shelter here till the contest is decided. In his prayers our follower suggested we enlist your aid. By temperament you are well suited."

"Leave my tailor out of this."

She scowled. She didn't get it. "We were considering bringing in a nonbeliever already. The Shayir must have gotten wind of you and so set a trap for you."

"Must be the bump on the head. I'm not understanding any of this." I asked again. "Who are you? What are you?"

The blonde giggled. That rogue Garrett. He says the cleverest things. However, the boss guy didn't find me amusing. Lightning crackled on his brow. Literally. He had grown a tad again, too. Should have clued me right then. His type don't have any patience.

"You've never heard of the Godoroth?"

" 'Fraid not. None of those other names, either."

"Ignorance was one point that recommended you." She didn't sound like she believed in ignorance, though.

Thunders pranced around the big guy's melon. The brunette flashed him a look that might have been disgust. Then she told me, "I'm Magodor. Collectively, we are the Godoroth. We were the patron gods of the Hahr, one of the first tribes to settle this region. They were primitive by your standards. They planted crops and herded cattle but were not very good at it. They lived as much by raiding as by agriculture. Almost all physical trace of them has vanished. Their blood still runs strong in the rulers of this city, but their culture is extinct. And their gods are on the verge of extinction."

That bad at agriculture—and the interest in institutionalized thievery sounded like a cultural aspect that had persisted amongst our rulers.

"The worship of the Shayir was brought into this region by the Ox-Riders of Gritn during the Gritny Conquest. The Gritny were much like the Hahr in the ways they lived. They did not last long. They were just the first wave in an age of great migrations. Every decade saw its raiders or conquerors. Each wave left its seed and a few settlers and their ideas. Of the Ox-Riders no physical trace remains. But their gods, the Shayir, are persistent and resilient. And now, brought low by time, we and the Shayir must fight for a place on the Street of the Gods."

Street of the Gods. That was the insiders' name for the avenue that runs the length of what cynical and undereducated types refer to as the Dream Quarter, that part of the South Side where TunFaire's thousand and one gods all have their main temples. Another legacy of the remote past, from an age when the temporal power reigned supreme and was totally paranoid about the worldly ambitions of priesthoods. Those old emperors had wanted every priest where he could be watched easily—and could be found easily at massacre time.

I looked around. Gods? Right.

"You know how it works on the Street? It's all marketing. If you win a good following, you migrate west to temples and cathedrals nearer the Hill. If you lose market share, you slide downhill eastward, toward the river. For three decades we have hung on by our nails, in the last temple to the east, while the Shayir holed up across the Street and one place west, with a monotheistic god named Scubs in the status niche between us. But Scubs won a family of converts last month. And immigrants from the Cantard have imported a god named Antitibet who has enough followers to seize a place a third of the way to the west. Which means a lot of shuffling around is due. And which also means that either we or the Shayir will have to leave the Street."

Yeah. I understood that. I knew how things worked in the Dream Quarter. I didn't have a clue why, or how, the priests worked it all out amongst themselves, but the results were evident.

Farthest west are the Chattaree cathedral of the Church and the Orthodox compound. These are feuding cousin religions that, with their various schismatic offspring, claim the majority of TunFaire's believers. These are rich and powerful cults.

And at the east end are dozens of cults like this one represented here, gods and pantheons known only to a handful of faithful. At that end of the street the temples are really nothing but worn-out storefronts.

I thought I understood the situation. Which did not mean I believed these characters were actual gods and goddesses. Didn't mean I didn't believe, either. You ask me, the evidence in the god business is always thin and, in most cases, thoroughly cooked by priests who survive by charging admission to heavenly attention. But this is TunFaire, the wonderful city where any damned thing can happen.

"You are a skeptic," Magodor observed. She looked very pretty right then.

I confessed with a nod. I did not confide my own be-
liefs, or the lack thereof.

Wisps of smoke trailed from the big guy's nostrils.
He was up to eighteen feet tall. If he got any more per-
turbed he would run out of headroom.

"We will explore your thinking another time. For the
moment let's just say that we Godoroth are in a situation both simple and desperate. We or the Shayir are
going to leave the Street. For us that would mean oblivion. The Street has a power all its own, a manna that
helps sustain us. Off the Street we would be little more
than wraiths, and that only transiently."

Maybe. The ugly boys looked as solid and eternal as
basalt.

She reiterated, in case her point had gone over my
head the past several times: "If we're forced off the
Street we are done, Mr. Garrett. Lost. Forgotten."

I'm not often accused of thinking before I open my
big yap. I could not be convicted this time, either.
"What actually does happen to gods who run out their
string? You have gods of your own to report to, stand
on the scales, be judged and all?"

Rumble-rumble. A crown of little thunderheads rode
the big guy's head now. He was over twenty feet tall.
Too tall for the cellar, even sitting down. He was bent
over, glaring at me ferociously. I got the impression
that, despite being the boss, he was not too bright.

Isn't that a lovely notion? Even in the supernatural
world it isn't necessarily the cream that rises to the top.

Lack of brilliance was a suspicion I had entertained
concerning numerous gods. Mostly their myths consist
of vicious behaviors toward one another and their worshippers, spiced up with lots of adultery, incest, bestial-
ity, parricide, and whatnot.

"Some just fade till even the ghost is gone. Others
become mortals, prey for time and the worm." I cannot
say that she sounded entirely convincing.

The big guy closed his eyes, breathed lightning. His
companion had better control. She had gotten herself
down to six feet tall and was quite attractive in a ma-

ture, country sort of way. I had no trouble picturing her galloping across the sky on a stormy night, wearing an iron hat with horns, scattering ravens while harvesting the fallen heroes. Trouble was, she eyed me like she had no trouble picturing me dangling across the neck of her mount.

My head still hurt. My stomach kept rolling over. I wanted desperately to go back to sleep.

I said, "I'm not comfortable here." I was also, still, very confused, completely distrusting of my senses. "Is there somewhere we can sit down, just you and me, so I can get a handle on this without being distracted?" If I wasn't trying to keep from stepping on my tongue when I looked at the blonde I was worrying about the big guy's temper or about the ugly brothers taking a notion to bang me around again. I did know I was in one bad spot, whatever these things were.

The big guy spat from the side of his mouth, like those country boys who chew weed instead of smoking it. A ball of fire hit stone a few yards from my hand, melted right down into the slate. Charming.

8

There was another cellar above part of the one where I had awakened. It was more normal, used for wine storage and lumber rooms. Lots of dust and spiders. Plenty of rats. Refreshingly mundane. My companion illuminated our way with a light from within herself. She seemed fuzzy but appeared solid once we climbed into a kitchen where a dozen women were cooking and baking. They paused to stare, baffled. Who was this guy coming out of the cellar?

Apparently they didn't see Magodor. Nor did they seem inclined to challenge my presence. They went back to work. That was not reassuring. It meant they were used to strange doings and to minding their own business.

Their number meant I had to be way up the Hill. And that meant the house probably belonged to one of the great and most wicked of the sorcerers who are the true powers in Karenta.

I hate it when I get noticed by those people. That never is good for me.

Magodor led me into a small drawing room apparently set up just for us. She told me, "You will have to manage without refreshments. We're not allowing ourselves to be seen by mortals."

I dropped into a chair so overstuffed I sank almost out of sight. I caught an arm and saved myself. In moments I was so comfortable I was ready to sleep. I knew I had a concussion, so I fought the drowsiness. "How come?"

"Our enemies would find out where we are."

"That's a problem?"

She offered me a sour look. Must have been my tone. "You've never seen a war of the gods. Pray you don't." The woman with all the teeth and arms and the snake problem shone through momentarily. "Neither we nor the Shayir need worry about injuring mortals under our protection." But wasn't that sort of thing supposed to be bad for business in general?

The nasty side faded. Lovely. Yum!

"That wouldn't be smart, Garrett."

"Huh?"

"Your thoughts are obvious. They were with Adeth. They were with Star. They are with me. You should know that my lovers seldom survive. I offer the warning only because we need you healthy. I am Magodor the Destroyer."

Into my head flooded images of famine and pestilence, of acres of bones, of cities burning and ravens darkening the sky. Boy, would she be a fun date. When the visions cleared, Magodor looked her loveliest yet, a make-the-celibate-monks-howl-at-the-unfair-moon sort of girl.

"Resist me."

"Will do." I was not sure that these Godoroth were not just slick con artists with a little hedge wizardry, aiming to use me as a stalking-horse. But why take chances?

"Until we triumph over the Shayir." If anything, she grew more desirable.

"Uh," I said, wondering if I ought not to hold a hand over my eyes. "Let's have some details. Like who was who down there and what you expect me to do."

"Meaning, if we really are gods, why not handle our problems ourselves?"

"Something like that." She talked too much for any god I ever heard of.

"Even gods are constrained."

"How?"

"We cannot, for example, invade the temple of the

Shayir. More will become evident in time. You haven't agreed to help."

I didn't intend to, either. I didn't tell her that. I don't have much use for gods of any sort. I figured what I needed to do was be polite, stall, ride it out, and soon enough I would be out of there. All the gods I had heard of had notoriously short attention spans. They all wanted to go boff their father's girlfriend or their brother or their pet three-headed dragon. Two hours after I was gone, these characters wouldn't remember me.

"Are you going to help?"

"You haven't told me anything. I don't even know who I would be representing. I know the name of one lovely who dotes on devastation. I know the name of a long drink of water who has feathered ears. That's not much."

"Jorken the Messenger. He is of no consequence."

"Then there are the big guys. Daiged, Rhogiro, and Ringo? What are they?"

"Avars. We inherited them. They were servants of the Old Ones. They have no attributes but strength."

"Don't forget ugly. They're really big on ugly."

"You have no idea. And of course, being you, you're really interested in Star."

"Star?"

"She has an older name, but it means Morning Star. She is the whore avatar of Woman, the Temptress, the temple prostitute who always comes across."

"How romantic."

"I could see the romance in your eyes whenever you looked at her."

"Some things we can't control."

"Or you wouldn't have followed Adeth."

"Adeth?"

"The one trying to lead you into a trap. You are lucky we were watching. You would not have enjoyed her company as much as Star's."

"The redhead? Some things we can't control."

"If you must lose it, concentrate on Star. She might

get interested. She hasn't turned it on for you yet, Garrett."

Wow. She ought to bottle and sell that indifference, then. Be a comedown from the god racket, but she would get rich and famous and maybe famous would put her feet on the ladder back to the top. I could get rich myself, managing her. Cut myself a percentage of the take and . . .

Sssss!

Snakes out of green hair. Magodor was irritated. I don't think she could read my mind, but she was bright enough to realize I wasn't paying attention. I came alert fast. They might not be gods, but they might believe they were and had every right to be vicious and capricious. I put on my killer grin, hoisted an eyebrow charmingly, said, "I'm awake! I'm awake!" same as I used to tell the sergeant of the guard when he caught me with my attention wandering back in those good old Marine Corps days, dancing with the Venageti in the islands.

"You don't seem especially interested."

"Consider the mortal's viewpoint. He's been kidnapped. He has a knife across his throat. Somebody supposedly wants to hire him, but he can't find out what for. You haven't said a word about payment. The one thing that does come across is that these would-be employers don't look any more trustworthy or stable than any other gods."

With every word sweet Maggie grew less attractive. I quit before she decided to drop me down a hole and interview elsewhere. "Why not finish telling me about the others?"

I basked in the pale green light of her disapproval. She wasn't used to backtalk. But she took control. Maybe she *was* desperate.

Doubtless, in the shadows of her heart, she put a tick beside "Garrett" in her book of destruction.

"How about the boss couple? Who are they?"

"Imar and Imara." I didn't have to be told. Both brother and sister and man and wife. "Lord and Mis-

tress of All, Skystrider and Earth Mother. Sun and
Moon, Scatterer of Stars and She Who Calls Forth the
Spring."

"And so forth," I muttered. When you have the habit
of backmouthing crime bosses and Guard chieftains, it
ain't easy to break the circle.

"And so forth. We tend to accumulate titles, of both
supplication and accusation."

That fit with what I knew about other gods. The
Church, where I was raised, didn't have a full crew of
gods like most religions. We had one God, No God But
God—and about ten thousand saints who covered the
same ground as lesser gods and goddesses. The Church
had a whole heavenly bureaucracy, with saints who
didn't do anything more strenuous than find lost but-
tons or keep an eye on the wine grape harvest. The
Church's supernatural establishment was so big the
whole thing would continue on inertia for ages after its
last believer perished.

"All right. Now that I know who you are, I have a
vague notion what your problem is. One temple. Two
bunches of gods. Whoever loses out loses big time."

"Exactly." She was all business now. As if a beautiful
woman can ever be all business, however much she
wants to think that. Nature does not care about the
clutter in the mind. Decorum is just another obstacle to
be surmounted by instinct.

I tried being all business, too.

Instinct could get me dead.

I reminded me that lady spiders eat their mates.

9

"Listen," Magodor snapped. "You get to hear this once."

Generous. "I'm all ears, Maggie." I tried to wiggle them encouragingly, but I just don't have that talent. What an unfair world. A big goof like Saucerhead Tharpe can wiggle one of his ears, but I am stuck with . . .

"Garrett."

Whoops. "I'm awake! I'm awake!"

"You may not accept it, but we gods have dealings amongst ourselves. Few of your priests are aware of this."

"Yeah. Mostly they're big on declaring their own gods to be the only gods."

"Partly. Some younger religions are intolerant that way. About rules. There is a set that governs the situation that exists now. Additionally, there are custom and past practice. It's not explicitly forbidden, but past practice is that pantheons don't fight over places on the Street."

"Bad for business, eh?"

"You have no idea. Customarily, a committee of more successful gods oversee a competition. Winner takes all."

"Ah." That was my polished professional ah, my ah of illumination.

"The competitions are unique each time so the contestants cannot rig the results beforehand."

"I'll bet they never even try."

Maggie smiled me a genuine smile. "Indeed."

"So what's the contest? Where do I fit in?"

"The prize temple has been sealed. Neither the Shayir nor we can get in. Somewhere there is a key. Whoever finds it, and recognizes it, can open and take over the temple."

I used my eyebrow trick. "Oh?" She wasn't impressed.

"It's supposed to be ordinary but rendered invisible to immortal eyes. The lock it fits cannot be broken. It will open only to the key. The Board probably expects us to rely on our faithful to do the legwork, but there is no specific prohibition against employing a professional. So we turned to you. And it seems that the Shayir, apparently having gotten wind of our interest, tried to lure you away."

"I see," I said, not sure that I saw anything. "I'm supposed to find this key, scoot to this temple, and let you in before the Shayir find it."

"That's the meat of it."

"Interesting." If I was not caught up inside some bizarre con. That would fit my luck. Time and again I get dragged in where nobody plays me even close to straight.

All part of the business.

I had questions. Were the contesting gods, though discouraged from bushwhacking each other, allowed to make life hard for the opposition's mortals? I have enough troubles.

Maggie looked at me like she meant to glare a hole through.

"It's worth thinking about. My weirdest case yet. Great for my references later." I had to get out without making commitments. I knew I could not get away with a flat no.

"There's a time limit, Garrett. The sands are running already. We have maybe another hundred hours."

Gah. "What happens if nobody finds the key?"

"These southern immigrants could bring more gods than Antitibet."

"Everybody loses?"

"It has happened before."

"Let's talk money, then."

Her face tightened. Prospective clients never want to talk about money.

I told her, "I have a household to support. The usual story stuff—like maybe a night with Star, like a night in Elf Hill, wonderful as that might be—won't put food on the table."

10

"I have hovered above a thousand battlefields, Garrett. I can tell you where the treasure of a hundred vanquished armies are hidden."

Handy trick. "Excellent. Then clue me about one small one that's close by."

Her green began to rise. But she nodded abruptly. "Very well. The workman is worthy of his hire. And it is necessary that we trust one another. There is no time for anything else." She stalked across the room, bad Magodor becoming luscious Maggie as she walked. My instinctual side was adequately impressed. "Come see, Garrett."

She indicated a hand mirror on the room's small mantelpiece. There was nothing mystical about it. The dwarves produce them by the thousands. Maggie passed a hand over the metal in a circular motion, as though polishing it. A mist formed between her hand and the metal. That faded. The mirror no longer reflected here and now.

Woodland scene with men who rode desperately, low upon the necks of lathered horses. Arrows fell around them. A rider fell. The rest swept on into forest so dense their horses could make little headway. The riders dismounted and fled on foot. One led them to a trail hidden in the growth.

"Amis the Third. In flight from the uprising masterminded by his brother Alis. He failed to make proper sacrifices. We turned our eyes away. We were strong in those times. Here. This is the treasure they were able to carry away. They buried it in a badger's den. It is still there." Her hand made that wiping motion again. The view backed off enough to give me a good idea where to look. Then the view changed.

Now the fugitives were cornered. Their guide had led them into a trap. Their pursuers showed no mercy.

"That's inside the wall now, isn't it?"

"Yes."

"Wonderful. That will do for a retainer if it's still there."

"I wouldn't have chosen something that wasn't. One thing more." She took a cord from around her waist, a cord that had not been visible till she unwound it. It was four feet long. She wrapped one end around her left hand once, let the cord dangle from between thumb and forefinger, drew the thumb and forefinger of her right hand along the length of the cord.

The cord became as stiff as an arrow. "Neat trick."

She jabbed it, swordlike, right into my breadbasket.

"Oof!" said I.

"Had I pinched the end down into a point, so, it would have gone through you."

"Uhn."

She swung the cord, hit me on the left elbow. Right on the funnybone. I said something like, "Yeow! Oh shining wondrous mudsuckers fingushing wowzgoggle! That hurts!"

"Pain is the best teacher. Watch." She reversed her fingerwork. The cord fell limp. She was a lefty. I was not surprised. Most artists and sorcerers I run into seem to be. So are most of the more successful villains. The really stupid bad guys, the kind who try to get in somewhere by sliding down the chimney without checking first to see if there is a fire burning, are always righties. But I am not a lefty myself, so not all righties are dumb.

Magodor grabbed the middle of the cord and pulled. It kept getting longer. "Just like this, Garrett. Hands extended, level, palms up, heels of your hands together. Pull outward from the middle. It will stretch as long as you need it to."

"That's one handy piece of rope."

"Yes. It is." She stopped when she had twenty-five feet of cord. "It can be used as a garrote, too."

"I saw that right off." It looked very much like the ritual garrotes the Kef sidhe use to carry out their holy murders.

"Pay attention. To shorten it you rumple it all up in a ball, so." The cord crushed up small. She rolled the wad around on her palms, grabbed the ends that were sticking out, pulled. The cord was four feet long again.

She stretched it to ten feet. "If you need more than one piece of line, tie a slip knot in the middle, so. Pull out a loop as long as you need. Cut the loop right at the knot." She held cord and knot with two hands. Another hand clipped the cord with a thin knife. Yet another hand dealt with the second piece of cord, which she handed to me. She dropped one end of what was left, grabbed the knot and slid it right to the end.

I had seen this trick's cousin before. It was in the arsenal of most street conjurers. Only it didn't seem to be a trick this time.

She took the cord back from me, wadded, rolled, had one four-foot piece again. "I will want this back."

"Darn! I was afraid of that."

She eyed me sharply. "I'll show you one more thing. For you this is likely to be its most useful facility."

She stretched the cord to six feet, tied a small bowline at one end, ran the other end through the resulting loop, forming a large noose. She set the circle of cord on the carpet, stepped inside, lifted the cord. Everything of her below the rising cord vanished. In a moment there were just hands floating in the air. Those disappeared as she pulled the loop shut. "Pull the cord inside but leave it hanging." I could hear her fine.

"That's astounding."

"There is still one little hole up high where someone can see inside. You must be careful about making sounds. You can be heard. If you take reasonable precautions neither people nor animals should be able to scent you." A knot appeared in the air. Fingers poked through, expanded the loop outward. It dropped.

Magodor stepped out. She untied the bowline, handed me the cord. Her fingers were soft and hot, but I jerked away from the prick of a talon as sharp as a razor. She raised a finger to her lips.

I pulled that cord around my waist the way she had worn it. It stayed in place without any special tucking or tying. I couldn't see it but could feel it. I observed, "The sands are running. How do I get out of here?" See? No commitment at all. Any she heard she made up herself out of wishful thinking.

"Abyss."

The guy who had driven the coach floated out of a shadow. I had not suspected his presence. Magodor was pleased by my surprise. "Show Mr. Garrett to the street."

Abyss looked at me from eyes that were leagues away inside his hood. The air grew cold. I got the feeling he resented being forced to bother with me. I thought of a couple of cracks but doubted he had the brain or sense of humor to understand. And I still had to get out of there.

As I left that room, Magodor said, "Be careful. The Shayir are desperate and dangerous."

"Right." The Godoroth, of course, were just playful puppies.

I encountered several servants before leaving the house, startling every one. None paid Abyss any mind, though one who passed close by suffered one of those unexpected chills that sometimes fall upon you for no obvious reason.

Abyss never said a word. I felt his eyes upon me for a long time after I got my feet onto cobblestones.

11

Just playful puppies, the Godoroth.

I moved fast for a few blocks, just to get some distance. Then I stopped to get my bearings.

I had been right. The place was right up there. I didn't recognize the particular house, but it wouldn't take much effort to find out who owned it. I wondered if I should bother. Knowing might be too scary.

Before I moved on, I charted a course unlikely to lead me into trouble. I had to get to the Dead Man. I needed some serious advice. I had fallen into deep shit if I was dealing with real gods. I might be into it deep anyway.

I moved fast and tried to watch every which way at once, sure that the effort was a waste because I was dealing with shapeshifters who could walk behind me and just be something else every time I looked around.

My head still hurt, though my hangover had faded. I was past the sleepiness, but I was starved and all I really wanted was a sample of Dean's cooking.

The streets were not crowded. Up there they never are. But times have changed. I saw several enterprising pushcart operators trying to sell trinkets or services. They would not have dared in times past. Used to be privately hired security thugs would send their kind scurrying with numerous bruises.

They still did, I discovered. I came on several brunos bouncing an old scissor sharpener all over an acre of street. They eyeballed me but saw I was headed downhill. Why risk any pain encouraging me to hurry? I guess those other cartmen were around because the thugs did not have time to get them all. Or they had purchased a private license from the guards.

Not long after I crossed the boundary into the work-aday real world, I realized that I had acquired a tail. She didn't give me a good look, so I could not be sure, but I suspected she might have had red hair when I was on the back end of the chase.

Sometimes you just got more balls than brains. You do stuff that don't make sense later. Especially if you blow it.

I was lucky this time but still can't figure out why I headed for Brookside Park instead of going home. If that was the redhead back there she knew where I lived.

The park was a mile out of my way, too. It is a big tract of trees and brush and reservoirs fed by springs that fill a creek running off the flank of the Hill. There are Royal fishponds and a Royal aviary and a stand of four-story granaries and silos supposedly kept full in case of siege or disaster. I wouldn't bet much on there being a stash if ever we are forced to tap those re-sources. Corruption in TunFaire is such that the offi-cials in charge probably don't even go through bureaucratic motions before selling whatever the farm-ers bring in.

But, hell. Maybe I am too cynical.

The park police force, never numerous nor energetic nor effective at their best, had worse problems than the thugs up the Hill. Whole tribes of squatters had set up camp. Again I wondered why they found TunFaire so attractive. The Cantard is hell by anybody's reckoning, but a lot less so if you were born there. Why leave the hell you know, walk hundreds of miles, plunk yourself down in a town where not only do you have no prospects but the natives all hate you and don't need much excuse to do you grief?

On the other hand—and I don't understand why—TunFaire is a dream for this whole end of the world, the golden city. Maybe you can't see why if you are looking at it from the inside.

The woman gave me more room out there, off the

street, so she would be less obvious. I didn't get a better look.

I strode briskly, hup two three four. Up and down hump and swale, round bush and copse. I darted into a small, shady stand of evergreens in a low place, careful not to disturb the old needles on the ground. Hey, I used to be Force Recon. I was the bear in the woods.

I selected a friendly shadow, did the trick with the cord that was supposed to make me invisible. I waited.

She was careful. You have to be when you are tracking somebody and they drop out of sight. They could be setting an ambush.

I didn't plan to jump her. I just wanted to try my new toy and get a look at someone who seemed interested in me.

She was about six feet tall, dishwater blonde, sturdy, maybe twenty-five, better groomed than most gals you see on the street. She had an adequate supply of curves but wasn't dressed to brag. She wore a homespun kind of thing that would have looked better cut up and sewed up and used to dress large batches of potatos. From what I could see she lacked legs and feet. Her skirts were that long. She made me think of a younger version of Imar's wife, Imara.

She moved cautiously, as though she knew I had turned. She eased past not ten feet away. I held my breath. It was obvious she could not see me. It was just as obvious that she felt I was real close. She had the heebie-jeebies. I restrained my boyish side and didn't yell "Boo!" I studied her but didn't come up with a clue. She might be some nightmare in disguise. Whatever, she was no smouldering redhead.

She seemed human. Do devils get the heebie-jeebies?

She decided to get the hell out of there before bad things happened. Which suggested that bad things could. But that might only be because she was Shayir and knew something unpleasant about the Godoroth.

Some surprise that would be.

I do a good tail. I decided to put off seeing the Dead

Man, and suffering his wisdom, long enough to see where this mouse ran. I spotted her a lead.

I discovered that becoming invisible imposes limitations. Like I was enclosed inside some kind of sack I could see through. There was plenty of air in there with me. The walls of the sack didn't collapse. It was like being inside a big, floppy bubble that wobbled and tangled and toppled when you moved. You could get around, but you had to be careful. If you got in a hurry, you stumbled and rolled downhill into a soggy low spot. The bag didn't keep water from soaking your knees and elbows.

Rorjfrazzle! Mirking sludglup! Everything just has to have a down side.

Or three. It took me ten minutes to get back out of the sack. The loop in the cord has to line up with the closed hole just right. If you have been moving around, you probably didn't keep track of where that hole went. Rotten racklefratz!

As I stumbled out and crawled away and started undoing my bowline, I realized that the tittering above wasn't the gossip of sparrows. A tiny voice only inches overhead piped, "We seen what you done. We seen what you done."

A pixie colony inhabited the grove. Now that they were bouncing around and giggling they were obvious. I hadn't noticed a thing when they were silent.

I didn't commence my rebuttal till I was safely away from any branch likely to serve as an aerial outhouse.

12

I headed for my house. The girl was long gone.

Used to be whenever I was out I had to knock so Dean would let me in. Before he left town he looted my savings to have a key lock installed so I could let myself in. Being a bright boy, I had my key with me. I used it.

The door opened an inch and stopped. Dean had the chain on.

I closed the door gently, took a moment to collect myself, knocked briskly. The Goddamn Parrot started up inside. O Wonder of Horrors, the little vulture had made it home on his own. I tried to avoid worrying about what kind of omen that might be.

I stepped back while I waited, studied the face of my house. It was a very dark brown, built of rough brick. I saw several places where the mortar needed tuck-pointing. The upstairs window trim needed fresh paint. Might be a job for Saucerhead some time when he wasn't tied up cracking skulls.

"Damn it, Dean! Come on! If you've had a heart attack and I've got to bust the door down I'm gonna break your legs."

There was a horrendous squawl behind me. I whirled. A huge, ugly ogre had gotten too near a donkey cart. A wheel had crushed his toes. He was bounding around on one foot offering to whip all comers.

"Ah, shuddup!" an old granny lady advised. She hooked the heel of his good foot with the crook of her umbrella. He went down hard. Ogres are solid-bottomed fellows, as a rule. This one was no exception. His breath deserted him in a mighty whoof. The cobblestones buckled. I might have a traffic hazard out front for months now. Maybe years. Who knew when a city crew would come and actually do something?

The crowd howled and mocked the ogre. Ogres are not popular because they are just not nice people, generally, but this was an especially tough crowd. They would have laughed had he been a sweet little old nun. Times had the mob in a vicious humor.

I spied my new friend Adeth. She wore a darker, longer wig and had changed apparel, but I was sure it was her. She moved like a cat now, without wasted motion, absolutely graceful. Maybe while Dean made up his mind to answer the door I could stroll over there and invite her to dinner.

I hammered the door some more. Then I got my key out again. I would unlock the damned thing again, then kick the chain loose. I was in one bad mood.

My head still throbbed like a couple of pixies were in there waltzing in combat boots.

Dean opened up as I reached with the key. "We have to talk," I told him. "Let's rehash the argument over that damned lock that cost me more than most guys make working twelve hours a day for two months."

"What happened?"

"I couldn't get into my own house, that's what happened! Some damned fool put the chain on!" The God-damn Parrot was in fine voice. "When did that damned thing come home? How did it get inside?"

"Hours ago, Mr. Garrett. I thought you sent it." He nodded his head toward the Dead Man's room, scowled. "He told me to let it in." Dean shuddered.

On cue, I heard from Old Bones. *Garrett. Come here. I want to review events of the past few months.*

Him and his hobbies. "What you're going to hear about is events of the past few hours."

Dean shivered again. The Dead Man gives him the creeps. He has as little to do with His Nibs as he can.

"That dressed-up buzzard over there should of let you know I was having some trouble."

"I'll make some tea," Dean said, by way of offering a white flag.

"Sounds good. Thanks." When he gets those big hurt eyes it is hard to stay mad at him. "But you, you traitor, you deserter," I snapped through the doorway of the small front room, "you're going to star in an experiment to see if parrots make good hasenpfeffer." The shape my head was in, I was real short on tolerance.

I went into the Dead Man's room.

Pickled parrot?

"He must be good for something."

Do I detect a measure of crabbiness?

"Things are closing in on me. I was getting used to not having to deal with Dean's nagging. I was getting used to not having to deal with your outrageous demands. Then you woke up. He came home. I went out for a walk and a bunch of ugly wazoos bopped me on the head."

The picture the bird brought in had you lunging through a coach without the forethought to open the nether exit.

He has moments when he looks beyond the end of his nose. And an ugly nose it is, too.

The Dead Man has a human look to him. You glance into his room—the biggest in the house and poorly lighted at his insistence even though he cannot see—and your gaze is drawn to a wooden chair at the room's center. Maybe you could call it the Dead Man's throne. It is massive—but it has to be to support four hundred and some pounds. He has not moved in all the years I have known him. He *has* grown seedier. Though he can protect himself if he concentrates, mice and bugs do nibble when his attention wanders.

His outstanding feature, other than size, is his schnoz. It's like an elephant's trunk a little over a foot long.

Bad day?

"It was a bad day when I got woke up at a totally ridiculous hour, thank you very much. It has gone downhill ever since. Why don't you just dig into my head?"

I would prefer that you told it. I get more subtext examining the subjective side.

This from a guy who insisted I had to maintain my emotional distance when I reported to him. We might as well be married. You can't win with him.

This is not good.

"Hey, I hardly got started."

I read you. These are not friendly gods. These are old-style gods, all wrath and thou shalt not.

"You know them?"

Dean brought in a tray with teapot, honey, cup, spoon. What? Usually he just handed me a mug ready to go. Was he kissing up?

Only by reputation. They have been marginal pantheons since the beginning, deities of ancient nomadic immigrants. Both religions were too cold and hard to win many converts. They are much alike.

"Oh, your head!" Dean said. He was looking straight down at the top of my conk. "No wonder you're in a black mood. Don't move. I'll clean that up." He bustled out.

Apparently your skull is as thick as I have claimed.

"Huh?"

Your head wound is worse than you realized.

"What did I say? The good news just piles up." I reflected on what he had sent. "I got a question."

Yes? I felt a mental smirk.

"Back when we dealt with that crazy Loghyr you told me Loghyr never found proof of the existence of any gods and claimed logic suggests they can't exist. I believe you said 'They are not necessary to explain anything. Nature does not provide that which is not needed.' "

That is correct. There is no concrete proof that any of the deities worshipped in this city exist as independent entities, outside the imaginations of those with the will to believe.

"Who tried to toss me through that coach door, then? You telling me they were scamming?"

That is a possibility deserving of examination. But to your question. For the sake of argument, your interlocuters were indeed Daiged, Rhogiro, and Ringo. Magodor gave you your answer in her remarks.

Oh boy. Here came my favorite part of our relationship, the part where he tries to expand my horizons by forcing me to expand my intellect.

Dean came back with our first aid stuff. I keep a good home medicine cabinet. For a while I had a girlfriend who was a doctor. She fixed me up because I seem to get dinged up every time I turn around.

"I'm a little woozy here, Chuckles. How's about you just hand it to me this time?"

All the sport is gone out of you, Garrett. The very nature of their situation should shriek the answer. If they fall off the Street of the Gods, if they are forced to leave the Dream Quarter, if they lose their last True Believer, they cease to exist.

"Ouch!" Dean was dabbing at my head with a hot, wet rag. "You mean I wouldn't have this dent in my head if somebody didn't believe in the ugly boys?"

Essentially.

Dean asked, "Who sewed this up for you, Mr. Garrett?"

"Sewed what?" And to His Nibs, "But they exist on their own. Nobody dreamed what was happening to me."

Dean told me, "You have three . . . six . . . nine stitches here. You must have bled pretty bad."

"No wonder I'm so weak. I thought it was a concussion."

"Might be that, too."

They need only be imagined and believed in fervently enough, on the right level. They assume an existence of their own, within the attributes assigned them.

"Careful!" I snapped at Dean. "That's tender. They must have given me something to make it not hurt. Ouch! Damnit! . . ."

"Don't be such a pansy."

"You aren't digging for gold. Old Bones, your theory is absurd."

Gods are absurd, Garrett. And it is a hypothesis, not a theory. A theory is supported by experimental proof.

"I'm just looking to see if there's any infection," Dean grumbled, doing his hurt thing.

I ignored him, told the Dead Man, "There you go splitting hairs."

"Theory" is a much-abused word, particularly by those in the divinity trades. Be careful, Dean. If those stitches break, his brain may leak out. Have you formed any plans, Garrett? To deal with your situation?

My situation. "I take it I need to worry in a big way." When the Dead Man sets aside his own self-centered interests, I know he is troubled deeply. It was obvious that he had no problem believing that I could have fallen afoul of real gods and not just sleight-of-hand con folk somehow setting me up.

I answered his question. "I don't have a clue. That's why I came home. Are you going to pay your rent?" Though *he* insists he is a full partner, the most work he does is aimed at getting out of doing anything constructive.

"Right now I don't see any choice but to play along."

Indeed. Wriggling out of this will require intense self-discipline and long hours of work by all concerned.

"Don't whine. I hate it when you whine. You were way overdue to kick in around here anyway. You could've saved me a ton of grief with Maggie Jenn if you would've just woke up." He had unraveled the mystery at the heart of my most recent case before I had finished telling the first half of the tale. It was a case he had slept through stubbornly.

13

It was great to be in the righteous right so solid I could bury my spurs in the Dead Man.

"Will you hold still?" Dean snapped. "Looks like a little pus here. Let me clean it out so we won't have to cauterize later."

I had a vision of my handsome face set off by a strip of scar tissue skewed across my scalp. I held still, but it hurt.

Dean said, "Miss Tate was here while you were away, Mr. Garrett. She . . ."

"She must have been watching the place." To know he was home so soon after he arrived. Tinnie probably shouldn't be the ex-girlfriend. She was waiting for me to make the first move toward reconciliation. I liked to think.

"News travels fast, Mr. Garrett."

"Did it have some help?"

"It's possible." Dean is as stubborn as I am. He is determined to get me hooked up with Tinnie Tate or Maya Stubbs, both of them beautiful, squared-away sweethearts who deserve Prince Charmings who are the real thing.

The Dead Man sent, *Miss Tate was as charming, witty, and beautiful as ever and her companion, Miss Weider, cannot be encompassed by normal superlatives. Nevertheless, their petition will have to wait.*

"Alyx Weider?" Those two must have buttered him up big. He has no use whatsoever for the female of my species—or any other species, as far as I have seen. I'm sure that is why he tries to sabotage most of my romances. He doesn't think most women deserve me.

Them pigs were flying formation today.

Dean tends toward the opposing opinion.

He said, "I believe Miss Tate did introduce her as Alyx." He did something to my head that sent a ribbon of pain streaking from my scalp to my toenails.

"You're on my list, Dean. Someday I'll get my chance to patch you up."

I am on retainer as chief of security at Weider's brewery. My role is to drop in unexpectedly and check employee honesty. I saved Weider from being robbed blind a long time back. The job was my reward. Old man Weider has been trying to get me on full time ever since. There are times when a regular job looks real good, even if I would have to call somebody else boss.

Alyx was the old man's baby, much younger than the rest of his sprats. I had not seen her for some time. She had been a lovely but shy girl at sixteen. I was surprised to hear that she had come to the house. Her dad wasn't the sort to let his baby girl out, especially in today's TunFaire.

Miss Tate brought her. There is something happening within the Weider family, possibly having to do with The Call and other radical fringe human rights groups. We owe them an interest but this mess must take precedent. Gods! Garrett! Garrett! At best you are an agnostic. But still you become entangled with a clutch of redundant deities.

"Like I went looking for them? I'm not agnostic, though. I'm indifferent. My philosophy is, you leave the gods alone and usually they'll leave you alone."

"Another one bites the dust," Dean said.

"Huh?" He find a nit?

"Another of your adolescent fantasies."

Dean is a religious man. I never pressed him, but I do not understand his blind devotion to his peculiar monotheistic mythology when we are plagued by a thousand other deities and, obviously, those gods occasionally really do mess around with mortals. The human capacity for selective blindness appears to be infinite.

For me the religion business becomes problematic when the gods outnumber their worshippers.

Well, in some cases. One of which I seem to have stumbled into. I told the Dead Man, "You sound like you're actually interested. Maybe I ought to be suspicious. But I don't think there's time."

Exactly. Long hours and rigorous self-discipline lie ahead. Your first chore will be to visit the Royal library and sweet-talk your friend into loaning us whatever books they have devoted to these religions.

"Uh . . . that might not be so easy."

Make peace.

"It's not that. Linda Lee and I get along fine. I found some rare books she let get away."

Find me some books. Dean! Put aside your prejudice for a moment. Go to Mr. Dotes' establishment . . .

"That may not be any good either. Morley has gone upscale. He might be trying to put his whole past behind him."

Must you interrupt? He rooted around inside my head. He never does that unless he is seriously provoked or concerned. He reviewed my experiences during his nap. Usually he is overly careful to respect my privacy.

His behavior was troubling. I had to suspect that he knew something that had not occurred to me.

Who do we know who has the ability to read? Other than yourself?

"Playmate," I replied, puzzled. "But not real good. Winger, a little. Morley. Barking Dog . . ."

Winger? Astonishment.

"She's been learning. The better to con you with, my dear. Always a surprise, Winger is."

Not good enough. Try to get your librarian friend to come in.

"Why?" Talk about astonishment. The Dead Man asking for a woman to be brought into the house?

Any books you do obtain will have to be read to me. It is too difficult for me to do it by myself.

Turning the pages is a bitch when you're dead. Though he could manage it if he had to.

"I got you."

An even bigger problem is that he has a hard time seeing if he can't use somebody's else's eyes.

Once you have dealt with Linda Lee I want you to go to the Dream Quarter. Examine the temples involved in this business. Move carefully. Waste no time but take all the time you need to study the places right while maintaining your personal safety.

"What? Shouldn't I look for this key?"

That is of no concern now. Information is. If you collect the available information I will sift the clues. I am not as powerful as these gods, but I am far smarter.

"No self-image problem over there," I told Dean, who had made no effort to leave

Much the same can be said of you, Garrett. I do not recall the Godoroth well, but do believe Magodor may be the only one smarter than a four-year-old.

Wonderful.

Time is wasting, Garrett. To the library. Then to the Dream Quarter.

"What about the Shayir?"

What about them?

"Apparently they were on to me even before the Godoroth. What do I do if they close in on me?"

Use your wits, guided by experience. You have your weapons and your physical skills. In any event, you will achieve nothing standing there. Dean. After you have spoken to Mr. Dotes, locate Mr. Tharpe. If Mr. Tharpe is unavailable, find Mr. Playmate. As a last resort, call upon Miss Winger. Then return here quickly. I will have more for you to do. Garrett.

I paused at the door. I will say this about the Dead Man. It is blue-haired hell getting him started, but once he is into something he is a take-charge kind of guy.

"What?"

Take the parrot.

"What? Are you crazy? I got lucky a while ago, but you know my luck ran out. He'll get me killed before I walk a block. He'll tell some giant his mother does trolls, and they'll find parts of me all over town."

Take the parrot. Put a lanyard on his leg if you feel the need. I believe he will be more cooperative than usual.

"Dead would be more cooperative than usual."

Garrett.

He was impatient. He had no time to play. When he is in a mood like that it is best to humor him.

The Goddamn Parrot offered me a black look but only nibbled my fingers once when I moved him from his perch to my shoulder. Hell if I would tie him down. Anytime he wanted to escape I would stand there grinning and waving bye-bye. But I knew how my luck would run already. Just like before, he would beat me home.

"I need an eye patch and an earring," I muttered. "Yo ho ho."

14

I stood on the stoop wishing for a beard to go with the earring and eye patch. I growled, "Argh! Prepare to repel boarders."

T. G. Parrot squawked, "Awk! Shiver me timbers!"

I tried to give him my best jaundiced look, but he couldn't get the full benefit perched as he was on my shoulder.

Neighborhood kids materialized out of the crowd. "Can we feed your parrot, Mr. Garrett?"

"Yeah. To one of those flying thunder lizards." A pair were circling high above, shopping for plump pigeons.

The kids didn't get it. Short attention spans, I guess. It had been a while since their elders had worried about trouble with thunder lizards. Now we had centaur infestations and whatnot.

As my old Aunt Boo used to say, "It's always something."

I looked up the street. Mrs. Cardonlos was out watching. I waved. Always a neighborly smile, that Mr. Garrett. It drove her crazy. Made her *sure* I was up to no good.

I'd barely entered the crowd when Dean left the house. He was pale. He didn't look at me. He headed downhill, toward Morley's Joy House, which now masquerades as The Palms.

I went the other way, amidst the fastest traffic. I didn't make much effort to see if I was followed. If I had gods on my case they would have resources better than mine. I headed where I had to go, wondering why the Dead Man was taking this so seriously.

I think I was followed by the same woman, only now she seemed taller and had a fall of white on the right side of otherwise raven hair that hung quite long. I didn't get a good look at her clothing, but it had a foreign air.

The Royal Library has a side entrance that isn't well known to those without friends inside. You do have to slip past an ancient guard who uses his job to catch up on naps he lost while he was off to war. Once he is behind you, all you have to do is avoid notice by the senior librarian. That isn't hard, either. She is ancient and slow and stumbles into things when she is moving around. Once you are inside, you have to decide whether to see your friend or load up with rare books to sell.

Turned out that was the way it used to be. Changes had been made. All my fault for returning the stolen books I had happened upon the other day.

The old man had been replaced. A hard young veteran manned his desk. He was snoring. A liquor bottle dangled from his hand. Sneaky was wasted on him. I was tempted to leave the parrot on his shoulder. Let him wake up and find himself infested. He wouldn't take another drink for hours.

I resisted. We must not dishonor our public servants.

I found Linda Lee in the stacks, peering intently at worn and flaky leather spines. She had a stylus in her mouth, bitten crosswise. She carried a wax note tablet and a small lantern. Her sleak brown hair was pulled back in an old maid's bun and, damn me, a few gray hairs showed on her temple. She might have a few years she hadn't mentioned.

Even so, she was the cutest bookworm I'd ever seen.

I asked, "What do you do when you have to make a note?"

She jumped. She whirled. Sparks danced in her eyes. I never knew how she was going to greet me. "What the hell are you doing here?" She had no trouble talking around the stylus.

"Looking for you."

"Can't get a date?"

"It's professional this time . . ." There you go shoving one of those big old dirty hooves of yours right down your throat, Garrett. You slick talker. "My mouth just won't say what me head tells it to today."

"Surprise, surprise. What the hell is that on your shoulder? You trying a new look?"

"You remember Mr. Big."

"Unfortunately. That's why I asked. Why haven't you drowned it? What's wrong with it?"

"Huh?" She wasn't herself. I wondered who she was. That might clue me in about who she wanted me to be so all four of us could get along.

"It hasn't said anything. Usually it's criminally obnoxious."

"The Dead Man did something to him."

Linda Lee shuddered. The Dead Man gave her the creeps. That might be a problem.

"So ignore the fact that I haven't seen you since I was a girl."

"Three days?"

"What do you want?" For all she apparently wanted to fight, she kept her voice down. Her superiors and coworkers didn't like me wandering in and out. It shook their confidence in their safety and the security of the Royal collection. If I kept it up, someday they would have to do something. Maybe even put out money for a real guard.

"Three days isn't long enough for you to turn into your own grandmother . . . Damn! Now I'm doing it."

"It hasn't been a good day. Time is flying, Garrett."

No need to cause more difficulties. I told the story, quick and straight, giving the most detail in the least time. I left out a few details she didn't really need, like how exciting some of those goddess types were.

She grew thoughtful before I finished. "Really? Gods? I never? . . . You don't think about them actually getting in your way, do you?"

"No. They're like another remove beyond the fire-lords and stormwardens. They may shape your life, but you don't figure on banging into one going around a corner. Given my druthers, I'd never run into either one."

"Too much potential for disaster."

"Absodamnlutely. You know anything about these gods?"

"Only their names. There are a lot of old mythologies. They aren't my area. I could get Mad."

"I thought you were. I just couldn't figure out why."

"Mad is Madelaine. She handles our scriptures."

I recalled a harridan of satanic disposition old enough to have written the first drafts of most of her charges. "That's not necessary. I just need whatever I can get on the Godoroth and Shayir over to the house so somebody can read them to the Dead Man."

"You can't take books out of here."

"I thought I explained. I've only got a few days and I don't have a clue where to start." I touched the high points again.

She understood, all right. She was negotiating. If she was going to take risks she wanted something more than a kiss and a thank you. Maybe some yellow roses.

"All right. All right," she whispered, throwing a troubled glance over her left shoulder. She placed a finger against her lips. I nodded. Her ears were better than mine. First thing they check when you apply at the library is your ears.

She gestured "Go away!" with finger still to lips. I went. She would do me the favor. She might even read for the Dead Man. He could charm them when he wanted. But she was going to make me pay.

I eased into shadow at the nether end of the stacks as the mother of all librarians materialized at Linda Lee's end. The way she moved, she could have run the hundred-yard dash in slightly under a decade. She leaned on a gnarly, ugly cane notched once for every time she had caught someone talking. Her hair was white and thin and wild, and she was bent way over. She wore cheaters, which suggested she had wealthy relatives. Spectacles cost a fortune. But she still could not see her hand more than a foot from her face. I could have danced naked where I was and she would not have had a clue.

She croaked, "What's all the racket down here, child?"

On the other hand . . .

"Mistress Krine?"

"The noise, child. The noise. I heard it all the way upstairs. Do you have one of your men down here again?"

One of? Well. You devil.

"Mistress! I was only whispering to myself. I can't read the lettering on these spines. The gold flake is almost gone."

"And that's the project, isn't it? Find the volumes that need restoration? In future, restrain your expression of frustration . . . What was that? Is someone there?"

Not anymore. I was gone, down the back way to the back door, with less sound than a mouse on the run. I floated past the guard. His sleep remained untroubled.

What the *hell* was wrong with the Goddamn Parrot today? He just blew the opportunity of a lifetime. He hadn't made a whimper.

15

It was still daytime outside. I know because they took a couple of bars of sunlight and tried to drive my eyeballs out the back of my head. It wasn't morning anymore, but it looked like one of those days when the rest of the world would insist that it stay morning all day long.

Once the pain faded, I surveyed the immediate area. The library stands amid an infestation of official buildings, both municipal and royal. Traffic is different there, being made up mostly of functionaries. I saw nothing unusual—which meant only that I couldn't see any watchers.

I headed out.

The afternoon remained so relentlessly pleasant that I began to give in despite the state of my head. Infected by a lighter mood, I paused at the Chancellery steps to listen to the crackpots rave. Any wacko with a goofball grievance or a fanciful cause can use those steps as a forum. Never kindly, the rest of us use them as free entertainment. I know some of the less bizarre, habitual speakers. In my line, knowing people is a major asset. I didn't nurture my contacts enough anymore. Today I didn't have time. I gave Barking Dog Amato a thumbs up and dropped a groat into his cup, waved to a couple other howlers. I moved on. My head throbbed. My parrot never cracked his beak. The Dead Man must have destroyed his brain.

Around and down and off for the south side. I wasn't going to like this thing because of all the walking. There are less strenuous ways to get around, but none faster. Even the great wizards with their big coaches and running footmen and outriders and trumpeters can't get around as fast as a man on foot. Walking, you can cut through alleys and climb over fences.

I didn't shortcut much. I don't climb unless I have to, and alleys often harbor people or prospects best left unchallenged. Still, when the choice is a hundred yards straight or half a mile around . . .

I had used Slight Alley often. A lot of people do. It stays relatively clean. Heavy traffic discourages both squatters and the forces of free-lance socialism. It is difficult to manage what is essentially a privacy-oriented one-on-one transaction when at any time somebody troublesome may wander between you and your . . . er . . . client.

I risked Slight Alley.

The ramshackle frame half-timber structures popular in the neighborhood leaned in overhead, reaching out to one another like drunks in need of mutual support. Most of the afternoon's intense sunshine failed to penetrate, but there was more light than normal. The paving bricks were cleaner than usual, too. You could see their dark red. On the other hand, there were squatters in residence. Not only the ratmen you expected, but families of refugees.

The times they change.

I wondered how we would feed all the immigrants. If racist groups like The Call had their way, the refugees would eat the dwarves and ogres and elves already here.

I stopped. "What?" I had caught a strange smell. There was no describing it. It was neither awful nor particularly pleasant. Mostly it was startling.

It was gone in an instant. I couldn't catch it again. Happens all the time. I resumed walking, ignored the sleepy-eyed stare of a drunken ratman trying to decide if I was behaving strangely.

I was. At the first hint of the unusual my hand had darted to Magodor's cord. My habit is to face sudden threats with an eighteen-inch oaken nightstick into which has been introduced, by way of providing additional encouragement to the customer, a pound of lead at the business end.

Slight Alley has a couple of jags and an offset where it crosses another alley stretching east and west. I noticed that the light had a golden, autumnal cast. Though diffuse, it sent shadows crawling over the walls. Some of those seemed to assume almost recognizable shapes.

Then there were the whispers behind me, like the whispers of mocking children, perhaps speaking a foreign tongue. I felt a lot better when I reached a real street filled with real people.

As I hurried the last mile, I tried to think of somebody I knew in the religion racket who wouldn't run me off on sight. Most religious leaders are paranoid about their privacy. They feel especially threatened if they suspect an investigation of their finances. They have me run off just on the chance somebody might want me to check them out.

Playmate was the only religious character I knew. And he was just a wannabe preacher.

Then how about somebody who would answer my questions in order to get rid of me? Somebody who had no use for me at all. I tried to recall who all had been involved that time that Maya and I had straightened out the feud between the Church and the Orthodox over their missing Terrell Relics.

Hell. I didn't even have useful *enemies* down in the Dream Quarter.

I hit the Street of the Gods farther to the west than I had planned, but Slight Alley had given me a case of the willies. There was no reason not to feel safe now. The Dream Quarter is the safest neighborhood in town.

I hustled past Chattaree and other huge places belonging to successful cults, recalled from past cases. Back then, though, I was dealing with flawed holy men, not the gods themselves. What was Maya doing now? I could ask Dean in a few days. He would know. They stayed in touch.

The weather must have melted the stone hearts of the older priests because the acolytes and postulants and what-have-you were all out fluttering like mayflies. The scenery was positively brilliant around the female-oriented temples.

The first four or five people I approached had not heard of either the Godoroth or the Shayir. Farther east I got a couple of bewildered "I ought to know what you're talking about but don't" responses, like the guy seven and a half feet tall, pale as death, wearing a black robe and lugging an ivory staff topped by an angry cobra's head. This character had no more meat on him than a skeleton. He mused, "Shayir? Those the people with the squid gods?"

"I don't know." Squids? I'm not even fond of mortal cephalopods, let alone many-armed critters with delusions of being masters of the universe.

"No, wait. Those are the Church of the Nameless Unspeakable Elder Outer Darkness From Beyond the Stars folks. I'm sorry. I should know, but I don't. But you're headed in the right direction. They must be right on the bottom end, ready to fall into the river."

How you going to learn anything when nobody knows anything?

I thanked him, accepted a small card good for one admission into one of his snake-worshipping services, said I sure would stop by, I just plain loved snakes. The bigger the better. I had a few for breakfast in the islands.

He guaranteed me they had a serpent that was a genuine kick-ass god snake big enough to snack on horses.

"Excellent idea. Round them all up and let him get fat." Then feed him to the ratmen.

A block later I met a guy who knew about both cults. He was a free-lance guide and street sweeper. He did little odd jobs, and the temples fed him scraps and let him sleep in warm spots out of the way, as long as he didn't spook the marks. He was raggedy around the edges, so probably didn't get a lot of work at the high end of the street.

"Name's No-Neck," he told me, proud of the fact that once upon a time folks thought enough of him to hang a nickname. "Had a little muscle on me when I was young."

"I figured. Marine?"

"Hey! Fugginay! How'd you know?"

It might have been the tattoos. "You can always tell a Marine. Got that special attitude."

"Yeah. Ain't dat da troot? You too, eh?"

"First Force." I added the years, so he would know there was no chance we had acquaintances in common. I hate it when people play that game. They find out you are from a particular neighborhood, whatever, they spend an hour asking do you know this one or that like all you ever did with your life was keep track in case somebody asked.

"Good. Dat's good. You come wit' me. I show you where dey hang. What you say you want to know for?"

"I didn't, No-Neck. But I'm supposed to check up on some changes going on down here." I told him about the Antitibet cult coming in.

"Yeah, yeah," he said. "I'm gonna help wit' da moving. Dese here Dellbo priests from da Cantard, you ask me, dey got no business taking over from honest TunFairen gods, but rules is rules and the gods made dem demselfs. You can only have so many temples and stuff or pretty soon you lose control and have dem loony churches wit' only tree members where nutsos worship killer radishes and stuff."

I am no heartbreaker, so I didn't let him know there were some off-Street storefront temples where minuscule congregations really did worship holy rutabagas and snails and whatnot. If the mind of man can come up with a screwball god, however bizarre, a god will arise to answer that lunatic appeal. At least in the imagination of man.

Many of the nonhuman species have their religions, too, but they do not go for diversity and cuckoo. Only us humans need gods crazier than we are.

And we are the future of the world. The other races are the fading past.

Makes you wonder if there isn't a god of gods with a really nasty sense of humor.

16

For a couple of sceats No-Neck showed me both the former Shayir temple and the Godoroth.

"Couple of real dumps," I said. "Tell me what you know about these gods." Thought I would catch him while he had a grateful glow on. I glanced around. Once you have experienced Chattaree it is hard to imagine such squalor.

"Cain't tell you jack, pal. Wisht I could. But it ain't smart even ta name names, like Strayer, or Chanter, or Nog the Inescapable. Dey is nasty as hell, all a dem."

"That's no surprise."

The Shayir and Godoroth were competing for the last hovel on the Street. It was beyond the levee, leaned out over the river on rotting piles fifteen feet tall. One good flood surge and it would be gone. But it was home to the Godoroth, I guess, and nobody wants to get kicked out of their own house.

No-Neck told me, "Bot' places is closed down. Dey'll open back up in a couple days."

"Under new management?"

No-Neck frowned. He didn't have a lot of brain left over to untangle jokes and decipher sarcasms.

I asked, "Any reason I can't go in and look around?" There were no physical locks on the doors.

"You'd be trespassing."

Right on top of it, my man No-Neck.

"I wasn't planning to touch anything. I just want to see the setups. For my client's information."

"Uhm." He focused his intellect, frowning, investing heavily for a small return. The No-Necks of the world are great for getting work done as long as they have somebody to tell them what to do.

"I don't tink I unnerstand what you do."

I explained, not for the first time since we teamed up. I said, "It's like being a private soldier. A client hires me, I'm his one-man army, except I don't bust heads or break arms, I just find out things. The client I have now wants to find out as much as he can about these two cults."

No-Neck made a connection. "Like dat might be somebody what has to help decide who gets dat last temple."

"There you go." Far be it from me to disabuse a man of an erroneous intuition. Not that he was entirely off the mark.

"I guess it cain't hurt. You ain't involved wit' dem. If you was involved wit' dem I'd hafta raise a holler on account of some of dese gods would do any damned ting to stay on da Street."

"Ain't dat da troot." If you are big time, going off with the holy rutabagas won't get you no respect at all. Better gone than playing out of the Dream Quarter.

"Well, den let's look in dat dere place where da Shayir got bounced. But I guarantee you ain't gonna see nuttin' exciting."

We went into the Shayir place. Always quick on the uptake, I muttered, "Not going to find anything exciting here."

"Cleaned it out." No-Neck had a trained eye, too.

The dump was as bare as a thousand-year-old thunder lizard thigh bone, emptier than No-Neck's head. He said, "We done took all da stuff down to da place at da end. Goin' ta paint and fix up here."

I glanced right. I glanced left. I didn't stand all the way up because the ceiling was too low. The place was barely fifteen by twelve, last stronghold of an ancient religion, first bridgehead of a new one. It seemed touched by the same sad desperation you see in middle-aged men and women who can't let go of a youth that has long since stolen away.

"So let's stroll over there and count the silver."

"Silver? Dese is small gods, Garrett. Dey probably didn't even have no copper. Down here dey're da kind we call pewter gods. Petty pewter gods. Da pot metal boys." He leaned close, ready with a garlicky confidence. "You never say dat where dey might hear you, dough. Da fard'er dey slip da more dey demand respect, got it coming or not. You go on up dere to da high end of da Street, dem gods you don't never see no proof dey even exist. Dey ain't got time to be bodered. Down here, dough, dey might be running deir own bingos. And you better not cut dem where dey can hear it."

That sounded like a notion worth keeping in mind.

"I been front wit' you, Garrett. Tell me something straight."

"I'll try."

"How come you got dat stupid stuffed bird on your shoulder?"

The Goddamn Parrot. T. G. was being so good I'd forgotten him. "He isn't stuffed. He's just pretending." What the hell. I plucked the bird and studied him as we climbed crumbling steps on the face of the levee. They were the conclusion of the Street. No repairs had been offered them in recent lifetimes. The smell of river mud hung like an all-pervading mist. The air was thick with the flies that breed in the mud. They were nasty, hungry little flies.

The Goddamn Parrot was breathing, but his eyes were milky. "Hey, bird. Show some life. Got a man here wants to hear one of your jokes."

That flashy jungle chicken didn't make a sound.

"Just like a kid, eh?"

"How's that?"

"Clever as he can be when dere's nobody dere but you. Clams if you want him to show off." Maybe No-Neck was not as dense as he let on.

"You got it. Most of the time you got to hold him under water to shut him up. Got a mouth like a dock walloper. Gad! This place is a dump." The Godoroth temple hadn't been cleared, the movers had just piled the Shayir stuff inside where it could be unpacked or chunked in the river if things turned out that way. All the rats and roaches and filth were still on the job. No broom had gotten past the threshold any year recently. Definitely a place with character.

No-Neck chuckled. "Way I hear, da Godoroth got only one worshipper left, some old goof on the Hill wit' so much juice he's kept dem on way past dere time already. Say he was around when dey built dis burg. Been in a wheelchair more dan tirty years."

"And the gods won't sully their fingers cleaning up around here."

"You got it. Won't even run a message to dis dink when I want to offer to take care of da place for a reasonable retainer."

"Sounds like they're their own worst enemies." I put the Goddamn Parrot back on my shoulder. All that vulture was going to do was breathe.

"You just said a mout'ful. I been working da Dream Quarter twenty-eight years. You tink people fool demselves, you hang out down here, see what da gods do."

"You actually see them?"

He gave me a funny look. "You don't know much about how tings work here, do you?"

"No. I'm perfectly happy to let the gods ignore me, same as I ignore them."

"You cain't see dem. Not unless'n dey done gone to a lot of trouble to touch you, or you been working here a long time, like me. Den you maybe see shadows and glimmers or hear whispers or get chills and the willies. We could have a whole gang of dem standing around here right now. . . . Well, way I hear, dey wouldn't actually be standing. Shapes like dem little idol tings, dat's what dey might do if dey decided to come out and be visible a while."

I picked up a statue that had to be Magodor. Maggie was not a pretty girl. Her idol had more snakes, more fangs, more arms and claws than she had shown me. "How would you like this for a girlfriend?"

"Way da myts go, I wouldn't get dat close. Dat one's like a spider. Any mortals what do survive her, dey say she ruins for any mortal woman."

I examined one statuette after another. The ugly guys were even uglier, too. "Fun-looking bunch."

"Dem idols don't do dem justice, what da myts say."

"Bad?"

"Very. But dis one, she's da one I dream about. Call her Star."

"I've heard about her. I know what you mean. What about the boss couple? Imar and Imara? Big and dumb is my impression."

"Imar is your old-time always-pissed-off kind of god, real pain in da ass, loves da smell of burnt flesh, which is maybe why da Godorot' don't got dat many worshippers anymore."

"How about the Shayir? I know nothing about them. Who are they? How many of them are there? They have any really special attributes? Are they different from other gods? These Godoroth, overall, aren't anything special. There are gods or saints like them in most religions."

"Da Shayir ain't dat unusual neither. Well, Torbit the Strayer and Quilraq the Shadow, dey're weird. And Black Mona. But da All-Father god is Lang. He probably hatched out of da same egg as Imar. Dey even look alike."

No-Neck was not shy about digging in the boxes filled with Shayir relics. I wondered if he had rummaged through them before, supplementing his income. "Here. Here's all da idols." He held up one that did look just like the Imar idol up where the altar was.

"Let me see that." I upended Lang, probably an act of deadly disrespect. Sure enough, there was a dwarfish hallmark on the base, along with a date. That was dwarfish, too, but no mystery. Most scholars use the dwarfish dating system because human dating is so confusing, especially back a few centuries when every petty prince and tyrant insisted on setting dates based on his own birth or ascension.

I handed Lang back, went to the altar. The dust was thick. I sneezed, grabbed Imar, treated him with the same lack of respect that I had shown Lang. "Well. What do you know." Imar had the same hallmark and some of the same mold markings, though an earlier date. I could see the dwarves snickering. Stupid humans. Maybe there were thirty gods in the Dream Quarter who all looked exactly alike.

I wished I knew a good theologian. He could tell me how much a god's idol influenced his shape and attributes. Be funny if the gods headed downhill were on the skids because some mass-market idols of dwarfish manufacture didn't distinguish the little quirks that made an Imar an entirely different menace from a Lang.

"Can you read?" I gave a thousand to one in my mind.

"Never had da time to learn." I win. "Even when I was down to da Cantard and dey was trying to teach guys, just to keep dem out of trouble in da waiting time, I never got da time. How come you ask?"

"These idols came out of the same workshop. Out of the same mold. If you could read I'd ask you to look through the records, maybe find me something there."

No-Neck snickered. "You gonna tip me a reasonable tip for helping you out, Garrett?"

"Yeah. After I finish looking through this Shayir stuff." The Shayir were rich compared to the Godoroth. And even homelier, if their idols were accurate.

"You give me a good tip, you come on over to Stuggie Martin's, we can toss back a couple. I'll tell you how silly dis all gets around here sometimes."

"Sounds like a winner. If Stuggie Martin can draw a decent pint of dark."

"Top o' da line. Weider's."

Wouldn't you know?

17

After a few mugs, No-Neck and I had become friends for life. I told stories about my more outrageous cases. He told tales about his war days. I told stories about mine. Now that their hell is far enough away, I find that there are some memories worth saving. No-Neck told stories from his years in the Dream Quarter, and we giggled and laughed till the proprietor asked us to keep it down or do a stand-up so the whole place could enjoy our good humor. Sourpuss. Surprise! His name wasn't Stuggie Martin. The real Stuggie Martin did own the place once upon a time, but nobody living remembered him. It was easier and cheaper to stay Stuggie Martin's than it was to get a new sign.

All that fun and the Goddamn Parrot never horned in once. It was unnatural. I was beginning to wonder. Everybody in Stuggie Martin's thought he was some kind of half-alive affectation till I got him his own mug.

I was a little dizzy and it was getting shadowy outside when I told No-Neck, "Man, I got to get going. My partner will be having fits. Da way dis ting scopes out, I can't afford time to have a good time." It *was* time to get away. I was starting to talk like him.

The Goddamn Parrot was on the table, working on his beer, showing more signs of life than he had for hours. The bird was partial to the Weider Dark, too, which is all I can say positive about that animate feather duster.

What had the Dead Man done? That devil bird talked in his sleep.

Something was going on, I didn't have any idea what, and so what else was news?

An attraction that made Stuggie Martin's a popular and upscale neighborhood hangout was an actual real glass window that let its patrons see the street outside. The window had lattices of ironwork protecting it inside and out, of course, and those didn't enhance the view, but you could watch the world go by. The name of the street out there was regional, after a province, typical of that part of town. I wouldn't remember it or be able to find it again, but that didn't matter. What did matter was that when I glanced out the window into the provincial street, amidst evening's shadows and oddly golden light, I spied that damned redhead whose twitching tail had lured me into this mess in the first place. She had taken station in a shadow across the way. The light didn't play fair. She stood out like a troll at a fairy dance contest.

I beckoned Stuggie's current successor, who had proven a fair keeper of the holy elixir, if short on good humor. "You got a back way out of here?"

He glanced at No-Neck, who put his seal of approval on me with a nod. "Sure. The back door."

Will wonders never cease?

I sucked down my beer, planted the Goddamn Parrot on my shoulder, said good-bye to No-Neck, scarfed the rest of the bird's beer and headed out. My navigation was unstable but under control. I looked forward to getting home and taking a nine-hour nap. I was a little less than fully alert. For some reason I had become preoccupied with significant persons not of the male persuasion. That can be the downside of a few good mugs. You start thinking about serious stuff and don't pay enough attention to what is happening around you.

I slid along the alley feeling totally cunning. If anybody was after me they would be watching the front door. Autumnal light illuminated the walls of the alley. Shadows played. I didn't pay much mind. It was late in the day.

I slipped around a corner, said "Awk!" at the same

time as the Goddamn Parrot, pranced to one side and started running.

A guy had been waiting for me. He looked more human than troll or giant, but he was twelve feet tall and carried an axe with a handle as long as me. It had a bizarre double head, *big* curved blades, some kind of runes worked into the metal, a spike on the end of the handle. The handle itself looked like ebony or ironwood also deeply worked with runes. Some were inlaid with paint or metal. The guy had a wild long red beard and, probably, equally wild hair, but his head and the top half of his face were hidden inside an iron helmet that Dean could have used for an oven. He must have ridden in on a dragon or a big blue cow.

Maybe he didn't want me annoying his sister, following her around.

His clothes were not the height of fashion. Oh, maybe a thousand years ago, when people lived in caves and the badly-cured-hides look and smell was in. But not today, brother.

I had a hunch he was what I had smelled on my way down to the Dream Quarter.

The Goddamn Parrot came to life now. He flapped away. He squawked something outrageous at the big thing, distracting him for the moment I needed to get my rubber legs pumping. I banged into somebody. "What's the matter with you, buddy?" I was lucky. He was just some guy headed home from work, who hadn't had a bad day and was not in a belligerent mood.

"Sorry." I glanced back. The big character was slapping at the Goddamn Parrot like the bird was some annoying insect and his axe was a flyswatter. I probably couldn't have lifted the damned thing. He got a fix on me and started getting all that beef organized to head in my direction.

"Maybe keep an eye out where you're going." The working stiff headed right for the monster man, obviously not seeing a thing.

"Oh my," I told me. "I guess I just met one of the

Shayir." I kept on moving as fast as wobble legs would allow.

Shadows and golden light ran with me. I suspected that meant something that might not be good.

A woman stepped into my path, possibly another version of the redhead I had tracked when the world was simple and gods were just bad practical jokes on the credulous. I faked left, got her off balance, and cut right. The Goddamn Parrot ripped past, flapping all out and cussing his fool head off. I would've cussed myself but needed to conserve my wind. I juked around a startled dwarf peddler and his cart full of knives, hurdled a water trough, zigged around an extremely short, fat character who might have been the world's only bald and morbidly obese dwarf, banged into an alley, and did quick and wonderful things with my piece of rope. I vanished.

I tried to hold down the racket I made huffing and puffing as I worked my sack of invisibility back into the street and kept on moving.

The Goddamn Parrot screamed past again, not seeing me. Right behind him was the world's biggest owl. A shadow flickered past. I looked up. Another owlish overachiever cruised at a higher altitude, watching. Neither owl was real maneuverable. The Goddamn Parrot cut a tight turn. The owl behind him didn't make it. It banged into the side of a building, fell, looked foggy for a moment, like it was having trouble deciding what it wanted to be. The owl overhead took up the chase. It kept up easily on the straightaways.

Screeching like a sailor just awakening to find that last night's sweet luck not only had vanished with his whole fortune but had left him a nasty rash as a memento, T. G. headed for home, abandoning me to my fate again.

A gang gathered. The big character with the axe rumbled like a pissed-off volcano. The redhead stood by herself in some shadows and looked pretty. The fat bald dwarf guy looked puzzled. The owl that had hit the wall wobbled through the air, alighted, fuzzily changed into

a perky lovely who looked about seventeen and wore
nothing but thin lavender gauze. Golden light and
shadow coalesced to become a guy about seven feet tall
who was naked to the waist and from the waist down
was mostly shaggy brown fur and goatlike legs that
ended in hooves. He and the reformed owl must have
been in love. They couldn't keep their hands off one
another.

Nobody else could see them, but nobody walked
through them either. Not that there was much traffic
anyway. It seemed some message had gone out at an unconscious level and most humans were staying away.

The guy with the weird legs pointed to where I had
been when I slipped into my invisibility sack. I couldn't
hear what he said, but his gestures gave me the gist.

He had seen me disappear. They all understood my
limitations, obviously. They spread out and started feeling around for me. All but the young number. She
turned into an owl and flew away, not in the direction
the Goddamn Parrot had gone. My impression was that
she was going after reinforcements.

I couldn't outrun them without becoming visible
again, where I couldn't outrun them anyway. So I slid
into the damp under a watering trough and got uncomfortable. I would try to wait them out.

They were stubborn. I guess you become patient
when you are immortal. They knew I wasn't moving
fast or going far. Soon enough, too, I began to suspect
they were only interested in keeping me contained
while they waited.

That didn't boost my confidence.

An owl arrived. She misted down and became another
tasty delicacy wearing not much of anything. This was
not the same sweetmeat as before. This one wore a different shade of purple.

The blind guys on the street were missing one hell of
a show.

The faun guy—who actually bore only a passing re-
semblance to the faun tribesmen of the Arabrab
Forests—seemed to bear no prejudice against this owl

girl, nor she toward him. They engaged in a little heavy petting the others apparently failed to notice.

I began to study the lay of the land.

I wondered if the Goddamn Parrot had gotten away.

18

Soon I began to suspect that I had outwitted myself. I should have covered what ground I could. The Shayir lacked no confidence in the help that was coming.

I eased out of hiding, checked myself. Good. Mud had not clung to whatever surrounded me. I studied the Shayir. They had stopped poking and chattering, were looking out of the corners of their eyes or squinting like that might help them see me better. I guess they could sense that I was moving.

The first owl dropped out of the sky, changed, immediately started slapping the other girl away from the faun guy, who didn't apologize at all. The huge guy rumbled like a volcano getting ready to belch, waved his axe. The air shrieked. Passersby heard and looked around nervously. The owl girl relented long enough to deliver whatever message she carried. The others looked smug.

Big trouble, Garrett.

What could I do to fool them?

I didn't have a clue. Motion seemed the best course at the moment. I got over against a wall and drifted northward. Unlike the gods, I discovered, people who could not see me did not avoid me. Luckily, the guy I bumped was far gone. He mumbled an apology and stumbled on for another dozen steps before his jaw dropped and he looked around. I hoped the Shayir were not alert.

Just then some fool opened his front door but paused to yell back inside, reminding his missus of what a melonhead she was. The lady made a few pithy remarks by way of rebuttal. I took the opportunity to slide past the guy and invite myself into a tiny two-room flat that had to be the place where they made all the garlic sausage in the world. I felt a moment of sorrow on behalf of the couple who lived there. They hadn't had time to pick up after the Great Earthquake yet. You know how it is. The centuries just slip away. There was stuff in there that had mold growing on its mold.

The woman sprawled on a mat on the floor. That mat had been chucked out by more than one previous owner. She didn't care. She had one arm wrapped around a gallon of cheap wine while she soul-kissed its twin brother. She seemed accustomed to having invisible men move through the gloom around her. I positioned myself where I could watch the street through the peephole in the door, which was the only window that place had.

Right away I discovered that the skinny geek with wings on his head was peeking out of an alley half a block to the north. The Shayir spotted him about the same time, became agitated. The whole bunch surged toward that alley.

Winghead moved out.

The term "greased lightning" does not do him justice. He was a shadowy flicker moving between points. The weird herd rumbled after him, hollering and flailing bizarre weapons.

He had their full attention. I took my cue. I got out of my bag, so startling my roommate that she actually spilled a precious cup of wine. "Take it easy, lady. That stuff costs money." I waved good-bye, stepped into the street like her man before me, walked off like I was just another local going about his business. I made believe I had a stone in one shoe. That altered my way of walking.

It worked.

Three blocks later I could not see an immortal anywhere. I settled into a trot, headed for home.

With a whoosh Winghead settled in to jog beside me. "Thanks," I told him. He offered an enigmatic look and flickered into the distance ahead. He was not hard to track when you were behind him. He just dwindled fast.

I slowed to a pace that didn't mark me out from the crowd. I started feeling smug.

19

Owls have always been birds of ill omen, particularly when they fly by day. Owls were my first clue that I was, perhaps, premature in my self-congratulation. But the owls themselves were preceded by the uproar of a crowd of crows.

Crows are common, and they get rowdy when they get together, like teenage boys. They get triply rowdy when they find a feathered predator to pick on. Or two. Two familiar owls in this instance. And the crows were so numerous they attracted the attention of everyone in the street.

I listened to people talk. Nobody but me and the crows could see the owls. There was a lot of chatter about omens. It was a trying time. People would look anywhere for guidance. That ought to make religion and divination growth industries.

Maybe crows have better eyes than people, or maybe they just can't be fooled. Of course, they could be semidivine themselves. They and their cousins turn up in a lot of myths and religious stories.

They kept the owls on the move, which was dandy by me. They wouldn't have time for aerial spotting.

I continued my jog, wondering if I might not have done better running back to the Dream Quarter. I could have taken refuge in one of the big temples where these small-timers couldn't come after me.

I cut across Gravis Convent Market, where they had torn down an abandoned convent and used the brick to pave a square that became a flea market, thieves' market, farmers' market, haymarket, so people in the neigh-

borhood would not have to walk miles to do their
marketing. There must have been scandal and corruption involved, a construction scheme that fell apart, else
the square would have been gone long since. Corruption and scandal are always involved in any public works
scheme, sometimes so much so that they poison the
well.

The square sinks a little toward its middle, probably
settling where the convent's vast basements had been
filled with rubble. It is two hundred yards across. I was
about twenty yards in when old Jorken Winghead
zipped up. I was puffing heartily. He wasn't breathing at
all.

He suggested, "You should move faster."

A genius. I glanced back.

He was right.

"Good idea."

But not entirely practical. The square was packed ear
to elbow with buyers and sellers and pickpockets and
sightseers and people who just plain couldn't think of
anything else to do or anywhere else to go.

I glanced back again. Jorken was for sure right. New
players had come onto the pitch for the Shayir. A
woman on unicorn back, not wearing much but showing muscle tone on muscle tone, probably six and a half
feet talk, dark as eggplant, iron helmet with a crescent
moon up top, herself festooned with weapons and stuff.
Ropes. Nets. A falcon. Dogs cavorting around her
steed's legs, critters that looked like half wolf and half
whippet and were maybe big enough for dwarves to
ride.

Well. Your basic huntress goddess. Probably with a
list of nasty quirks, like most of the older deities. Ate
her firstborn, or whatever.

Amidst the barking and yelping and galloping another form stood out, something like a haystack of black
cloth with tails fluttering, dripping an occasional wisp of
dark smoke, more floating than running. I saw no limbs,
nor any face, but when I looked directly at it I staggered. A voice thundered inside my head. *Nog is inescap-*

able. The voice was like the Dead Man's, only with mental bad breath.

Jorken showed up again. He seemed exasperated by my lack of progress. "Follow me." He started to pull away but did keep it down to a mortal pace. The crowd parted for him without seeing him. I zipped along in his wake, making much better time.

The effort only delayed the inevitable.

20

The huntress wasn't thirty yards behind me when I fled the north side of the square. The voice in my head told me, *Nog is inescapable*. The black thing fluttered and flapped amidst the hounds. It seemed bemused by my attempt to get away.

I ducked around a corner and into a narrow breezeway, readying my magic cord as I went. Jorken didn't like that. He shook his head violently, snapped, "Don't!"

I popped into my sack of invisibility anyway and kept moving through the breezeway. There wasn't much light back there, but enough for me to see the huntress and her pets race past the breezeway. I chuckled. "There, Winghead." But Jorken had taken a fast hike, last laugh choking him.

The bundle of black appeared, hesitated, drifted into the breezeway behind me. The horsewoman returned. Her four-legged pals climbed over one another, trying to sniff out a trail that wasn't there. But everybody trusted Nog's nose. Or ears. Or whatever.

I kept humping that sack but never got out the other end of the breezeway. I was trying to slide into the cavity at someone's back door, without making a racket, when Nog caught up. I heard a slithering snakes sort of sound, like reptilian scales running over scales. Something like black worms, nightcrawler size, began oozing into the sack through the little hole left by the knot when I had closed up. The voice in my head reminded me, *Nog is inescapable*.

Old Nog knew his limitations.

Old Nog smelled pretty damned bad. I didn't get a chance to offer him any man-to-man advice on personal hygiene. Paralysis overtook me. I felt like a stroke victim. I was fully aware, but I couldn't do anything. Nog slipped back out the hole, content to leave me in the sack. I saw nothing that looked like hands or arms, but he took hold anyhow and dragged me back into the street, to the huntress. She leaned down, felt around, grabbed hold of my arm, hoisted me like I was a doll. She flipped me down across the shoulders of her mount. She let out an earsplitting shriek of triumph, hauled back on her reins. Her unicorn reared, pounded the air with huge hooves, then we were off at a gallop, hounds larking around the great white beast's pounding hooves, Nog the Inescapable floating alongside. Owls passed overhead, still fleeing the crows but finding a moment to send down hoots of congratulations. The huntress laid a silver-tipped arrow across her dark bow—weapon and shaft both just materialized in her hands. She sped the arrow. A monster crow became an explosion of black feathers. The missile flew on through, took a big turn, came back home. Mama snatched it out of the air, on the fly.

The crows got the idea. But they didn't back off entirely. Whither the owls flew they followed, waiting to flash in and rip a few more feathers off heavy wings. The owls were looking pretty ragged.

Not that I got a real good look, sprawled in that undignified position. But it was a long ride, out of the city completely, into the region of wealthy estates south of town. I don't like it out there. Every time I go I get into big trouble. This time didn't look like it would be any exception. I was in trouble before I got there.

I wondered why nobody remarked on me floating through the streets.

Along the way we accumulated the rest of the Shayir crew, some of whom had real trouble keeping up—especially that wide, stubby guy. None of his pals seemed inclined to make any allowances. Sweethearts, the gods.

21

The place was huge and well hidden by trees and a stone wall ten feet tall, a quarter mile before you got to the house itself. There were guards at the gate, in keeping with the spirit of the times, but the gate stood open and they didn't notice our entrance. I realized that nobody saw me floating around because I was still inside that damned invisibility sack. All I had done was make their job easier for them.

It was dark when we reached the manor house. I couldn't see much of it from my position. I wondered if I would recognize it in the daylight. I wondered if I wanted to. I wondered if the Dead Man had any idea where I was or what was happening to me. I wondered why I was doing so much wondering lately.

The huntress dismounted, tossed her reins to a lesser deity of some sort who looked like a pudgy kid with the world's foremost collection of golden curls. She dragged me down and tossed me onto her shoulder. Into the house we went. The pudgy kid flew away on impossibly small wings, leading the unicorn.

I hit the floor on a bearskin rug in front of a merrily crackling fireplace at one end of a room they could have cleared of furniture to use as a ball field on rainy days. I lay there looking up at my captor, who was as beautiful as any woman I'd ever seen. But there wasn't an ounce of warmth in her. Cold as ebony. No sensuality whatsoever. I was willing to bet a mark she fell into the virgin huntress subcategory.

Nog crackled. The owl girls passed near the fire, as lovely as ever but sadly tattered. Hardly a thread re-

mained of their wispy apparel. In better times I would
have applauded the view.

The dogs, the stubby guy, the giant, all stood around
staring at the bearskin. I didn't think they were trying
to bring Bruno back to life.

I spied other faces great and small, humanoid and
otherwise, all with a definite mythological caste. Shadows played over the walls. The faun guy began consol-
ing the owl girls. A pleasant, avuncular sort of voice
said, "Might I suggest, Mr. Garrett, that as an initial
gesture you come forth from that pocket clipped out of
reality?"

I wiggled and rolled and looked at a guy who was sitting in a big chair, facing the fire. He had his hands extended to the flames as though he had a circulation
problem. He did look enough like Imar to be his
brother. Maybe Imar's smarter twin brother, since he
could articulate a civilized sentence.

Straining and groaning—I do not recommend horses
in any form as transportation—I wobbled to my feet
and fumbled with my cord till I was able to step out
into the room with my hosts. None of them seemed interested in the cord. I made it disappear, hoping nobody
would have second thoughts.

But why should they care? They had Nog, god of lit-
ter piles.

"I apologize for the less than genteel means by which
you were brought here, Mr. Garrett. You have made it
difficult to contact you."

I stared for maybe fifteen seconds. Then I said, "I
guess you're not one of them."

"One of what?" Puzzled.

I waved an inclusive hand. "The Shayir pantheon."

He frowned.

"I've never heard of a god who has manners, let alone
one who treats mortals with respect."

Shadow touched his face. It wasn't one of the shadows that infested the place, it was a shadow from
within, a shadow of anger. "Would you prefer to be
treated the way you expect?"

I am, I thought. "Actually, I'd rather not be treated at all. I ignore you, you ignore me, we're no problem to one another."

"But you are a problem. Of the worst sort. You threaten our existence. You cannot possibly expect us to overlook that."

I swallowed about three times. The guy in the chair projected a furious temper, restrained only with great effort. I must have some power in the situation, though I couldn't catch a whiff. "How am I a threat?"

"You have been enlisted by the Godoroth to find the Temple Key. That simple name doesn't tell you that the group who fails to take possession of it will perish."

"I think you got the wrong guy. I don't know anything about any Temple Key."

A whispering filled the air. Ice formed on my tailbone and crawled northward.

"Curious, Mr. Garrett. Torbit says you are only partially lying. But." He rambled through an eyewitness review of my visit with the Godoroth. Maybe he was Imar in a good mood.

I searched the crowd, trying to get a good picture of faces. The Dead Man would want every detail—if ever we met again.

I said, "You got all the details, then you know I didn't agree to do anything. I just slid on out of there."

"There was an implication. You did not refuse."

"Won't stand up in court. Duress and coercion." Which got me a blank look. Duress and coercion? Wasn't that what being a god was all about? You could make people do what you wanted? Weren't mortals toys?

He took it his own way. "Granted, you did not swear allegiance to the Godoroth. That is good. But why, then, were you on the Street of the Gods asking questions? Why were you visiting temples?"

"I was pretty sure it was a con of some kind. Those Godoroth characters didn't convince me that they were real gods. They just told me that they were. They hadn't shown me anything a clever conjurer couldn't manage." If you overlooked my magic rope. "I figured somebody wanted to set me up."

My audience stirred. Most probably didn't understand me. The guy in the chair had to mull it over before he got it. Give him that. He could step out of his own viewpoint. Not that he credited the mortal viewpoint with much value.

That chill whisper filled the air momentarily.

"It appears that, once again, you are telling most of the truth. Very well. I believe you understand the situation. Foreign gods have come to TunFaire. They have been awarded a place on the Street of the Gods. This means great inconvenience and dislocation for many gods, but for us and the Godoroth it means one group or the other has to go. For my part, I do not care to fall into oblivion."

"Me neither."

"You still believe you are being hoodwinked?"

"It's starting to look like the real thing."

"I want that key, Mr. Garrett."

"I'll say a prayer for you."

Teensy thunderbolts crackled at his temples. Maybe it was something I said. He regained control. "You fled from my friends. If you are not in the service of the Godoroth, why run?"

"Give them an eye, chief. Most of them look like nightmares come true."

More teensy thunderbolts flickered. I wasn't doing too good here. I looked around. Things moving in and out of the light *might* have lurked under my bed when I was a kid. This was a much bigger crowd than the Godoroth. And not real friendly. Bad cess to the infidel, I guess.

"Where will you look for the key?"

"I'm not interested in any key. I just don't want to be between gangs of divine sociopaths who have no interest whatsoever in my welfare."

Crackly whisper in the air. Stir in the crowd, which seemed larger every time I checked. They were not all nightmares, either. This pantheon was well supplied with attractive goddesses, not one of whom had trouble with her hair and all of whom had normal teeth and the usual complement of limbs.

I didn't need the whispers translated. Torbit the Strayer—whatever he, she, or it was—had reported the truth of my lack of interest. No grail quest for me. Forget that Temple Key. Garrett has no desire to save any holy bacon. I said, "I have friends in the beer business who do care and who do need my help. I'd rather be solving their problems."

"There is little time, Mr. Garrett. We need a mortal to rescue us. Our remaining worshippers are few and of little value because of their age. Belief is not a requirement. Free will is. I see no more likely candidate than yourself. You work for hire. We have resources beyond your imagining."

Yeah. Everything but loving followers eager to bail your asses out.

22

I'm sure I didn't say that out loud. Must have been my body language. Dumb, to be twitching and aggravating the gods like that.

The head guy growled, "Put him into the lockup room. Some time with his thoughts should help him develop a new perspective."

I liked my old one fine, but several unpleasant fellows disagreed. I had seen them on their day jobs as gargoyles. And not only did they have heads like rocks, they had muscles of stone as well. We took a vote. The majority elected to go along with Lang's plan for an attitude adjustment. They lugged me through the house, up various flights of stairs, past a scattering of antique humans who had no trouble seeing us and who kowtowed to anything that moved. My companions chucked me into a large closet containing one ragged stolen army blanket (I knew it was stolen; otherwise it would still be in the army), one feeble fat candle, and two quart jars, one full and one empty. I presumed I was to be the middleman between jars.

The door closed. I gathered I was supposed to ruminate and quickly conclude that signing on with the Shayir was preferable to the alternatives. At the moment it looked like that could be true. I might have gone with that option had I not become distracted.

The dust hadn't settled when the door popped open and the owl girls invited themselves in. They hadn't bothered finding fresh clothing. They had mischief in their golden eyes, and "Uh-oh!" was all I got to say before they piled onto me.

They weren't great conversationalists. In fact, I didn't get anything out of them but giggles. I did my best to remain stern and fatherly and aloof, but they just took that as a challenge. I am nothing if not determined in my pursuit of information, so I continued to ask questions while I endured the inevitable.

After a while I began to fear the interrogation would never end. Those two only looked like girls.

Then they were gone and I was collapsing into exhausted sleep while trying to figure out what that had been all about. They hadn't tried to worm anything out of me or to get me to promise a thing. They were very direct, very focused, and very demanding.

The door opened. The woman who had gotten me into this mess stepped inside. She was in her redhead phase, and a very desirable redhead she was. She sniffed. "I see Lila and Dimna have been here." Her observation was as neutral as a remark about the weather.

"I don't know what they wanted . . ."

"What they wanted is what they got. They are direct and simple."

"Direct, anyway."

"Simple." She tapped her temple. "You find this form attractive?"

"I'll howl at the moon." Though she made no effort, she exuded sensuality. "But that won't get you anything."

"You're sated."

"Got nothing to do with it. I'm being pushed and bullied. I don't take to that much. I get stubborn."

"You have to understand something. If the Shayir don't get what they want, neither do you."

"And the Godoroth will think the same, so I can't win. But I can stay stubborn and take everybody with me." Damn. I didn't like the sound of the slop gushing out of my yap. I don't know if I believed it. I hoped that Torbit thing wasn't listening.

"What do you want?" she asked.

"To be left alone."

"That isn't going to happen. And you know it. A sensible man would cut himself a deal."

"I've already referred to the fatal flaw that renders that idea specious. Based on the record, it's only reasonable to assume that you all will fail to keep your half of any deal. Promise the fool mortal all the gold and girls he can handle, tell him he gets to be ruler of the world and several provinces in hell as soon as he delivers this nifty key that will save some divine butts." Speaking of divinity of the foundation, she knew the nature of perfection. "When we're done we'll turn his mortal ass into a catfish or something."

"You're certainly a cynic."

"I didn't create myself."

She appeared thoughtful. "You may have touched on a real problem. I'll think about it." She looked straight at me, radiating that heat but not extending any invite.

"What?"

"You're a true curiosity. I've met believers, unbelievers, fanatics, skeptics, and heretics, but I don't think I've ever met a man who plain just didn't care." She did not, however, seem displeased by my indifference.

"I do care. I care a whole bunch about being left alone."

"Only the dead are left alone, Garrett."

"And even that depends on which gods they chose while they were alive."

"Perhaps, stubborn man." She left me with an enigmatic smile and a philosophical conundrum. She seemed content with my attitude.

TunFaire has innumerable clots of gods. Each bunch anchors a different belief system. Some of those are as crazy as pickled cats. If competing groups of gods, like the Godoroth and the Shayir, actually revealed themselves to mortals and confirmed not only their own existence but also that of their enemies, by implication, the existence of all the rest of the gods would be validated. In my skewed view it further implied that any given value or belief system must be just as true as any other.

Maybe I should start my own Church of the Divine Chaos. Everything is true and nothing is true.

I had no trouble with the idea that all the gods might be real. I'd always liked the notion that gods will exist as long as there is someone who believes they exist. The solidity of my intuition was now at the root of my difficulties. What troubled me was the possibility that the dogmas surrounding various really wacko religions might bear equal validity while there were true believers. If the general population reached that conclusion, there would be a big winnowing fast. Some belief packages just look a whole lot better than others. I would much rather kick off and fall into a paradise stocked with wild women and free beer than just become part of a ball of light or shadow, or become some dark spirit that necromancers would summon, or be gone to eternal torment, or, as had always been my personal suspicion, be just plain dead.

Deserved some thought.

23

I didn't get time. I had too much on my mind. And I kept getting interrupted by one god person after another, each with the same mission: convince Brother Garrett to scare up that precious key. I had several truly intriguing offers from a couple of goddesses who looked like I had made them up. Maybe I did, come to think. One side of me wished I had a really remote deadline so I could take advantage of all these wonderful offers.

I dozed off at last, started sighing my way through a marvelous dream wherein all these randy goddesses decided I should go in with them on starting a new paradise. We would forget all those stuffy, weird shadow lurkers and hammer pounders and generally unfun, gloomy-gus guy gods. Then the bane of my existence raised its ugly head once again.

Somebody tapped on my cell door.

Something buzzed like the world's biggest bumblebee. Voices clashed in whispers. The buzzard-size bee went away.

Somebody tapped on the door again.

I did not respond, probably because I was so amazed that anyone here would have the courtesy not to walk right in. I decided to play possum. I cracked an eyelid and waited.

The door opened.

This one was a girl. Surprise, surprise.

At first watery glimpse she seemed chunky and plain, and at second glimpse she seemed vaguely familiar. She had the glow of a peasant girl lucky enough to have enjoyed good health, with a body designed for serious work and frequent childbearing. As lesser gods went, she might be some sort of spring lamb or crop planting specialist.

She poked my shoulder. She was between me and the candle. Nothing insubstantial about her. My earlier visitors, however determined or enthusiastic, had not been entirely impervious to the passage of light.

I opened my eyes completely, startling the girl. I frowned. I did know her . . . Ah. She looked like a young version of Imara, Imar's wife. But the head god here looked like Imar, too. Maybe Lang had a kid. No! Hell. She was the girl from Brookside Park.

"What?" I asked.

She didn't seem to have in mind using woman's oldest tool of persuasion.

"Hush. I'm here to help."

"Funny. You don't look like any royal functionary I ever met." I touched her. She flinched. Earlier visitors had felt just as solid but had seemed awfully warm. This one was a normal temperature and lacked the absolute self-confidence the others had shown.

"You're mortal." Clever me. Now I was sure she was the girl I had seen in the park. The pixies had seen her, too.

"Half mortal. Come on! Hurry!" An angry buzz waxed and waned in the corridor outside. "Before they realize there's something happening outside their set pattern."

I debated it for a long time, six or seven seconds. "Lead on." I couldn't see her getting me into the hot sauce any deeper, whatever her scheme.

Sometimes you just got to roll the bones.

"Who are you? How come you've been following me? Why are you doing this?"

"Hush. We can talk after we get out of here."

"There's an idea I can get behind." And right in front of me was a behind I could get behind. She wore the peasant skirt again, whitish linen under a pale blue apron. I liked what I could see.

This mess had its aesthetic up side. I could not recall

ever having run into so many gorgeous females in such a short time.

So some were a little strange. We all have our moments of weird, and life is a series of trade-offs anyway.

Blonde braids trailed down the girl's back. "Wholesome" was the word that came to mind. Generally, wholesome is the last thing most guys find interesting. But . . .

She beckoned. I rose to follow. She opened the door a crack, beckoned again. I caught a bit of that buzzing racket again. It had an angry edge. Or perhaps it was impatience.

I don't think the Shayir ever posted a guard. I guess when you have a Nog on staff you don't much worry about prisoner escapes. Or maybe it was just divine hubris.

I wondered how my new pal planned to cope with the owl girls and Nog and his girlfriend with the dogs and weapons and no sense of humor.

"Come on!" She was intense but would not raise her voice above a whisper. Which was a good plan, probably.

She was flesh for sure. The floorboards creaked under her, ever so softly. They groaned under me. My earlier visitors had not made the house speak.

"This way, Mr. Garrett."

Her chosen route was not the one the Shayir had used when escorting me to my spacious new apartment. It was not the route I would have chosen to make my getaway. It led down a narrow hallway only to a small, open window. A chill breeze stirred the thin, dirty white cotton curtains there. Outside, an almost full moon slopped light all over and made the whole manor look like a haunted graveyard. Maybe it was. How were we going to deal with that?

There was a whole lot of buzzing going on out there, suddenly. Somebody said, "Come on, babe, getcher buns moving." Outside. Stories and stories up.

The girl went right out the window, indifferent to the fact that she was not dressed to play monkey on the wall. I stuck my head outside—and discovered that the big darling was not going downward. Gulp! What the? . . . Where was the rope? There wasn't any rope. I had expected a rope from the moment I'd realized her plan included us climbing out that silly little window.

Buzz overhead. I looked up in time to glimpse just a hint of movement vanishing behind the edge of the roof.

Meantime, the girl had gotten herself onto a ledge that was not much wider than my palm. She was sidestepping industriously, headed I couldn't tell where.

I then noted that the ledge was not a ledge as such. It was the top side of some kind of decorative gingerbread I could not make out because I wasn't out there in the moonlight. I drew a deep breath, meaning to tell the young lady that I preferred my adventures at low altitudes with solid footing. Somebody behind me spoke up first. "Here, now! You! Who are you? What are you doing there?"

The speaker was a real live human old man, possibly of the butler calling. He wore only nightclothes but was armed with one truly wicked-looking meat cleaver. A door stood ajar behind him. Feeble light leaked into the hallway. If he had pests in his room the way I'd had them in mine that might explain why he slept with kitchen utensils.

The old man didn't look like he was interested in conversation. He began slicing the air. I considered using my magical cord to climb down. But there was no time to stretch it. Nor did I see any handy place to tie it off.

Why not just jump? Falling would be less unpleasant than an encounter with a slab of sharp steel. The ground wasn't more than a mile down.

That bumblebee buzz whirred off the roof and dropped down behind me. "Why you want to waste your time on this candyass pug, sweetheart?" I caught a strong whiff of weed smoke.

I looked back. Floating behind me was a pudgy baby with a thousand-year-old midget's head. The critter wore what looked like a diaper but was actually a loin-cloth. "What you gawking at, Jake?" it snapped. And, "Get your lard ass moving." He yelled upward, "Hey, babe, this one's a fourteen-karat dud."

The critter carried a teeny little bow and a quiver of little arrows and had the world's biggest weed banger drooping from the corner of his mouth, smoulder-ing. Here was the source of the buzz. And of the weed stink.

I managed to stand myself up on that ledge. A dud, huh? Look here. Sometimes a military education *is* use-ful in civilian life. Watch me now.

The old man leaned out the window and took a swipe at me. Rusty iron dealt the air a deep, bitter wound en-tirely too close to my nose. For a moment it looked like pappy was going to come outside after me.

The buzz changed pitch. I glanced back but kept my feet moving. The little guy doing the floating and cuss-ing slapped a little arrow across his little bow and plinked the old man in the back of his meat-chopping hand. "Get moving, ya drooling moron!" he growled at me. "If you'd hauled your ass from the start they'd never have seen me."

"I wouldn't have missed you."

Sometimes it's wonderful to be young and dumb. A stunt like this would not have bothered me ten years ago.

About twenty feet from the window a bit of rope hung over the edge of the roof, which at that point de-scended to within eight feet of our footing. However, the roof did overhang us by several feet. Young and dumb, my new friend just leaped, grabbed the rope, clambered right up, skirt flying. Although he was busy cursing his wound, the old man caught that action. His eyes bugged more than mine did.

As the girl's feet vanished, the flying critter soared up after her with the same sort of ponderous grace you see in large flying insects, the sort of stately defiance of gravity of a thing that don't look like it ought to get off the ground at all. He filed various verbal complaints as he went. What a team the girl and I would make, her with her chattering whatisit and me with the Goddamn Parrot.

I shut my eyes, took a deep breath, considered the racket the old man was raising now, opened my eyes, offered the old boy a salute, took the plunge.

That sort of thing was all very well when I was nineteen and only one of a bunch of lunatics who tried to outdo one another in the face of an implacable enemy and almost certain premature death, but I was thirty now. I had a reasonably ordered and comfortable life. Well, sort of. Why the hell couldn't I remember the moments like this when Old Man Weider made one of his pitches aimed at getting me to work the brewery full time?

I grabbed the rope, found arm strength I had feared was not there anymore, scrambled toward the roof. No longer did I possess the liquid grace of youth, but I did manage to get the job done.

"Can ya believe it, toots? The wuss actually dragged his lead ass up here."

"Hurry!" The girl beckoned from the top of a slope of slate. "The alarm is spreading."

Wouldn't you know. I hurried. After bellying up twenty feet of steep and treacherously dew-slick slate, I dragged myself onto the flat part of the roof, which was large enough for a battalion's drill ground. You could farm there if you wanted to haul the soil up first. I got to my feet. The girl beckoned anxiously. Beckoning had to be her top skill. I got the notion this was going slower than she'd planned.

The flying baby with the hallucinogenic stogie watched sourly from the back of a horse big enough to haul ogre knights around. The little guy had wings sprouting out of his shoulder blades. They looked just about big enough to lug a pigeon around. I guess he had to work hard when he flew.

There were two horses. "Oh no," I said. "No. I've done all the riding I want for today." Me and horses never get along. My ribs informed me that Black Mona's mount had made every effort to ensure that my immediate future was one filled with misery. And that thing was only related to horses. Did I really want to escape badly enough to put myself at the mercy of these monsters?

"Look at this clown, babe. He don't . . ."

"Please stop horsing around, Mr. Garrett." The girl was exasperated.

"You don't understand. They have you fooled."

The house shuddered underfoot. Somebody big had begun to stir downstairs.

"See ya later, Sweet Buns." The little thing's wings turned into a blur. He buzzed off into the night.

I started climbing the one horse that didn't already have a blonde on top. It was a monster the color of old ivory, maybe even big enough to haul a troll into battle. For a while there I thought I would need ropes and pitons to make it to the top.

I completed the long climb. I swung my right leg over, was pleased to discover that the horse and I both had our heads facing the same direction. The extra altitude gave me a fine view of the roof.

The roof?

It occurred to me that I was about make my getaway on horseback from a rooftop. How far could I get? Was I the victim of an all-time practical joke? I do have friends who would consider this kind of situation a real howler.

I didn't see anybody standing around snickering behind his dirty elven hand.

I didn't have any friends who would, or for that matter could, spring for the cash a setup like this would cost.

The girl howled like a merry banshee. The child was happy. She kicked her horse in the ribs. It took off down the roof, chasing the baby whatisit. My horse was exactly as treacherous as I expect every equine to be. He took off, chasing his pal, without ever consulting me.

24

Those goddamned horses were stupider than I thought. They decided to race. The girl's mount had shorter legs but a head start. When mine got up to speed it started to gain. All I could do was howl and hang on as my brave but terminally stupid steed pulled even. The girl grinned at me and waved.

We ran out of roof.

Neither horse blinked. Neither horse slowed down either, though they did angle away from one another at the last second.

The shapeshifting started well before the leap into space, but it was only as we ran out of roof that I noticed it. In scant seconds huge wings burst from my mount's shoulders. Those broad shoulders narrowed dramatically. The beast's whole back slimmed down until it was barely wider than a trim woman's waist. All that bulk turned into wings. Those great wings hammered the air.

I hoped my whimpering wasn't loud enough to hear.

We climbed toward the moon. The girl's laughter tumbled back toward the manor like the tinkle of celestial windchimes. Possessed by the confidence of youth, she thought we were safely away. I was too busy not falling off to worry about owls and fluttering shadows and whatnot.

We went up and up till all TunFaire lay sprawled below us, more vast than ever I had imagined. To my right the great bend of the river shone like a silver scimitar in the moonlight. Lights blazed everywhere, for the city never sleeps. It boasts almost as many nocturnal inhabitants as daytime ones. It is several cities coexisting in the same place at the same time. It changes faces with the hours. Only in the hour before dawn is TunFaire ever more than coincidentally quiet.

I buried my hands in horse mane and hung on for dear life. I didn't pray, though, if that was what they were trying to get me to do. Soon I became engrossed in that remarkable view of the city I call home. When I saw it from up there I didn't wonder that half the world wanted to come here. From up there you could see only the magnificence. You had to get down on the ground to capture the stench and filth, to see the pain and poverty and cruelty, the irrational hatreds and the equally mad occasional senseless acts of charity. TunFaire was a beautiful woman. Only when you held her close and buried your face in her hair could you see the lice and scabs and fleas.

Not even in my most bizarre dreams had I ever drifted above everything like some great roc of darkness. I boggled while moonshine turned reservoirs into glimmering platters and drainage ditches into runes of silver. The earth seemed to wheel as the animals turned in flight. Amazing! My hands were cramped from holding on so tight, but I knew only the awe.

The girl shrilled, "Isn't this wild, Mr. Garrett?"

"Absolutely." I would tell her that Mr. Garrett was my grandfather after I got my feet back onto solid ground.

I looked back the way we had come. Trouble, if it was after us, was not yet close enough to pick out of the night. Trouble was sure to follow, though. That could be the title of my autobiography. *Trouble Follows Me.* Though usually it ambushes me. I wondered if Nog was capable of tracing me through the air.

The girl let rip a wild yodel, swung one hand violently overhead. Lilac and violet sparks flew off her fingers. Her mount pointed his nose down. He plunged toward the earth.

Mine followed. "Oh, shit!" The bottom fell out.

Mine wanted to race again. TunFaire hurtled toward me, getting less enchanting by the second.

My stomach stayed back up there among the stars. Good thing I'd had no supper. We would be racing it to the ground, too.

The winged horses actually descended in a great circle, tilting slightly, moving their wings no more than buzzards on patrol. The streets and lights turned below. Soon I could make out individual structures, then individual people, none of whom looked up. People seldom do, and I take advantage of that fact occasionally, but seeing my world from the back of a horse cruising above the rooftops gave that concept new dimension.

My fright had ebbed. I was thinking again. I was proud of me. I wouldn't have to change my underwear. I must be getting used to these bizarre adventures.

What were these winged horse things? What was the little flying thug in the diaper? He was around somewhere. I couldn't see him, but his voice carried altogether too well. The only place I had seen their like was in old paintings of mythical events.

Unicorns, vampires, mammoths, fifty kinds of thunder lizards, werewolves, and countless other creatures often deemed mythical I had seen with my own eyes. Too often they had hammered bruises into my own flesh. But these flying horses and the bitty bowman constituted my first encounter with a class of critters I thought of as artists' conventions. Symbols. These guys, griffins, ostriches, cameleopards, cyclops. All of them supposedly as uncommon as lawyers driven only by a need to see justice done.

We dropped lower. The horses glided wingtip to wingtip. The little guy buzzed, but I could not spot him. We seemed to be headed back into the heart of TunFaire, down toward Brookside Park.

I still had not gotten a name out of my demigoddess benefactor, nor did I have a ghost of a notion of her true motive for helping me. She offered up another amazing yodel. I began to fiddle with my amazing cord. We could amaze one another. "Hey, girl! Who are you?

You got a name or not?" There was a lot of wind noise in my ears, not to mention the powerful hum of the little guy's wings. I couldn't spot him no matter how hard I looked.

Crystal laughter rang out off to my right. It looked like the horses were thinking about landing. The girl was pulling ahead to go down first. "Call me Cat, Mr. Garrett. Bad Girl Cat."

"I like bad girls." I would have said more, but my throat tightened up. We were down so low the peaks of buildings with pointy roofs were at eye level. My mount started using his wings to slow down, but still structures whipped past at a speed beyond my imagining. I could not believe anyone could travel so fast and still be able to breathe.

My mount reared back and presented the entire undersurface of its wings to the onrushing air. We slowed violently, shuddering, air roaring. The beast's wings shrank. Its shoulders began to bulk up. Its speed dropped. Then it hit the ground galloping. And there was nothing upon its back. Or so I hoped the casual observer would conclude. The horse had to sense my weight.

I had strained my courage to its limits to get myself inside my sack of invisibility.

Actually, initially I pulled the noose up only to my armpits. I needed my arms free. Once the horse touched down and began slowing its run, it trotted in amongst some trees. It promptly lost two hundred pounds as I grabbed a sturdy branch. Oof! Rip the old arms out by the roots, why not?

I dropped to the ground, pulled the sack of invisibility over my head, moved along before my self-proclaimed rescuers had time to realize that I had disappeared.

Pixies laughed and yelled, "We saw what you did. We saw what you did." But if you were not listening for them they just sounded like sparrows complaining about having been wakened in the middle of the night.

25

"Mr. Garrett? Where are you? Are you all right? Answer me if you can."

I could but I didn't. She could not be sure I hadn't fallen during our landing. Damn! If I had kept my mouth shut, if I hadn't asked her her name, she couldn't have been sure I hadn't fallen earlier, when she was having too much fun to concentrate.

The bumblebee whir of the runt's wings came toward me, wordlessly putting death to my maunderings. He knew I hadn't fallen. He was on patrol now, running a slow search pattern. The little rat couldn't shut up. And everything he said was less than complimentary toward my favorite working stiff. Me.

To know me is to love me.

I headed for home full speed, encouraged by a racket behind me that suggested a welcoming party might have been waiting. Sounded like lots of folks were in a sudden bad mood, including a nation of pixies untimely rousted from their sleep. Over what sounded like a henhouse disturbed I heard Cat shout at one of her horses. She wanted to get airborne again.

The little winged guy buzzed up to within a few feet of me. He settled his plump rump onto the outstretched bronze palm of one of the few nonmilitary statues in the park. He had an arrow across his bow. His moonlighted expression said he meant to use it. "Know you're around here somewhere, Slick. Know you're close enough to hear. That was a nifty stunt, turning sideways to reality to give the kid the slip." Weed smoke had begun to cloud up around his head. He ought to be too

stoned to breathe. "But fun is fun, and I don't think
you're gonna have much more if you don't come in
now. You don't got no other friends."

I figured the Godoroth crew had tried to reel me in,
irked because I had been trafficking with the enemy,
and now they were triple irked because I had done a
fade. I considered taking advantage of my invisibility to
get a closer look at them. But I was worn out. I just
wanted to go home. Reason told me home was no safer
than out here, but the animal within me wanted to believe otherwise, wanted to slide into its den and lick its
wounds. I kept the sack of invisibility around me till I
was sure the flying runt had gotten lost.

I caught his buzz again as I was about to leave the
park. I stepped into deep shadow and froze. Thus I was
out of sight and motionless when two huge owls flapped
over moments later. Though they were talking owl talk,
the girls were bickering virulently.

I chuckled. To myself, of course.

Let them go butt heads with the Godoroth.

Knowing the Shayir were around put some extra hus-
tle into my step. Good thing, too. Wasn't long before I
began to feel a chill. It grew. I found another deep
shadow and shrank down into it. I was crouched there
when Abyss the Coachman floated across my backtrail
like a black, wind-tossed specter. Looked like he had
been sent to patrol the routes from the park to my
home.

Had that been set up ahead? Had they expected an
escape attempt?

You get paranoid.

I'd always thought gods were big on omniscience and
such. Maybe as your followers become fewer you have
less ability to draw on the power leaking over from the
old country. Certainly if either bunch had any way of
knowing things for themselves they would have no need
for me. And I wouldn't be running around loose.

Paranoia. I had a bad feeling that when the smoke
cleared and the earth stopped rocking and the dust settled, neither bunch would have much use for a mortal

pug who had gotten his nose into too many divine secrets.

Something to keep in mind.

I heard a rustling. It came from the south. It grew louder quickly. Nog? No. Not Nog the Malodorous. Marvellous. I crouched in another shadow. Something passed overhead like a flight of bats but was not bats. More like fluttering paper shadows in a big hurry, moving with great purpose, hunting. Might that be the thing called Quilraq the Shadow? I wasn't inclined to hang around and find out.

I stuck to alleys and breezeways that would not have been graced by my presence at any other time. I even crossed the Bustee, the deadliest slum in town, where nine of any ten inhabitants would have cut my throat for the shoes I was wearing and the gods themselves would walk in peril. Twice I turned to Maggie's wonderful cord to fend off overeager shoppers. That was one handy tool, but I was getting reluctant to use it. It could be no coincidence that every time I did one of the Godoroth turned up soon afterward.

No exception in the Bustee, either. Each time it was one of the ugly guys that came, too, like the Godoroth knew those mean streets well enough to send only their meanest and most expendable. The streets emptied quickly after that, even though the locals could not see what was scaring the bean sprouts out of them.

I tried to see the bright side. The Shayir were not turning up at the same time. They were, apparently, only running random patrols in areas that interested their opponents.

The ugly guys were not Nog. Nor were they especially powerful other than in the scary department. I ducked and dodged them with little difficulty. On the other hand, I suspected everyone now had a solid idea of where I was headed. Whole platoons of divine beasties might be setting up camp near my house.

Owls and paper shadows, flying horses and flying babies who smoked weed crisscrossed the night, possibly taking their bearings from Godoroth on the ground. It was a wonder they didn't collide.

I changed course the minute I cleared the Bustee, skirting its eastern edge as I headed north. I mean, what would Mrs. Cardonlos say if I brought this all home and the gods themselves started duking it out in Macunado Street?

It seemed a better strategy would be to go where the gods wouldn't look, then stay put till their deadline passed. Put them all out of business.

Faces and figures flickered through my memory. Such a pity I couldn't pick and choose. There were some divine ladies amongst those gods, and the world might become a lesser place for their absence.

26

I drifted more than a mile north and east of my original course. I attracted no attention but never made up my mind where to go, either. Then I changed my mind.

This was like being back in the Corps. The people in charge didn't know what they were doing. I cussed the guy giving me orders. I told me to shut up and do what I was told.

I'd decided that I did have to go home. I needed to see the Dead Man. He needed to know what had become of me. Maybe he could find a thread of sense in this madness. There was more going on than I had been told, and I still had only a glimmering of the rules of the game I was being forced to play.

Surely both god gangs had my place staked out. I needed to draw them away. So give them a sniff of the false trail, Garrett.

Out came that cord. I turned it into a poking stick and swished it around, relaxed it and trotted a third of a mile northeast, toward TunFaire's northernmost gate, then I played with the rope in an alley infested with snoring drunks. I hurried on, used the cord one last time on the street that leads directly to the gate.

TunFaire's gates all stand open all the time. Only once had they closed, when some thunder lizards from the north had been ravaging the countryside. A guy with the need could make a high-speed exit anytime of the day or night. I suspected the gates would be of particular interest to the new secret police.

The street to and from the northeastern gate is always busy. I tied my rope around my waist and plunged into traffic headed south. I didn't think the Godoroth and Shayir, busy tripping over one another, would become sure of where I wasn't for a good while yet.

My plan worked like they write them up in a book. For a few minutes.

I was preoccupied. The texture of the night changed, and I failed to notice because there were no mad little gods weirding around me. The street grew quiet and tense and the crowds thinned out, but I caught on only after a howl arose ahead and I discovered the street blocked by a bunch of guys carrying angry red-and-black banners. They were armed with clubs and staves and were whipped along by drums and trumpets. They sang some really vicious racist song.

Startled, I stopped to take stock.

More human rights guys came from cross streets. They appeared to have a specific objective, attainment of which required the physical battery of everyone in their way, human or otherwise. It seemed that, for the purposes of the moment, anybody not actively marching with them was deemed to be against them.

People on the street fought back. The nonhumans went at it with great verve. The rightsists didn't care if those folks were apolitical and there by accident. They were not human. That was guilt enough.

I saw banners from several organizations. The demonstration would be something unusual, then. These groups fought one another over subtle points of dogma more than they battled their declared enemies.

Up ahead, where the rightsists were thickest, the northbound side of the street dissolved into ferocious turmoil. The center of violence appeared to be a caravan intent on slipping out of town under cover of darkness.

Stones flew. Clubs flashed. People hollered. I ricocheted back and forth, banged around, finally came to rest in a pile of mixed casualties. The cobblestones exercised no favoritism toward anyone. I got back onto one knee, muttering curses on all their houses. My headache was back. How could I douse all the streetlamps? But they would keep fighting anyway.

A knot of nasty-looking rightsists drifted my way. Ever flexible, I dived down and liberated an armband from an unconscious guy who didn't really need his right now. I put it on fast. Then I did what I have been doing so well lately, which was act like I'd just had my brains scrambled and couldn't quite get myself put back together. "Garrett? Hey, Wrecker, is that you?"

"I think so." I knew that voice but couldn't place it. It was a voice from long ago and far away. I faked an effort to get up that failed and left me down on my face.

Somebody else asked, "You know this guy?"

"Yeah. He was in my outfit. In the islands. He was our wreck."

I got it. "Pappy?" That was the voice. Pappy Toomey, also known as Tooms. The old man of the outfit at twenty-seven, a lifer, like a father to the rest of us, like a sergeant without official authority. Pappy never got out but never wanted to advance either.

"Yeah, Garrett. Help me get him up, Whisker." Hands hoisted me. "Who you with, Garrett?"

I didn't know who he was with, so I wobbled a hand vaguely, muttered vaguely, "Them."

A piece of brick whizzed by. They ducked, nearly dropping me. "What's wrong?" Pappy asked me.

"Somebody whacked me with a log. Everything keeps turning around. My knees won't work."

"Lookit here, Whisker. Already got his head sewed up once today. Right in the thick of the Struggle, eh, Wrecker?"

I tried for a grin. "Hey, Pappy. Butter and bullshit to you, too. How's it going? I thought you was dead."

"I heard that rumor, too, Garrett. It's almost all horse puckey. You gonna make the big rally?"

"I'm still walking," I said, knowing that was the answer Pappy wanted. "I got to roll, Tooms, catch up with my crew. Nice meeting you, Whisker." I took a couple of steps and glommed onto a lamp post that already supported two addled lovers against the seductions of gravity. Why does my luck run this way? On the lam from my personal armageddon and I stumble right into a guy I haven't seen in a decade and he recognizes me and throws my name out where anybody with an ear can catch it.

What next?

Aunt Boo was right. It's always something.

Nothing dropped out of the night or poured out of an alleyway. I saw no sign that anybody but Pappy and his pals had any interest in me. I held a conference. My feet agreed to stay under the rest of me. We all got going. My head hurt bad. I cursed softly and steadily, a vision of my own bed the carrot that kept me moving.

And still nothing plopped out of the night or boiled forth from the sewers while I was still in a part of town where they have those.

27

I was bone-tired. I wasn't smart, but I was lucky. It was a quiet night. Everybody with a taste for trouble had gone to the riots. My own brush with those, I learned later, was little more than a glance off the fringes of a minor skirmish far from the center of conflict, where matters grew serious. The push and shove and shouting escalated into massacres when real weapons came out. Nonhuman shops got plundered by the hundred. Refugees and squatters got tormented and beaten too often to number.

The scary thing was, the men responsible were out of control now but were all trained soldiers and combat veterans. If they reclaimed military discipline and organization, TunFaire could witness some real bloodshed.

I wondered what Relway and the secret police were doing to stem the tide. Maybe nothing. Serious bloodshed might serve Relway's personal agenda.

Bad as I wanted to get home to my bed, I entered my neighborhood with care. The temptation to make myself invisible was almost overpowering. Instead, I took my mind back in time, again became the company wreck. "Wreck" was what the regular grunts called us recon types when we were stuck with an infantry outfit. Wrecks got lots of training in sneakery and the mental skills important to the recon mission. I retained the physical skills, but getting to that place in my mind where there was no uncertainty, no nervousness, no worry, no lack of self-discipline, eluded me. That was something you had to work on every day. I had been slacking for years. I felt all the things your master wreck is supposed to set aside.

But I was quiet. I was one with night and shadow, never mind that big moon up there. I was fluidity itself, illusion flowing over the faces of walls in silence of stone. I passed sober but sleeping ratmen and they stirred not a whisker as I ghosted through the alleyways they called home.

I jumped about nine feet high when a sudden weight plopped onto my shoulder, grabbed hold like the cold, clawed hand of something risen from the grave. Every damned time I start telling me how great I am doing.

I returned to earth without screaming, having realized that the clawed hand was two bird feet. Attached to those feet was the ugliest duckling that ever lived. This one couldn't even swim or honk like a swan.

It said, "Do not approach the house yet. There are watchers. They must be diverted. Do not move at all until I give you the word." The voice did belong to the Goddamn Parrot, but there was only one horrible possible source for its dialogue.

I froze, the sheer horror, the terrible implications, leaving me completely blind to the fact that my venture northward, which had cost me such pain coming back south, had not broken the stakeout around my place. "No!" I whined, envisioning a future wherein there was no escape, no safe place. "Tell me it isn't so." He would be able to nag me anywhere.

"Awk! Garrett?"

"I understand and obey, O babbling feather duster." He was doomed. He had to go. If he could be used to follow me around carping, his fate was sealed.

It was him or me or the nightmare. Him or me. Heh heh. Accidents happen, Morley. Terrible accidents. Every day.

"Garrett! Please respond."

I was so involved in scoping out Mr. Big's short future that I had forgotten to keep my eyes and ears open. But luck looked the other way. No evil happened. "I'm right here. Right under this stinking vulture."

"Do not talk that way. The creature could have feelings, too. Hurry home. This diversion will not last long."

"On my way, Old Bones." I could sell him into slavery. Plenty of big-time wizards wouldn't mind having a dead Loghyr on staff. Well, a tame one anyway. Maybe I could give him away. Anybody wanted him, they could just come by and haul him off. I was not going to endure having him looking over my shoulder and criticizing me all over town.

28

I sensed the Dead Man's presence long before the house came in sight. He was wide awake and totally involved, which was a little disconcerting.

"Hurry!" the bird muttered. "Hurry!" *Hurry*! echoed inside my head.

I ran, still horrified by the possibility that there might be no escape from the Dead Man ever again.

My block of Macunado was filled with smoke. A few neighbors were out asking the night what the hell had happened. Seemed a waste if this was the Dead Man's doing. Gods, even of No-Neck's petty pewter stripe, were without doubt capable of seeing through smoke screens both physical and metaphorical. But I soon discovered that this smoke was full of specters flittering hither and yon, like the ghosts of childhood nightmares conjured for but an hour.

I scrambled up my front steps. My front door popped open just as a bumblebee hum grew in the darkness. I dived through. It popped shut behind me, hopefully before that banger-smoking runt caught a glimpse. For once Dean was on the job.

He was pale, frightened. I said, "Maybe you should have stayed another couple of days. You would've missed all this fun."

He gulped and nodded, but said, "I will have your supper ready in a few minutes. Meantime, Himself insists on seeing you."

Now didn't that dovetail sweetly with my own master plan?

I let myself into Himself's room, rehearsing some

choice remarks. "We're into some really deep shit, Old Bones, and it isn't going to be good enough to just tread water."

"I am aware of the peril . . ."

"Can it with the talking bird, will you? Let's do it the way we always have. No! Wait. Stay awake . . ."

Sarcasm is inappropriate, Garrett. We will proceed as you wish.

"I figure you can see how my day went with one glance at the inside of my head. I hope yours was better."

Indeed. I had a very instructional evening with your friend Linda Lee, once she gained the upper hand on her prejudices. That child has potential, Garrett. I approve.

Uh-oh. He never approves of any woman. "Don't let her image fool you, either. She knows exactly what to do with all that potential."

I fail to see any humor in your insinuation, Garrett. Linda Lee is that rarest of all mythical beings, a woman of reason and . . .

I burst out laughing. "I don't believe it. She got to you." I chuckled some more, telling me I would have to look out for my librarian. If she could turn the Dead Man's head she was dangerous. "Of course you don't see any humor. You don't have a sense of humor. Come on. What's the word on these gods? They the real thing? How do I get out from under?"

The Word is Trouble. In your vernacular, trouble in a big way. From the sheer scope of events around you we have to conclude that this is not an elaborate confidence game.

"No shit."

He failed to catch my sarcasm this time. Or he ignored it, which he will do.

Not even a government would go to the expense and trouble of staging something this difficult to manage.

"You're kidding. Imagine that. No government willing to fool me?"

Not in this pinpoint fashion. The expense anti-militates.

"Not to mention that I'm completely unimportant in the mortal scheme. A little nil."

Not to mention that no one on this earth has to work that hard to fool you. Some long legs, a bit of jiggle, some flouncing long hair, perhaps red for extra effect . . .

Sigh. "Great, Chuckles. We're really getting somewhere here, aren't we? We are really getting diddled by gods?"

They believe they are gods. And almost certainly they are within the liberal definitions employed by your primitive ancestors.

"All right. Whatever, they're bad. I'm a fly and I see the flyswatter coming. Do I get philosophical and suffer it? Or can I do something?"

There are several somethings available as options. Perhaps the most attractive is to lie low and do nothing at all while the situation runs its course. I would not be repelled by this option were it possible to sustain it. Your world and the Dream Quarter would be no poorer for the loss of these pantheons.

"The trouble is, they don't plan to go quietly into that gentle night."

Not at all. And since you have been given the opportunity to save them, any disaster is sure to come to roost here swiftly, whether or not they are able to discern your presence.

"They want a key, Chuckles. And I don't have a clue where to look for one. Or what it would look like if I tripped over it. Did Linda Lee help us out there?"

With her invaluable aid—and I cannot overemphasize just how much the child impressed me—I reviewed the available literature both on these pantheons and on those mechanisms used to determine presence, place, and status in the Dream Quarter.

"Wonderful. Does all that wind mean you figured something out?"

Restrain yourself. You are not safe here, nor is time ours to squander.

I rolled my eyes and beat back the urge to head upstairs right now. I was more than ready to get intimate with my bed. "I'm not the one blowing like the wind."

Based upon available information, supplemented by reason, I have concluded—albeit with a reluctance approaching despair—that you yourself are the anointed key. Additionally, it seems improbable that the interested parties have yet entertained that possibility.

"Say what?" I squeaked.

You are it, Garrett. They do not know yet. That has been your grand piece of luck to this point.

"No shit." If he was right. He couldn't be right. I didn't want him to be right.

They would break my legs so I couldn't run, then clap me in irons and toss me into a cage and rivet it shut, then surround that with magical spells.

I have no doubts whatsoever.

"Shit," I said again. I was going through one of those vocabulary droughts that set in after a really bad shock. "Shit. It's me? I'm the key? How the hell does anybody fit me into a lock?"

You have to begin from the fact that where religion is concerned, as is the case with magic, much of what you deal with is metaphor and symbol. In this instance metaphor and symbol have taken life.

That kind of babble usually sets me off. This time I was too tired and achy to squabble.

Dean brought a tray. I stared at a gigantic lamb chop, vegetables, cherry cobbler fit for the king and a mug of beer big enough to suit one of the divine thugs making my life miserable.

"Is there some metaphorical way to kick symbols in the ass so they leave you alone?"

Doubtful. They are gods—albeit as petty as they get. You are not. In all the histories of all the races of this world there have been only two methods proven efficacious in dealing with the gods. You must appease them or you must befuddle them.

"There you go stating the obvious again. Let's back it up some. What makes me the key? How and when did I get hung with it?"

I cannot offer an informed answer. I have a theory, but it is too tenuous and unsettling at this point.

"Bullshit." My buddy, my pal, who don't like getting caught being wrong so won't say anything till he is certain he is going to be right. "I'm not buying any of this premature . . ."

Though time is indeed precious, your best option now is to rest. It should be possible to maintain the illusion of your absence for a time. Sleep. And, henceforth, please do not resort to any of the options offered by the cord given you by that Magodor creature.

"I done figured that one out for myself, Smiley."

I suppose you have, at that. Sleep, Garrett.

My bed felt like a little slice of heaven, with whipped cream on top.

29

It was a night too short. Some thief of time ripped off the four best hours. Cruel wakeup arrived with a crueler sunup. Somehow, my curtains stood open. Sunbeams flailed around like whips in the hands of morons. I faced away, tried to den up like a groundhog under the covers, but there was no escape. There is no enemy so relentless as the sun.

I know I shut my door before I collapsed into bed. It stood open now, perhaps betraying the first feather-stroke of Dean's vengeance campaign. My struggle against a return to the realm of the waking suffered savage reverses at the beak of the Goddamn Parrot, who was perched atop the open door and deft enough of wing to evade a flying shoe traveling at high speed.

This was the last straw. He was gone.

I was not likely to fail to remember who was operating him, either. The very bone-lazy bonehead who had helped so little with my recent cases, the deadbeat who would not wake up if you set a fire under his chair.

To hell with him. I packed my blanket tight around my ears.

Stubbornness gained me nothing. I stayed in bed, all right, but didn't get any more sleep. I just lay there wishing. While the Goddamn Parrot preached sermons.

"Bird, your life expectancy is minutes. You don't shut up you're going to be creamed chipped squab on toast." Dean would put together a championship gourmet experiment.

The bird got the message. His inclination toward self-preservation overrode the Dead Man's low, practical joke kind of humor. For the moment. That was one stupid bird.

All right. I could tuck that triumph in my pocket. So how come I couldn't get back to sleep? How come some sadistically self-abusive part of me kept insisting it was time to get up and get at it?

"Get at what?" I muttered. I dropped my feet into the same abyss as yesterday. "There ain't nothing, but nothing, out there that can't get through the day without me."

Good morning, Garrett. Please exercise emotional caution today. The house is being observed. I believe I have your presence adequately masked. To maintain the illusion I must have you remain placid. Please refrain from these unproductive outbursts.

"Then don't provoke me," I grumbled. I staggered around and fell into some clothes I found lying around, mostly what I had shucked in the middle of the night. They were not completely ripe. They would do.

I took my life in my hands, peeked out my window. "Damn!"

Garrett! Calmly, please.

"It's *bright* out there." Whatever happened to all those gloomy, overcast days we'd been having? The world seemed to be getting warmer.

Stay away from the window. Someone might see the curtain move and reason that you are here after all—particularly since the movement came at your window.

It was going to be one of those days, was it? Nags punctuated by nagging? I reconsidered my bed. It had been so nice in there, so toasty warm. My dreams had been of a paradise where the motives of all the beautiful women were blatant and straightforward and the "me key, you lock" symbolism was direct and obvious. There were beer taps everywhere, and you would gain five pounds a day on the food if you ate it in the waking world.

By jingo june, as Granny used to say—I *did* hear her say that once—I ought to get my buddies together so we could cook us up our own religion. Most of them

believed in booze and bimbos, and some enlightened
religions already considered that sort of stuff important
enough to rate its own underling gods and goddesses.
Star was one example. Maybe we could get Star to jump
the Godoroth ship by offering her a better contract.

A diffuse wave of disgust emanated from downstairs.
"You don't like the way I think, quit poking around inside my head."

*I was not seeking adolescent fantasization. I was trying to
reexamine your experiences of yesterday.*

"You were playing voyeur because you can't think
that stuff up for yourself. The best you can come up
with is bug parades and goofball political theories."

*I cannot deny what is self-evident. I am a creature of in-
telligence and intellect, disinclined toward obsession with plea-
sures of the flesh.*

"You can't deny what is self-evident, which is that
you couldn't do anything about it if you wanted, so you
just sit there making sour remarks about those of us
who still have a little fire in our blood."

While we amused ourselves, I negotiated the stairway,
an epic adventure any morning early. I trudged into the
kitchen and drew a mug of tea from the pot. Dean was
at the stove. He offered me a look of exasperation, like
I had ruined his whole day by not staying in bed so he
could experience the enjoyment of rousting me out. I
tapped every reservoir of contrariness within me, put on
my brightest Charlie Sunshine face, chirped, "Good
morning, Dean. Did you sleep well?"

He glowered a deep black glower, sure I was putting
him on. "Breakfast will be a while yet."

I poured myself a refill. "Take your time. Me and the
big guy got schemes to scheme and cons to crack." I
was sure that, immortal players or not, there were cha-
rades going on in this temple squabble. Overall, the
Shayir probably were more straight with me, and one
sex of them sure was friendly, but I was sure we didn't
have the full map in front of us yet.

"Dean?"

"Sir?"

"Did the wedding go well? Was the trip worth it?" I could not recall having asked before.

"It all went quite well. Your gift was received with considerable pleasure. Rebecca expressed amazement that you even remembered her, let alone thought so well of her."

"There was a time when neither one of you let me forget for a minute. That gift was a sigh of relief." Back then Dean's whole mission in life, it seemed, was to get me married to one of his numerous nieces.

A hint of a smirk pranced around the corners of the old boy's mouth. He said, "It was an interesting journey. We even fell afoul of highwaymen on the return leg, gentlemen so inept they didn't know what to do when they found out that everyone aboard the coach was stone-broke. I enjoyed myself a great deal, but it's good to be back home."

"Yeah. No place like." Especially for me. "Sounds like somebody pounding on the door."

Garrett. Please step into your office and close the door.

"Huh?"

Our visitors are Mr. Tharpe, Miss Winger, and an associate of Mr. Dotes' known as Agonistes. They will leave shortly. I should like them to depart convinced that you are not on these premises.

That sounded like a reasonable idea, but who would want to admit it to Himself?

Who was this Agonistes? I didn't know anybody by that name in Morley's crew.

"Agonistes" is what you people call a street name.

"Oh. Silly me. I really thought somebody's mother would hang a tag like that on him."

Dean passed me, headed for the front door, wiping floury hands on a dishrag. I ducked into my office, which is a large, messy closet across the hall from the Dead Man's spacious suite. I swung the door most of the way shut. I left it cracked both so I could hear what was said in the hall and so I could peek at the Dead Man's visitors. "Dean, remember to keep an eye on Winger. She'll try to kype something."

"I always do, sir. All of your friends."

He started fumbling with locks and latches and chains, taking away any chance I would have had to speak on behalf of my friends.

The man's birth name was Claude-Ned Blodgett.

I didn't know that name, either, but I could see why he would take up just about anything else. Who was going to be scared of a gangster named Claude-Ned Blodgett? Was he going to pop you with a farm implement?

Agonistes, though, had a kind of self-selected sound to it. Names picked up on the street don't usually come that dramatic. Pretty often, they really sound plain stupid. Our great wizard lords on the Hill pick their own business names, and they always choose something like Raver Styx.

Winger started barking before Dean got the door all the way open. I hoped the Dead Man just had her doing legwork. She could complicate things real bad if she got in far enough to get ideas for some scheme.

30

"Garrett here?" Winger demanded.

"I fear not, Miss."

"I'd swear I heard his voice."

"Holy hooters!" the Goddamn Parrot squawked. "Look at them gazoombies!" He managed a creditable wolf whistle. Winger is blessed. Nobody will ever doubt that she is female, despite her six-foot stature.

"If Garrett wasn't my best friend I'd throttle that critter," Winger said.

I wanted to jump out and tell her not to hold back on my account, go for it, turn the little vulture into mock chicken soup.

Though he knew I would do no such thing, the Dead Man did brush me with a cautionary touch. Up front, the Goddamn Parrot continued to flatter Winger. Saucerhead's rumbling laugh filled the hallway. "I think he's in love, Winger. I bet you Garrett would let you take him home." He knew.

"Shee-it."

"Think of the advertising. That bird around wherever you went."

"Double shee-it."

I leaned in an effort to look through the narrow crack by the door hinges. I wanted to see this Agonistes character. I didn't get much of a look, though he waited for Winger and Saucerhead to go into the Dead Man's room first. He didn't look like a thug. He looked like a lawyer, which is a whole different species of villain. But, then, Morley is trying to polish his image these days.

I listened carefully. I couldn't catch a sound from the

Dead Man's room. Dean went back to the kitchen, prepared a tray with tea and muffins. My mouth watered. I was hungry. I resisted temptation. Those three did have to leave the house convinced I was still on the run.

Dean wouldn't be able to go out at all now. We would have to survive on whatever we had on hand. Unless Dean had managed some marketing, that would not be much. I had eaten out while the old boy was gone.

On his way back to the Dead Man's room, Dean stepped in and quietly handed me tea and several hot muffins. He winked, crossed the hall. Before the Dead Man's door shut I heard Winger carping about me being so cheap I wouldn't serve a decent breakfast.

Winger is one of those people you love because they have style. Anyone else who did the things she does would have no friends. Winger does it and you just sort of sigh and chuckle and shake your head and say, "That's Winger."

That kind of person always irritates me—along with guys who never get dirty or rumpled—but I fall under their spell as easily as anybody.

I munched a muffin with one hand and felt the stitches in my scalp with the other. They were tender. Surprise, surprise. But when I didn't touch them they itched. At least my hangover was long gone. I wished I could sneak into the kitchen for a brew. But there wasn't a drop in the house.

Oh my. No beer. And I couldn't go out. And Dean couldn't go out. Even having Dean have Saucerhead bring in a keg wouldn't work. Nobody out there would believe the keg was for Dean or the Dead Man.

That led to the really uncomfortable question. Were those god gangs likely to come play rough? Would they bust in here just to poke around?

"They're gods, Garrett," I reminded myself. "Maybe they aren't as powerful and all-knowing as they want people to think and most people usually think gods are, but they're still a long way up on us mortals." I could not see them having much trouble figuring out where I was.

And that being the case, why shouldn't I just cross the hall and hand Saucerhead a few marks and a nice fee for fetching me a keg?

Continue to assume you are the focus of a mighty confidence scheme, Garrett. It will help if you believe we are not powerless in this.

I jumped. For a moment after the touch opened, I expected it to be *Nog is inescapable.* I'm not sure why.

What was that all about? He did not expand upon his remark, which only indicated he was monitoring my thoughts, something he wasn't supposed to do except in extreme circumstances.

Dean stepped in. "More tea?"

"If you can manage. What's going on over there?"

"He has them collecting rumors so he can compare and collate them and test some theory about the true intentions of Glory Mooncalled."

My expression scared Dean. He grabbed my mug and platter and scooted. I squeezed the edge of my desk so hard I ought to have crushed fingerprints into the wood.

I wanted to blow up in a shrieking rage. I wanted to stomp around the house breaking things. I wanted to use words my mother would have disowned me for even thinking. I wanted to grab a certain humongous sack of petrified camel snot and drag him into the street, where he could become snacks for homeless and otherwise disadvantaged vermin. I couldn't do any of that without giving myself away, so I sat there rocking back and forth and making weird, soft noises that could get me committed to the mental ward at the Bledsoe Imperial Charity Hospital.

I had a feeling Dean had just let slip the real con going on around here. My esteemed sidekick was using my concern about my own dire situation to gull me into thinking I was getting something for my money when it was really him getting something else.

Child and Loghyr, living and dead, I have been in this

*world more than a dozen centuries, Garrett. Never have I
encountered a creature as cynical and selfish and penurious as
you. There are great changes stirring. True marvels and
wonders are transforming today into history out there. And
you insist we all focus completely on a squabble that may
work itself out just fine without you or me.*

I didn't shriek. I didn't foam at the mouth. I didn't go
over there and choke him. For what good would that do
me? It would not have any effect on him. And until his
guests departed, I could do nothing but fume and paint
mental pictures of vast, complex, and exquisite torments
to try out on the Dead Man.

*Were you to distract me so, I might not be able to maintain
the webs of deception I have woven to keep your presence here
concealed.*

He could deal with me and his guests both because
he has more than one mind. Which mainly means he
can be a pain in the butt several places at the same time.
Not what I count as a big plus talent.

The fact that I could fight back only in the darkness
of my heart only made my situation more unbearable.

*Perhaps you should spend less bile upon me and invest
more thought in the situation you fancy has engulfed you.*

Standard fare from the self-declared brains of the
outfit. Tell me to figure it out for myself.

Not easy. The situation was unlike any I had faced
before. With me identified as the divine key, there was
no mystery involved—unless it was why I had gotten
trapped in the first place.

I did not like being the key, but I believed the Dead
Man was right. Though No-Neck had made nothing of
it, I was able to stroll right into a temple that was supposed to be sealed so tight that gods couldn't get inside.

How had I become the key? When had I? How come
I hadn't been consulted? The virgins who give birth to
the children of gods, the men compelled to beat into
those sprats the principles of offering accounting and
believer manipulation later, those folks always got an
advisory visit from a messenger angel before the fact.
Just to smooth the road, you know. Me, I'd gotten

diddly. Squat. Zilch plus zip. Hell, I was out of pocket on this thing. And I could be helping people I actually liked to handle problems I actually cared about.

Not that I wanted to dive into the Weider family troubles. That just looked less treacherous than where I was at now.

The Dead Man may have been amused by my quandary, but he was preoccupied with his visitors. He spared me no more attention while he extracted whatever it was he wanted from the crew, then filled them up with new instructions and sent them on their way.

Winger was the last to leave. Of course. Dean shepherded her carefully, stopped her from entering my office, then stayed between her and anything valuable that she might find too tempting.

31

You do overestimate Miss Winger's cupidity and amorality.

The front door had not yet closed behind the overestimated lady, who had started swapping compliments with the Goddamn Parrot. I had to wait till the door slapped her behind before I could respond.

"I really doubt that."

She has a code of right and wrong. She sticks to it firmly.

"Yeah. Her code is, If it ain't nailed down it's hers to carry away. And if it can be pried loose it ain't nailed down."

You do the woman an injustice. But, then, you feel you have been through trying times and are justified in demonstrating a foul temper.

"It's no feeling, Smiley, it's fact. And my temper is going to turn even more foul if you keep indulging your hobbies while I'm getting batted around by characters who actually make you look attractive."

I stormed across the hall, burst into the Dead Man's room. Dean entered behind me, stood around nervously waiting to find out what was going on. He was scared. However casual or indifferent the Dead Man seemed, Dean's intuition told him we had big trouble. Usually he copes with big trouble by going wild in the kitchen.

Though you want to believe otherwise, I have given your god problem some attention. Your friend Linda Lee brought a cartload of books here last evening. She and your friend Tinnie and her friend Alyx and their friend Nicks spent hours reading for me. I learned very little that you do not already know. Neither the Godoroth nor the Shayir pantheons represent golden examples of the brilliantly absurd natural imaginings of humanity. If some unimaginably great beings were to be connoisseurs of absurdities, these would form the centerpieces of their collections. These pantheons slithered from the bottom depths of lowest-common-denominator minds. Thud and blunder, sex and scandal, and afflict your mortal followers with pestilences and famines, disasters and humiliations, for fun, is what they are all about. And in that, of course, they mirror the souls in their care. All gods are shaped by the hearts of their believers.

What a sight that must have been, the Dead Man surrounded by beautiful women reading aloud, him absorbing the information they provided while smugly ignoring the fact that I was flailing around on the bottom in the deep smelly stuff somewhere else. And he had been aware of my plight—the Goddamn Parrot, having abandoned me to my fate, had flown home to him.

There is one aspect in need of deeper consideration. The girl who brought you out of Shayir captivity does not appear in any recorded account of either pantheon. Nor does your air-mobile infant. Which, by the by, is usually called a cherub.

"Hell, I remember cherubs now." They were part of the mythological hardware of my mother's religion. Mostly they just appeared in religious art.

They are part of the background populations of divine beings common to most religions springing from the same roots as the Church.

So he still had a spying eye inside my head.

For efficiency's sake only, Garrett. About the girl. It is your feeling that she is the by-blow of either Lang or Imar, her mother having been a mortal woman?

"She didn't tell me a whole lot about herself."

No. She did not. And you were too taken by the imaginary possibilities of your circumstances to try to elicit any useful information.

"Hey! . . ."

I reiterate. She does not figure in either mythology. The cherub springs from another family of religions entirely.

"I heard you. Give me a break. Imar and Lang are both the kinds of guys who grab whatever and whoever wherever and whenever they think they can get away with it. And probably don't much care if they get caught."

Stipulated. That is not in dispute. It is beyond dispute. But it may not be relevant. What troubles me is this anomaly, these players who do not fit the game. This girl, the cherub, even the winged horses. Anomalies always worry me. Your better course may have been to stay with the girl until you learned who she was and what she wanted.

"Maybe." Hindsight makes geniuses of us all. "And maybe if I had done that, right now I would be the meat in somebody's stew."

We really are contrary this morning, are we not?

"Damned straight. The whole crew. Me, myself, and I. Happens every time I find my partner blowing my hard-earned in order to collect political rumors. Wasting it on people like Winger, that we know too well, and on that Agonistes, that we don't know at all."

Both are entirely trustworthy within the limits of the tasks they were asked to perform.

"Yeah? What happens when somebody out there starts wondering why you're asking questions? Political people are born paranoid. If they interrogate Winger, she'll tell them anything she thinks they want to hear to get herself out of it. We could end up with Relway's thugs all over us, or The Call, or somebody out of the Cantard, or the for gods' sake Pan-Tantactuan Fairy Liberation Army . . ."

You are becoming excited. Please restrain yourself.

Grumble grumble.

You fail to appreciate the real magnitude of the crisis gripping TunFaire. And you fail to accept my ability to protect myself.

"It ain't you looking out for your butt that I'm worried about, Old Bones. You've always done a truly outstanding job of covering number one. It's my ass ending up in a sling that worries me."

Always the self-centered, demanding . . .

"Don't play that game with me, Chuckles. It's time

you paid your rent. I'm calling. Tell me how to deal with this gods mess."

What do you know about the rash of strange fires in the Baden neighborhood?

"Huh?" Talk about your blindsider. But he does that. One of his minds will be mulling over something not remotely related to anything under discussion and it will pop right out. "I've been busy. You would have noticed if you weren't worrying about things like fires and Glory Mooncalled. What about these fires?"

I do not know. Several of my visitors have mentioned a series of unexplained, fatal fires. Not arson. Nothing burns but the victim himself, apparently, unless he sets fire to something himself.

"Sounds grisly."

Perhaps. It is only a curiosity, of course, but I gather there was no connection between the victims, none of whom were the kind of people who get themselves assassinated.

"Great. Sounds like the perfect puzzle to keep you out of my hair on a long winter's day. So put it on the shelf till the snows come back. Give me a hint here. What about these gods? Are we even dealing with gods?"

Again, the amount of energy being expended and the number of players involved militates against it being a confidence action. Indeed, it would be possible for a cabal of wizards to produce the effects you have encountered. But to what purpose such effort? There is no hint of any stake other than that proclaimed by the principals. This appears to be a straightforward struggle for divine status.

"Status?" Got me again. Another blindsider.

Of course. Do you accept as absolute and literal their expectation of total oblivion if they are driven from the Dream Quarter?

"Pretty much. They were real intense about it. You're right, though. They could set up in a storefront somewhere. Plenty of crackpot outfits do."

And there you have it. If you are not established in the Dream Quarter, yours is not a serious religion. You are a fo-

cus for lunacy. A bad joke. Even if you have a hundred times the followers of a respectable cult.

"But that would win you a place in the Dream Quarter."

True. Although you would carry a stigma for generations. Like new money amidst old. You see my point?

"Theirs, too. You got only a couple, three followers left and you get the old eviction notice, then you try to set up shop in an abandoned sausage cookery, your followers maybe won't show up for services anymore. Too embarrassing. They might sign on with some other crew who knew the right people and worshipped in the right place. So maybe you are dead if you're out. It's just not sudden."

They might see it that way.

"So suggest me a plan. Sit tight?"

I am applying some thought to the matter. I feel it is unlikely that the pantheons remain ignorant of your whereabouts, despite our precautions. It remains to be seen if they will accept inactivity—especially once someone realizes that you are the key.

"You think they will?"

I reasoned it out easily enough. They are less able, constitutionally, to consider a mortal closely, but eventually it will occur to someone that you entered that temple as though there was no seal upon it.

"Could have been No-Neck. He was with me."

No doubt he will pay for that.

"He deserves a warning."

He does. I will see to it. He seemed to mull something over. I let him ferment. *Events could become exciting, I fear, once that conclusion is reached. Particularly if one of the Godoroth reaches it first.*

"Huh? You want to explain?"

He *was* in a mood. His usual response would be to tell me to work it out for myself. *You suggested that Lang had eyewitness knowledge of your visit with the Godoroth. I suggest we seriously entertain the possibility that, in fact, he did hear from an eyewitness.*

"You think one of the Godoroth is a traitor?" There

was a boggler. Not that treachery isn't a favorite divine sport *inside* any given pantheon.

And perhaps the other way as well. During your encounter with Magodor there were hints. In fact, you were, apparently, intercepted on your way to a rendezvous with the Shayir, though there is no mention of any Adeth amongst them, according to Linda Lee.

"The more you complicate this the worse it smells. It could get real nasty."

Indeed it could. That is why I have devoted such a great store of energy to ferreting out potential twists before we find ourselves caught in the claws of an unexpected turnaround.

Although he was probably blowing smoke and wasn't really doing anything, it was refreshing to hear him claim that he was.

"Sit tight?" I asked again.

Sit tight. And keep your hands off that rope.

"I'd say something about grandmas and egg-sucking, but it would fly right over your head."

Like a child who cannot focus its attention long, you require frequent reminders. It is inevitable that some will be superfluous or redundant.

Was that a put-down?

Yes. It was. He was in full command of his powers, which meant there would be no getting any last word.

I jerked my hand away from my waist. That rope was damned seductive. It was hard not to fiddle with its ends.

A pity that we cannot interview the Cat person. She might be a sizable gap in these gods' wall of secrecy. It is possible she is knowledgeable but unable to protect her knowledge.

"Guess I should have turned on the Garrett charm and sweet-talked her right on home here. Eh?" His opinion of my ability to cope with women has no connection with reality.

He responded with an unfocused mental sneer.

I countered with another grumble about him spending my hard-earned, then retreated to my office.

32

When the going gets tough the tough guy takes his problems to Eleanor. "What do you think, Darling?" Hell, Eleanor might be more use than the Dead Man.

She was all the way Over There.

Eleanor is the central feature of a painting of a frightened woman fleeing a dark mansion. Shadows of evil tower behind her, suggestions of wickedness hunting. The painter had a great talent and incredible power. Once his painting had been possessed by a dread, drear magic, but most of that had leaked away.

Eleanor had been a key player in an old case. I had fallen for her, only to learn that she had gotten herself murdered while I was still wearing diapers.

It isn't often the victim helps solve her murder, then breaks a guy's heart when she's done.

It had been a strange case.

It had been a strange relationship, doomed from the start, only I hadn't known until the end. The painting, which I seized from her killer, and some memories are all I have left.

When I have a problem that cuts deep or just tangles my brain I talk it over with Eleanor. That seems to help.

The Dead Man doesn't have any soul. Not the way Eleanor does.

For an instant she seemed thoughtful, seemed to have a remark poised right behind her parted lips.

Take charge. Start acting instead of reacting.

"Right, Honey. Absodamnlutely. But clue me. How do I grab Imar—or good old Lang—by the gilhoolies while I kick his butt till he starts talking? Tell me. I'll strut out that front door with my ass-kicking boots on."

Which was the crux, the heart, the soul of my problem. And ain't it always, when mortals deal with the gods? Almost by definition, Joe Human has no leverage.

Dean appeared. He carried a big platter of stew. He set that in front of me while he frowned at Eleanor. Me talking to her makes him uncomfortable. There is enough residual sorcery in the painting to set his skin crawling. "I saw Miss Maya while I was doing our marketing last evening."

That explained why there was food in the house. He had wasted no time. I don't like stew much, and his latest effort didn't look even a little appetizing but it smelled tempting. I dug in and discovered the stew tasted way better than it looked. It was lamb. We hadn't had lamb for a long time.

Dean has his weaknesses, but bad cooking isn't among them.

"That's amazing, Dean."

"Mr. Garrett?"

"I can wander all over town for months and never once run into Maya or Tinnie. I live here, but I never see either one of them come to the door. But let me take a walk around the block, when I get back I hear all about how Miss Tinnie or Miss Maya was around and I get all the latest news from their lives. How does that work, Dean? Do you hang out some kind of sign to let them know the ogre isn't in his cave?"

Dean was both taken aback and baffled. I had lost him several sarcastic snaps earlier. "I'm sure I don't know, sir." He looked like he thought his feelings ought to be hurt, but he wasn't quite sure why.

"Don't mind me, Dean. I'm not in one of my better moods."

"Really? I hadn't noticed."

"All right. All right. The stew is better than ever. You didn't think to order a fresh keg, did you?"

"I thought of it."

We were going to play that game, eh? "And did you follow through?"

"Actually, I did. It appears Miss Winger will be spending some time here, off and on, and Mr. Tharpe enjoys a mug when he comes by, so that seemed the hospitable thing to do."

"Better have the empties taken away. I forgot to take care of that while you were gone."

"I did notice that." Since he had to work around the stack in the kitchen. "I cautioned the delivery outfit to bring a wagon or an extra cart."

Smart aleck. He disapproves of my hobby. He doesn't have a hobby himself. He needs one bad. Never completely trust a guy who doesn't have a hobby. He takes everything too damned seriously.

Maybe he and the Goddamn Parrot could go for long walks together.

"I just had an idea, Dean."

He backed off a step, beyond the sink. Beyond the kegs.

I gave him a look at my raised eyebrow. "What?"

"You are at your most dangerous when you start having ideas."

"Like a newly sharpened sword."

"In the hands of a drunk."

"You would make somebody a really great wife. Here it is. We let it out that Mr. Big knows where there is buried treasure. We say he used to belong to a Lambar pirate, Captain Scab, who taught him the major chart keys. Somebody will hold us up for him next time we take him outside."

Dean chuckled. He doesn't like the Goddamn Parrot either. That parti-colored crow is as hard on Dean as he is on me. I owed Morley a big one. I ought to lug the Dead Man and his bug collection over and dump them in The Palms.

"It would be far easier and much less complicated just to wring its neck."

It would indeed, but we humans seldom pursue the pragmatic course. We let ancillary factors influence us.

For example, Morley would be offended if I murdered his gift.

Dean pulled a baking sheet out of the oven. I grabbed a biscuit while it was still smouldering, drenched it in butter, splashed on a little honey. Heaven.

Paradise has a way of running off faster than I can sprint trying to catch it.

Garrett. Presences have begun gathering in the neighborhood.

"My friends?"

Dean gave me a look, then realized I wasn't talking to him.

I cannot sense them clearly. It may be that most are not entirely present in this level of reality. I do sense a great deal of unfocused power out there, and barely restrained fears and angers. That is not a combination that bodes well.

"No shit. The master is back, folks. Do you get any sense of immediate intent? Can you make out any identities?"

No. In my youth I went to sea. You have been there, on a day when the storms stalk the horizons, balanced on slanted towers of dark rain, and the winds rise and die in moments. Sitting here sensing those creatures is like standing on the deck of a galleon watching those storms walk about.

"Very picturesque, Old Bones." I knew exactly what he meant. I *had* been there. "I didn't know you were a sailor."

I was not.

"You said . . ."

I went to sea.

"Probably one step ahead of the loan sharks. You mean they're just out there, hanging around, pissed off, but without any special villainy in mind?"

Yes.

I headed upstairs so I could peek out the windows. Excepting one barred one in the kitchen that allows Dean to get some air while cooking on a summer's day, we have none on the ground floor. That is characteristic of TunFairen architecture. We like to make our thieves work. "Are we under siege?"

Not as such. We are under observation.

"Don't go showing off."

In your own vernacular, Garrett, go teach your mother to suck eggs.

Grandmother, Old Bones. It's go teach your grandmother to suck eggs. You're going to talk like the rabble, at least try to get it right.

33

Bizarre. The street was almost empty. A brisk but confused wind flipped leaves and rubbish this way and that. It looked colder than it ought to be. There was an unseasonal overcast. Mrs. Cardonlos was out in front of her rooming house taking advantage of the light traffic to clean the street. For reasons that would make sense only inside her strange head, she was staring at my place like the weird weather had to be my fault.

She can lay anything off onto me.

While I watched, she put her broom down, went inside, came out wearing another sweater. She glared at the sky, daring it to darken any more.

"You using my eyes?"

Yes.

"Looks like late autumn, except the trees still have their leaves." Not that there is a lot of greenery around. My neighborhood isn't big on tree-lined streets, lawns, gardens, and such. Brick and stone, that is us. Brick and stone.

"Can you tell anything useful?"

No. Have Dean put the bird out the front door. Back him up but stay out of sight.

"Right." What the hell? Oh, well. Let *him* explain to Morley.

Mrs. Cardonlos stopped working. She stared malevolently, but not my way. Remarkable. I leaned so I could see the object of her wrath.

"See that woman, Chuckles? That's the redhead who led me into all this. Adeth." Curious, the old woman being able to see her.

She looks forlorn. A sad waif.

"What's gotten into you? You have bad dreams last nap?"

Sir?

"You usually take a more mechanistic, colorless view of the world."

Surely not. Please dispatch the bird.

"I'd love to if I could find a way to make somebody else take the rap." I went and told Dean what His Nibs wanted. Dean just shook his head, dried his hands on a dishtowel. He left the sink to its own devices, headed for the small front room. Mr. Big had no premonition that he was about to enjoy a new adventure. Dean collected him unprotesting while I checked the stoop and street through the peephole. "All clear, Dean."

He fiddled with locks and latches and chains. I take back what I said about him not having a hobby.

The Goddamn Parrot looked like he was about half alive. He was behaving himself. It was scary.

I hoped I didn't start missing his obnoxious beak.

Dean pulled the door halfway open, leaned out far enough to chuck the flashy little squab into the wind. A puff of that got inside and, yes, it was chilly.

Dean jerked back inside, started to push the door shut.

"Wait! No. Go ahead. I can look through the peephole."

Dean stepped aside. I peeped. "I was right. The beer wagon is coming. Get an extra keg if he has one. We may be locked up a long time."

Dean glowed with dark disapproval. Then, "Are we actually involved in something serious?"

All the activity had not clued him.

"We are. And it might be the most dangerous thing yet." I hit the highlights while we waited for Charanagua Slim to bring his cart to the foot of our steps. Slim was part elf, part troll, an improbable mix that had to be seen to be believed. He was short and hard as a rock, and both his parents had to have been the ugliest of their kind ever to reach breeding age. He

was a sweetheart when you got to know him, but he
made nails look soft when money was involved. He was
important in my life only because he was my main
source of fresh kegs of the holy elixir.

Dean slipped out to help Slim. Slim was going to be
irked. Not all of my empties carried his chop.

I denned up in my office. Slim didn't need to see me.
He might tell somebody later. Or he might insist we review my fickle relationships with beer haulers.

I heard the door close barely after I sat down. I never
caught a snarl of complaint from Slim. Something was
wrong. I headed for the hallway.

Dean had just passed my door. He had a pony keg on
his shoulder. That's hardly enough beer to wet your
whistle. "What's that?"

"All he could deliver right now. All he had left on his
cart. I took what I could get."

I followed him into the kitchen. The empties had not
stirred. "What about those?"

"He didn't have room on his cart. He'll be back, he
said. He said business is good, what with the soldiers
coming home. Said he's working fourteen-hour days."

Wouldn't you know? "I smell a beer shortage coming
on. Another of the unexpected horrors of peace." I went
scurrying toward the front door. Better have Slim bring
me a cartload all my own. I would become a beer
hoarder.

Garrett, please.

I gave it up, just took a peek through the hole. Slim
sure enough did have kegs and barrels practically dripping off his cart. "I guess those human rights guys need
a lot to keep them going." Beer drinking is an essential
part of the preliminary rituals of political demonstra-
tions.

"Hang on, Smiley."

Yes?

"Use my eyes. Take a gander up the street, past Old
Lady Cardonlos' place."

I see nothing but a somewhat substantial peasant girl.

"That's Cat. The one who gave me the ride on the flying horse."

I have her. Half a minute passed. *She is not quite mortal, Garrett. Ah. She is an interesting child. And this house is her destination. She is not aware that it is the center of a great deal of attention. She lacks some very basic divine senses despite being the child of a god.*

"She never struck me as any genius. Hey, Dean! We're going to have company. Take her in to His Nibs. We don't want her to know I'm here."

Dean offered me a look at his hardest glare. "I hope there is money in this somewhere. I have no interest in putting on a show for one of your prospects."

"It's all business. Just let her in. Offer her tea and a muffin and hand her off to the Dead Man."

"Yes, sir."

Thank you.

Both sounded as though no greater imposition had settled upon their lives before.

"You wanted to interview Cat, Smiley. Now's your big chance."

34

*Those things out there do not appear to be aware of her as
anything but another mortal. I sense no interest at all.*

"Intriguing."

Extremely.

Nobody knew who Cat was, but Cat was in the game.
"Old Bones, this may be more complicated than I
thought."

*Probably. And she may be more of a challenge than I had
anticipated. Her mind has a remarkably stout shell surrounding it. It conceals her memories and all but her surfacemost
thoughts. There is enough on the surface, though, to confirm
the notion that she serves neither the Shayir nor the
Godoroth.*

"That's hot news. Shucks. Recomplication wasn't
what I wanted right now."

Dean continued to grumble his way up the hall. He
had a pie in the oven and didn't think it was reasonable
that he be expected to watch the door as well. We were
turning into a bunch of cranky old men.

Had to be the Dead Man's wicked influence.

*Pshaw! Allow her to knock a second time before you open
the door, Dean. I need time to get the bird back here.*

Dean responded with select commentary worthy of
Mr. Big himself. I have to admit I felt a certain sympa-
thy for his position.

Go into your office, Garrett.

He was surly. Still had that one eye inside my head.
I went, but watched as long as I dared.

Dean stiffened, presumably getting instructions. He
really hates having the Dead Man get into his head. I

managed to get out of sight before he yanked the door open, not waiting for any damned second knock while his pie was baking.

The Goddamn Parrot blasted inside, staggering the old man, arriving with his beak going full speed. "Lay your glims on this bimbo! Hooters deluxe!"

"What is *that*?" Cat squeaked. My erstwhile traveling companion seemed a touch irritable.

Welcome to the house of aggravation, dear.

"A pet. Ignore it. Product of a wastrel youth. It doesn't understand that it is offensive," Dean replied. "It escaped some time ago, going out to search for Mr. Garrett, my employer. Mr. Garrett has vanished. Wenching again, no doubt. They were inseparable."

I considered what choke holds might best serve in a debate with a man Dean's age.

Garrett. The creature No-Neck has been warned. He recognized the bird but failed to take its message seriously. He seemed to think you were trying to pull some clever practical joke.

Great. "He didn't get the name No-Neck for no reason," I whispered. But would I have listened to a talking bird I had met only once, when both of us were drinking?

Probably not.

Unless it was a redhead. Dean. Please close the door.

"Cheap shot!"

The Goddamn Parrot kept yapping like he thought Cat was Winger. Maybe he couldn't tell the difference.

Near as I could tell from the racket, she kept getting in Dean's way, possibly because she didn't know how to deal with the Goddamn Parrot. No matter how obnoxious the critter gets it's never good manners to stomp somebody's pet in their own house.

Then the awful truth plopped like a great stinking lump falling behind the tallest herbivorous thunder lizards.

"Hey, Honeybuns, dig the weasel out of this dump and let's get going." Yes. Him. And his humming wings.

The Goddamn Parrot shrieked and headed down the

hall. Dean clumped after him, exercising his own vocabulary. The bumblebee buzz drifted. I heard rattling at the door to the small front room.

"Nothin' in there. Stinks, though. That bird. Let's look at this next one."

I went over behind my desk and picked up the spare headknocker. It was time to find out how much power a cherub had.

Calmly. Calmly.

The runt's mouth never stopped. Neither did his banger. The smoke began coming in under my office door.

The Goddamn Parrot's beak never stopped.

Dean kept swearing.

Cat kept after everybody. She sounded like she was about to break down crying.

Be patient, the Dead Man sent. *The girl is rattled. This is to our advantage. I see weaknesses in the armor around her mind.*

"Oh, excellent," I muttered. "And what about that stinking, banger-smoking cherub?"

Cherub?

"The one in the hallway with the rest of that baby riot? The half-bug little guy trying to get into everything?"

Cat shrieked, "Fourteen, stop that!"

Oh. That cherub. And, somehow, I knew he could not sense the little monster at all except through the senses of others. Presumably he was seeing through Cat's eyes, since I was not out there. Unchosen mortal Dean ought to be blind to the critter.

Would ordinary mortals smell the smoke even if they could not see the smoker?

"That very cherub," I said. "Since you've found these chinks, chip away." And good luck with the runt. You marvel, you.

Your attitude needs adjustment desperately.

"And you need to get back outside of my head, Chuckles." Gotcha.

I felt his withdrawal. He didn't do it as a favor to me.

He was going to need all his minds to deal with Cat and her pet.

I tried to commune with Eleanor. Eleanor wasn't interested. And who could blame her?

35

Garrett. I have attained control. You may join us if you so desire.

"Oh, I will. I've got to see this."

The Dead Man was smugly self-satisfied. Which was not an unusual state of affairs. When things go wrong for him that is always someone else's fault, but his triumphs are all his own, brilliantly unshared. Just ask him.

"A prime candidate for Amazon school," I cracked. Cat did look like a leading contender for future queenship of the women warriors. "Another Winger."

Not quite. This one is completely healthy and totally honest and wholesome. The girl you will want your daughter to be.

"There anything inside that handsome head?" Cat was that kind of girl when you got her out into the light.

I was paying her no mind, really. I was studying the cherub. It was perched on the arm of the Dead Man's chair, frozen solid as some stone gewgaw on a temple wall.

Handsome, by the way, is a physically pretty woman who has no attractive pizzazz whatsoever. Something like being your good-looking sister. A perfect match for your feebleminded cousin Rudolf from Khuromal. Give her a pat on the hand and a weak smile, then go find the girls who want to be bad.

"You accomplish anything with the runt there?"

I succeeded in extinguishing his smoke. The room stank.

The hallway outside stank. *I managed to petrify him. Otherwise he has proven intractable.*

"Shut up and put out is good enough for me. How about Cat?"

There is a great deal in there, but I cannot reach it without her cooperation. She is quite strong.

"Must be the blood."

Sneer. A mental sneer is a remarkable thing.

"Hey! This is a woman who rides flying horses and thinks it's fun."

The Dead Man relaxed his grasp ever so slightly. The light of awareness grew in Cat's eyes. She shuddered, shifted her gaze to stare at the Dead Man. Her expression became one of horror. "We didn't know that," she murmured. She looked at me. "So you are here."

"I are. I live here. What's your excuse?"

She remained cool under pressure. She reached out to the cherub, touched him gently. "Poor Fourteen. He'll be unfit to live with after this."

"He's fit now? Ratmen would run him off."

"I came looking for you."

I settled into the chair that we keep there for me. It doesn't see much use. I put my feet up on a stool and examined my left thumbnail. Yep. Still there. "Why? Do I know you? Do we have a relationship? I don't think so."

"You deserted me before I could . . ."

"Definitely. Before you could anything. Especially anything unpleasant."

"But I got you out . . ."

"I haven't forgotten. Last night wasn't that long ago. But I can remember rescuing a light colonel from the Venageti so the Karentine army could hang him. I walked before you finished haggling with whoever you were delivering me to."

"I was taking you to my mother. We argue all the time. That's just the way we are."

Maybe. It happens. I waited.

It may be true.

Cat said, "She was the one who wanted you freed from the Shayir."

"I appreciate that. She didn't have time to spring me herself?"

Gently, but continue. She is beginning to leak. This is very interesting.

"Mother doesn't dare stay away long. It might be noticed. They're all so paranoid these days. Because of the temple business. And she can't manage Chiron and Otsalom."

Was I supposed to have a clue here? "Hell. I have trouble with five-card pitch."

Chiron and Otsalom, it appears, are winged horses common to the myths of the peoples of the city states of the Lambar Coast a few dozens of your generations ago.

"Back around the time you went to sea?"

Cat looked baffled. The Dead Man ignored the remark. *Coincidentally, cherubs appear in those myths, none of them named. And that whole family of religions is a branch from the trunk that produced the Church and its local relatives.*

"Chiron and Otsalom are my horse friends, Mr. Garrett. Mother never learned to manage them. She never had time. It's very difficult for her to get away. And I have a knack. She asked me to get you out and bring you to her. I tried."

"I'm grateful. I wasn't enjoying captivity at all."

Then I suggest you get rid of that goofy grin.

Darn. He can see through others' eyes.

"Savage." I continued, "I just wish I knew who she was and why she bothered." I recalled that the Lambar Coast has been a Karentine tributary since imperial times. For so long that there is no separatist sentiment there anymore.

The ships and boats and barges that dock in TunFaire often carry Lambar sailors, Garrett. Working ships is what the Lambar peoples do.

"They do. And that's interesting. What's going on, Cat?"

She put on a stubborn face.

We live in a time of amazements, Garrett. Would you suspect the existence of a temple serving the needs of Lambar sailors, down in the Dream Quarter?

"Some of us are surrounded by amazements. Some of us are just too lazy to die. Of course there's a temple for Lambar sailors. I'd almost bet your life there's more than one. You're a soldier or a sailor, even a merchant sailor, you have to do something after you've spent your wages in the Tenderloin and they've thrown you out of your rooming house for not paying your rent. Come on. You've had time to dig. What's her story?"

Cat gaped at me. She moved nearer the cherub, though reluctantly because that put her nearer the Dead Man. Being able to touch the little guy seemed to boost her confidence.

You told me she looked like Lang and Imar. Not so? But the fact is, she looks even more like Imara.

"You're pulling my leg."

I am not. Her divine half comes from her philandering mother. She is unaware of her father's identity. She knows only that he is not Imar, for which she is grateful. She does not think this consciously, but she suspects that her mother may not know who her father is. Imar, by the way, is unaware of her existence and, it would seem, Imara is eager to maintain his ignorance. I suspect that, should he learn the truth, he would indulge in one of those infamous celestial rages that tear down mountains and sink continents. Or he would at least cause the creeks to back up and mice to get into the corncrib.

"Huh?" Whoa. Who was getting wound up now?

I didn't figure Imar and the horse he rode in on had much heavenly oomph left between them, but why thumb our noses? You ask for trouble and you're damned well going to get it. "That's ringing the changes on the old holy bed shuffle, isn't it? Where do I fit?"

I intended the last question for Cat. She didn't answer me. Neither did the Dead Man, really. *I am unable to reach that information, Garrett. She may not have it. She seems to be motivated mainly by a desire to be a dutiful daughter.*

"Don't look to me like she's all here right now." Maybe she was mentally allergic to the Dead Man. She seemed to be aging before my eyes, taking on that lost look you sometimes see in stroke victims. She had a firm grip on the cherub. I doubt I could have beaten it out of her hand.

Easy, Garrett. Calm yourself.

Sometimes you stumble without seeing it coming. My mother suffered a series of strokes. A stroke finally killed her. In between the first and last, my cousins took the brunt because my brother and I were in the Cantard. She outlived my brother, but I got home often enough to see it at its worst.

It will tear your heart out when your mom all of a sudden can't remember your name.

Easy, I say.

" 'The pain still remains,' " I told him, quoting a popular soldiers' poem. He would be hearing that a lot if he kept up his interest in current politics. The Call had set it to music. When the fighting is done and the long night is gone, the pain still remains.

Manage it, Garrett.

"Getting short-tempered, are we?"

We have an opportunity here. This child is the stone at the center.

"The fruit outside looks pretty tasty, too."

Mental sneer. *She cannot be reached. Not at her heart. And now I see that it is not of her own choosing.*

I'm a normal, red-blooded TunFairen boy, so I wasn't much concerned about her heart when I looked her over. I grumped, "You manage your own pain."

Cat was drifting, but she was not catatonic. She knew we were talking about her and probably did follow my half of the conversation. She did not appear to resent it. Assuming the Dead Man was right about her birth, she undoubtedly had had plenty of experience being an outsider.

Ah. A plan presents itself. Inasmuch as you find Cat such

*a delectable morsel, you might try doing what you do so well.
Charm her. See where that goes. She may lead you to valuable information.*

"Like we have that kind of time?" He dwells entirely
in the realm of fantasy when he pictures my abilities to
understand and communicate with the opposite sex. Old
Bones, they are way too opposite for me.

And it was not like him to give up on himself so easily. Let Garrett do it? Not when he thought so much of
his own ability to get inside another mind. Either he
overestimated Cat or he was sneaking around to get an
angle on me. This news could break his heart, but it
seemed to me that, as is the case with so many young
ladies her age, there just wasn't a whole lot in Cat's head
to find.

Faintly, faintly, like the remotest, most tenuous whiff
of weed smoke drifting from an alley, gone in a blink:
Nog is ines . . .

I shuddered.

That was not pleasant.

"You ought to smell him."

Not a problem for me anymore.

"Nice to know there are advantages to being dead."

*The watchers have begun to move in slowly as members of
each pantheon try to stay a few feet ahead of their competi-
tors. I need Dean to send the bird out again.*

From the kitchen came an uncommon construction
blurted in response to the Dead Man's touch. I heard
Dean stomp toward the front door. I heard him say
something very unpleasant to Mr. Big. The Goddamn
Parrot did not respond. Maybe he had discovered manners.

Maybe there were blizzards in the hot place and all
the young devils were sharpening their skates.

Dean stuck his head into the Dead Man's room. "Mr.
Dotes is headed this way."

"Morley?" It had been a while since I had seen
Morley Dotes, my sometime best pal. He was trying to
go high class, which apparently meant scraping old buddies off the soles of his shoes.

"Do we know another Dotes?" Dean does not approve of Morley. Of course, he doesn't approve of much of anything but marriagable nieces and his friends Tinnie and Maya. But not many other people approve of Morley, either. Morley is what discreet, gentle folk would call a thug.

In the real world Morley is known as one badass bonebreaker.

Who has developed delusions and illusions.

Please await Mr. Dotes at the front door, Dean. Bring him straight here. I am certain we will find his news enlightening.

36

Morley Dotes is part human, part dark elf. His elven side dominates. His choice. He seems embarrassed by his human side. Can't say I blame him.

He is short and lean and so damned good-looking they ought to jail him and lose the key. So the rest of us get a break. I have known him a long time. Sometimes we are best pals. Sometimes he does stuff like give me a talking buzzard that is possessed by an insane demon that causes diarrhea of the beak.

"Mr. Dotes," Dean said, showing Morley into the Dead Man's room.

"Egad," I said. I've always wanted to say that. The opportunity never presented itself before. "Your boys knock over a tailor shop?"

He was dressed to the nines. Maybe even to the tens or elevens. He had on a silver-trimmed black tricorner hat, a heavy, bright red-, black-, and silver-trimmed cutaway over a white shirt wild with lace and ruffles at throat and wrists, a skinny sword cane, natty cream hose, and incredibly shiny shoes with huge silver buckles. He even had a little twitch of a black mustache coming in.

"Some high-class Hill couches must have died to make that coat."

Morley removed a white silk glove, took out a scented little hanky, held it beneath his nose. He sniffed and eyed Cat speculatively, wondering if there was something between her and me. That is the one line he never crosses.

"Really putting on the airs now, isn't he?" I asked the Dead Man.

A man has got to do what a man has got to do. The Dead Man's sarcasm would have rattled the windows if the room had had any windows to rattle.

Morley took it in stride. We peasants could not be expected to appreciate his improved, refined station. "As you requested," he told the Dead Man, flouncing that damned hanky like he belonged in the West End, "I inspected the site you specified. In fact, I soiled a perfectly beautiful . . ."

Nog is inescapable.

This one was a lot stronger. Nog was close. And his thought did not touch just the Dead Man and me. Morley lost his color.

I told him, "That's not just another Loghyr. That's a for sure howling petty pewter god whose specialty is hunting people down. Right now he's looking for me."

Cat had caught it, too. She started moving around nervously. "I need to get out of here, Garrett. If Nog finds me here . . ."

Show the young lady to the small front room, please, Dean. Miss Cat, I wish to speak to you for a moment privately before you depart. In the interim, I need to consult with these gentlemen.

"Where will I be able to get ahold of you?" I asked Cat, as though I believed the Dead Man really did plan to cut her loose.

"I'll find you."

"Sure you will. Good-bye, then. Behave yourself."

She gave me a funny look, then went with Dean. She failed to take Fourteen with her. That had to mean something to somebody.

In the background Nog faded away, but he left no doubt that he was not far off and in a foul mood besides. His pals were bound to be around, too, and I couldn't see their tempers being any more pleasant.

I fear it will not be long before they come visiting.

Morley asked, "Are you into something weird again, Garrett?" He stared at the cherub like he half expected it to come to life and snipe an arrow right into his black heart.

"Me? Into something weird? The gods forfend." I told him all about it. And concluded, "It wasn't my idea."

"But then, it never is. Is it? I take it that was some other clown named Garrett who went chasing the skirt up Macunado."

"Here's the pot calling the kettle. You never saw a skirt you wouldn't chase."

"Technically incorrect, although true in spirit. If you will recall I was able to resist several of the old man's nieces."

"They're a pretty resistable bunch."

I remembered the owl girls. I chuckled. They would make a fine payback for the Goddamn Parrot. I could give him back birds with interest. If I could fix it so he couldn't get away from them for a month or two.

"Great story, Garrett. Real interesting. I'm sorry I can't help you with this one." Dotes shrugged. "And I didn't come over to trade insults." He pumped a thumb. "That one asked me to look into something. I came to tell him what I found."

That you have appeared in person leads me to believe that the treasure is, indeed, hidden exactly as Magodor suggested.

"There's one to wake up to in the morning, Morley."

When money was involved Morley trusted nobody. I have become so cynical I even wondered why he hadn't just grabbed the treasure and reported it nonexistent. I wondered why the Dead Man had chosen to send Morley. I would have used Playmate. Morley's ethics are not as flexible as Winger's, but they still have plenty of elastic in them.

Actually, he wouldn't do me that way. He might use me in a scheme without consulting me first, as he had done a few times already, and he might dump a God-damn Parrot on me as a practical joke, but he would not steal from me.

Excellent. Then there is a possibility Garrett's latest mis-

adventure will not turn up a complete loss. Will you contract to recover the treasure for a percentage?

"Hey! . . ."

You will be busy running, Garrett.

I caught just the faintest parting echo of Nog. How long before he passed this way again?

"Mr. Garrett?" Dean was in the doorway. "Slim is here for his delivery and pickup."

"Good." I hadn't gotten a chance to steal a sip off the emergency pony keg. Life is a bitch. "That gives me an idea. Go let him in."

37

Slim doesn't find my line of work believable, but the notion I tossed out captured his imagination. "All right, Garrett. I'll do it. Might be fun."

Might turn painful if some Godoroth thug got pissed off, but I forbore mentioning that. We need not trouble him unnecessarily. It might disturb his concentration.

"All right, Dean. Let's get the barrel up here."

I had a huge old wine cask in the cellar. It had been down there for ages. One day real soon now I planned to clean it up and fill it with water so we could withstand a protracted siege. I have all sorts of great ideas for that sort of stuff, like running an escape tunnel or two, but I never get around to working on them.

Slim removed a couple of beer kegs while Dean and I wrestled the barrel up from the cellar. Dean mostly kept his opinions to himself because he didn't have anything positive to say. He did bark at Cat when she dared peek out the door of the small sitting room.

The barrel was thoroughly dried out, which meant its ends and staves were not as tight as they would be when soaked and swollen. That left me worried that the damned thing might fall apart while they were carrying it out to Slim's cart. I wouldn't look real dignified falling out of an exploding barrel.

As soon as Dean shut me in, I knew I had made a mistake. I should have just walked out the door. The results would have been less unpleasant. This was like being trapped in a wino's coffin. And I am not comfortable with tight places. Smelly tight places are worse. Getting rolled down steps inside a smelly tight place is worse still. And no effort to make me unhappier was spared when the bunch of them tossed my conveyance onto Slim's cart. Vaguely, I heard Morley mixing complaints about what could have happened to his clothing with chuckles about my probable discomfort.

I should fix him up with Magodor. Maggie was just the girl for him. Snakes in her hair. Fangs. Claws at the ends of all those arms.

Matters did not improve anytime soon. The cart started moving. Slim did not ride it, he led his team. He had no need to ease the bump and bang of solid wooden wheels rolling over cobblestones.

It seemed I was in there for several infant eternities. Slim was supposed to head straight for his Weider distributor to get shut of me and my empties and reload with full kegs, but soon I became convinced that he was going the long way, looking for the princes of potholes. Every bump we hit made the barrel creak and move around the cart a bit.

Bang! We hit a big one. I thought I was going over. Slim growled at his donkeys. I swear one of them laughed—that honking bray they have.

Donkeys are relatives of horses.

Bang! again. This time we got the mother of all potholes. My barrel bounced off the back of Slim's cart. It fell apart when it hit the pavement. I staggered up dripping staves and hoops, looking around fast to see if I needed to run. I didn't see a cherub, let alone a full-fledged third-rate god.

"Sorry," Slim told me. "These damned donkeys seem to be taking aim at every damned pothole."

The animal nearest me sneered.

"Throw them to the wolves. Use them for thunder lizard bait. Don't suffer them a minute longer. If you do, someday they'll get you."

Slim gave me a really strange look.

"Thanks for the help," I told him. "You want what's left of this thing?" A barrel is a valuable commodity even if it requires some assembly.

"Yeah. Sure."

No danger greater than the bile of donkeys presented itself. I helped Slim get the barrel pieces into his cart. People who had watched me get hatched from a wooden egg just stood around and stared. They worried me only because they would brag about what they had seen and somebody somewhere sometime would realize that the clown in the barrel had been me.

Could not help that. Could get my feet to stepping.

The Goddamn Parrot swooped past, vanished without any comment.

I had my feet moving now but did not know where to let them take me. South seemed good. If I made the Dream Quarter, the Godoroth and Shayir would not be able to bully me without irritating all the other gods.

38

I got so close I began to think I was going to make it. But I hadn't put enough thought into planning. I took almost the same route I had followed before. All too soon I began seeing strange shadows in golden light. I heard whispers just beyond the edge of hearing, though some of those emanated from the Goddamn Parrot, who was trailing me.

The bird swooped in, plopped onto my shoulder while squawking something about changing course right now. I told it, "I've picked up something that I think is called Tobrit the Strayer. Shayir. It's more like a fear than anything. If it's the same one, the one time I saw it materialize it turned into an oversize and over-ugly imitation faun that was hornier than a three-headed horned toad."

I spoke in a normal voice. The Goddamn Parrot screeched. Naturally, people stared. I made the turn the bird demanded. I tried not to dwell on the nightmare that life could become if the Dead Man kept the bird on me all the time.

The Goddamn Parrot guided me to Stuggie Martin's. That swillery, for all its lack of glory, had seen a dramatic improvement in business. Overflow guys were standing around outside, drinking and muttering. Some of their buddies preferred to mutter and drink.

Having failed to get so much as a taste off the keg delivered to my house, I decided to stop in, maybe revel in the ambience for one beer. My spirits were flying too high anyway.

It did not occur to me that the Dead Man actually wanted me to visit the place.

Yesterday Stuggie Martin's had been depressing. Today it was like the dead of winter inside. I called for a dark Weider's, then asked Stuggie's successor, "What's with these guys? They look like they just found out rich Uncle Ferd croaked and left everything to the home for wayward cats."

"You ain't heard? Got to be that you ain't heard. It was your pal No-Neck, man. Most everybody 'round here liked that old goof."

"Did something happen to No-Neck?"

"They found him a little while ago. He was alive, but that wasn't 'cause somebody never tried to make it go some other way. They tortured him really bad."

I smacked a fist down hard on what passed for a bar in there. "We tried to warn him. He didn't want to listen."

"Huh?"

"He did a favor for somebody that was sure to piss somebody else off. We tried to tell him they wouldn't let it slide."

The barkeep poured me another and nodded. He had been sampling his wares, no doubt making sure he was serving only the best. He was having trouble keeping up.

Hell, I was having trouble and my first few sips hadn't hit bottom yet.

"You guys friends?" the barkeep asked, topping my mug for me.

"Not really. Just had things in common. Like the Corps." This guy had the right tattoos. He could be diverted.

When I arose a while later I was in a bitter, black mood. No-Neck had been tortured to death only because his precognitive sense had failed him and he had gone walking around with me.

Thus we rail, in vain, against the whims of gods and fates.

Unless his killers were really stupid, one god-gang would have it figured out and would be out of control.

Getting into the Dream Quarter, fast, sounded like a really good plan now.

The barkeep asked, "No-Neck have any people?"

"I didn't know him. Just met him yesterday. He never mentioned any."

"Too bad. He was a good guy. Be nice to let somebody know. So somebody could do right by him."

Had I not been at the bottom of a deep barrel with herds of gods out to get me I might have volunteered to find No-Neck's family. But I was so far down there the open top looked no bigger than a bunghole.

So No-Neck would be seen into the great beyond by the city's ratmen, who would cart his remains to the nearest public crematorium.

39

The Goddamn Parrot plopped onto my shoulder as I hit the street. "Shiver me timbers," I muttered. "Do I live a blessed life, or what?"

"Awk. Something is following you."

"Am I surprised."

"Many of the presences are coming this way."

People stared. It was not often you saw a man chatting with a parrot. "And I'm headed thataway." I began trotting toward the Dream Quarter. Shouldn't be that hard to make the safety of the Street of the Gods. Getting back off again might turn out to be a grand adventure, though.

Apparently the Dead Man had little trouble detecting gods once he took an interest. In fact, there was an amazing array of things he could do if you could just get him started. *That* was a secret I really wanted to crack. I might trade my keyness . . . Nah.

I wondered if the Dead Man being able to spot them meant that my divine acquaintances had chosen to manifest themselves especially strongly during their struggle or if, perhaps, TunFaire was always infested with petty gods and we were detecting this bunch only because we were watching for them. My guess was that these two gangs were obvious mainly because they were fighting for their lives.

The Goddamn Parrot fluttered up and away, off to I-don't-know-where, once again leaving me to dread a future in which the Dead Man could tag along wherever I went through that bird-brained feather duster.

I walked around a corner and there was Rhogiro, big-

ger than life and twice as ugly, holding up a wall like
your everyday garden-variety street thug. Obviously he
wasn't really waiting for me but was there just in case
something turned up. I never slowed a step. I whipped
across into a narrow breezeway. It dead-ended on me. I
put my back against one wall, my hands and feet against
the other. Up I went. Meantime, Rhogiro realized who
he had seen, came to the end of the breezeway and did
some holy thundering. He was too big to get into the
crack and too stupid to recall that he had divine powers.
At least in the moments it took me to get up top.

My luck, as always, was mixed. The climb was just
two stories. Good. The roofs up there were flat and
identical and stretched on and on. Excellent. They
could be run upon almost like the street. None of the
buildings were more than three feet from their neighbors. Fine.

But in this part of town the slumlords wasted no resources on maintenance. My foot went through a roof
almost immediately. I didn't get hurt, but I realized that
I had to slow down or get down.

Slowing down gave me time to think about what I was
doing, which, mainly, was heading *away* from the Dream
Quarter. I needed to get down and head the other way.

I got down rough, after jumping to a roof so fragile
I punched right through. I caught myself before I
plunged into whatever disaster lurked below. I stared
downward. My eyes were not used to the gloom there,
but the area immediately below me looked empty. I
lowered myself as far as I could, let go. The floor was
not that far. And it held.

The place had been abandoned. Only the masonry
was more substantial than the roof. Now that I was into
the gloom I could see light leaking through the overhead in fifty places.

The walls consisted of plaster crumbled till it was almost gone, the lathing behind it mostly fallen too. The
floor groaned and creaked. The stairway looked so pre-
carious I backed down on all fours. I was interested only
in getting out but did note that there was nothing left

worth stealing except the brick itself and some wooden bits that would end up as firewood.

I was surrounded by things on their last legs. My partner was dead already. My housekeeper had one foot in the grave. The city where I lived seemed ready to commit suicide.

The street out front was almost empty. That was an ugly omen. These tenement blocks swarm with kids playing, mothers gossiping, grannies whining about their rheumatiz, old men playing checkers and complaining about how the world is going to hell in a handbasket. Where was the Goddamn Parrot? I could use a good scouting report.

Didn't look like I had time for anything fancy. I ran toward the Dream Quarter. On the other side of the tenement row Rhogiro continued to bellow and blunder around. Maybe his displeasure was leaking over enough to have startled the locals.

I could not see that some gods would be much missed.

40

I almost made it. The story of my life. A lot of almosts.
I was almost king, except right at the last minute I got
born to the wrong mother.

I turned into Gnorleybone Street a few blocks short
of the Street of the Gods. Gnorleybone isn't much used
because it don't go anywhere, but it did offer a nice
look at the distance I still had to travel. I saw only normal traffic for the place and the time of day. No funny
shadows or lights, no big ugly guys, no pretty and
deadly girls, no huntress or hounds, nothing but clear
sailing. I slowed to a brisk walk, tried to catch what of
my breath hadn't gotten so lost it was out of the king-
dom.

They say it's always darkest before the dawn. *They*
ought to live my life. With me it's always brightest just
before the hammer of darkness comes smashing down.

I don't know what hit me. One minute I was just
a-huffing and a-puffing and a-grinning, and the next I
was crawling through a molasses blackness. Time passed
there, inside my head, but beyond me seemed a timeless
sort of state. Maybe I was in limbo, or nirvana, depend-
ing on your attitude.

I sensed a light. I struggled toward it. It expanded to
become a face. "Cat?" Fingers touched my cheek, ca-
ressed. Then pinched cruelly. The pain helped clear my
head and vision.

"No. Not Cat."

Cat's mom. Imara. The Godoroth had gotten to me
first. But when I looked around I saw no one but Imara.
We were in a place like the inside of a big egg furnished

only with a low divan draped with purple silk. The light
came from no obvious source. "What's going on? . . ."

"We will talk later." She laid a fingernail on my forehead, over that spot sometimes called the third eye.
Then she trailed it down between my eyes, over my
nose, across my lips. That nail felt as sharp as a razor.
I shivered nervously but found her touch weirdly exciting, too.

"You have a reputation." Her hand kept traveling. "Is
it justified?"

"I don't know." My voice was an octave high. I
couldn't move. "Whoa!" That was a squeak.

"I hope so. I seldom get an opportunity like this."

"What?" I wasn't putting up much of a fight. This
matronly goddess was about to have her way with me
and, incidentally, establish her husband as my mortal
enemy. There was no arrangement between them, only
the arrangement Imar had with himself. Gods are always jealous critters, turning their spouses' lovers into
toads and spiders and whatnot.

Which seemed of no particular concern to her. She
had one thing on her mind and pursued it with a single-
minded devotion more often associated with less than
socially ept adolescent males. I began struggling too
late. By then the inevitable was upon me. I had no heart
for a fight. I hoped she wouldn't turn into something
with two hundred tentacles and breath like a dead catfish.

I am one agnostic who got made a believer. I should
have brought help.

If they were all that way no wonder they were always
getting into trouble.

Panting, I asked, "You make a habit of just grabbing
guys and getting on with it?"

"Whenever I get away long enough. It's one of the
little rewards I permit myself for enduring that bastard
Imar."

The Dead Man hadn't said anything about Imar's le-
gitimacy. No doubt being a bastard was part of his divine charm.

"Please stop for a while. I'm only human." Imara seemed human enough herself, except for the scale of her appetites.

"For the moment, then. We have to talk, anyway."

"Right."

"Have you found the key?"

"Uh ..." I was at a serious disadvantage here. I was getting sat upon at the moment. "No."

"Good. Have you bothered looking?"

Good? I ground my teeth. She was a goddess of some substance. "Not really. I haven't been given a chance."

"Good. Don't bother."

"Don't?"

"Ignore it. Hide out. Let it go. Let the deadline pass."

"You *want* to get kicked out of the Dream Quarter?"

"I want Imar and his band of morons to get kicked out. I've made arrangements. I've wanted to get shut of that belching idiot for a thousand years, and this is my chance."

She began numbering Imar's faults and sins, which reminded me of the main reason I avoid married women. I didn't hear one complaint that I haven't heard from mortal wives a thousand times. Apparently, being a god is domestic and deadly dull most of the time. Pile it on for millennia and maybe some divine excesses start to make sense.

Those recitals are boring at best. When you have no particular desire to be with the recitee they can become excruciating. Despite my improbable situation, my mind wandered.

I came back fast when she decided I had recovered. "Ulp! So you're gonna dump the Godoroth and sign on with the Shayir?"

How could she manage that? Any honest historical theologian will admit that deities do move shop occasionally, but the mechanism by which they do so eludes me.

"The Shayir? That's absurd! Lang could be Imar's reflection. Why would I want more of that? And his household has nothing to recommend its survival. Let them sink like stones into the dark cold deeps of time." She said all that in a sort of distracted, catechistic manner. Her mind was on something else.

Maybe the wrong gal got the temple whore job.

"You haven't communicated with the Shayir?"

"No! Shut up." She pressed her fingernails into my forehead again. I shut up. She took charge. She had her way with me for about a thousand years.

That molasses darkness reclaimed me eventually. The last I knew, Imara was whispering a promise that I would never be sorry if neither Lang nor Imar ever got hold of the key.

Why do these things happen to me?

41

I ached everywhere. I felt like I had done a thousand sit-ups, run ten miles, then finished with a couple hundred push-ups to cool down. I had bruises and scratches all over me. I was thinking about finding a new hobby. My favorite was getting dangerous.

Then once again there was a face in my face. This one was uglier than original sin. It was the face of a ratman that not even a female of his own kind could love. I grabbed him by the throat. Ratmen are not real strong. I held on while I climbed to my feet.

I had been lying on a bed of trash in an alley I did not recognize. The ratman had been going through my pockets. I relieved him of his ill-gotten gains. He wanted to whimper and beg, but I didn't give him enough air. I was in such a bad mood I considered putting him out of my misery.

My headache was back.

Though the world would be better off for his absence, I just slapped him silly. Then an idea occurred. An experiment to try. I didn't have much to lose. The gods all had a fair idea where I could be found.

I did a quick stretch job on a bit of my mystic cord, cut that piece off, tied it around the ratman's tail. He was too groggy to notice.

I got my behind moving. My feet worked hard to keep up.

Maybe the Godoroth would jump on a false trail.

I found myself on Fleetwood Place, one of the many short and lightly trafficked streets that enter the Dream Quarter. Fleetwood Place runs right through the Arsenal. Even now, with the war gone moribund, the place was going full blast. I don't know how the workers there put up with all the rattle and bang.

I darted from cover to cover, confident that a few hundred yards would get me into the safety of the Dream Quarter. During one pause two huge owls hurtled overhead, tracking a blur up the far side of the street. I grinned. Had to be Jorken, going for my fake.

A trickle of golden light leaked over the brick wall back up Fleetwood. That rustling-paper sound passed overhead. Hundreds of black leaves fluttered in a minor whirlwind. Wolves howled in the distance. I'd like to say dragons roared and thunder lizards stomped, but it did not get that dramatic.

I resumed putting one foot in front of the other as briskly as I could. A remote, foul bit of mind breath reminded me, *Nog is inescapable*. Nog didn't have much of a vocabulary.

As I ran I rehearsed what I had done to frame the ratman. Maybe I would work the stunt again, if I had to. I kept glancing back, expecting Jorken.

A huge boil of dirty brown smoke burst upward back whence I had come. Lightning ripped through its heart. An owl came flying out, folded up on its back, following a high ballistic arc. A thunderclap reached me moments later. And these were not phenomena that only I could see. People ran into the street to gape.

The Godoroth and Shayir were butting heads. I didn't wait to see if they got down to it seriously. I kept sucking wind and pounding leather. A wolf, or maybe a dog the size of a cow, hollered behind me. It was a cry whose tone said, "I got the trail, boss." I put my head down and went for new records.

I sensed something in front of me, a picket of shadow forming out of nothing, right in front of the line where I thought I would get safe.

That thing howled behind me. It was gaining fast. I didn't even try to zig, zag, or stop. I went for the hurdle.

42

There was a face in my face.

"This is getting old," I muttered. I tried to move. The darkness held me tightly, except for my eyes. I realized that that was all I controlled. My ability to see. No other sense was working.

The face in my face drifted back. It seemed to be a metal mask, its features stylized. Nothing but darkness appeared through the mouth, eye, and nose holes. It dwindled to a point of light.

Countless similar points materialized over what seemed like several minutes. A few began to drift, loop, swoop toward me, pursuing some pattern I did not recognize. These few became faces and even figures. Some resembled our better-known local gods. No two sprang from the same mythology.

Oh boy.

I grew up in Saint Strait's Parish of my mom's peculiar religion, so wouldn't you know the Strait Man himself would come shining up night center? "Are you with us, Mr. Garrett?"

"Wouldn't be smart to be against you."

Saint Strait was the patron of seekers after wisdom. And he looked out for fools, drunks, and little kids, which shows you that divine bureaucracies lump stuff together as rationally as do the mundane.

Saint Strait didn't get sanctified for his heavenly sense of humor or his divine tolerance for alternate viewpoints, but he was too preoccupied to indulge his famous temper. "If you will restrain yourself we can resolve several questions swiftly."

"Who is we?" I was in a mood so black I didn't much care if I was toe to toe with the gods themselves, including a leading saint of the religion that I had disdained and mostly disbelieved from eleven years old onward.

"We are The Commission, also sometimes called The Board, a permanent standing committee tasked with mediating and refereeing any arguments or contests between deities of different religions. Commission makeup changes continuously. Board service is a duty required of everyone. The Commission's mission is to ensure peace in your Dream Quarter. We arbitrate entries and exits of the mainstream religions there."

"I've always been content to ignore the gods. How come you can't return the courtesy?" These Commission types would be the clowns who had stuck me with being the key to divine nightmares—probably as a reward for past slights.

"There was no better candidate than you. However, we did not anticipate your being so much at risk. Apologies. Estimates were that you would become wealthy off the interested parties."

"Thank you very much. That sounds great. There'll never be another black day in my life. When does the bribing begin? I'd really like to get those bars of gold stashed away. And what sort of protection will I be getting?"

"Protection?" The concept was so alien he had trouble pronouncing the word. Him who looked out for our less-capable folk. How can you be labeled a hopeless cynic when your cynicisms prove valid all the time?

His response was an answer all by itself. But I soldiered on. "Protection from those lunatic Godoroth and Shayir who have started figuring out the fact that I'm the key they want. You guys set it up winner-take-all—including me. But the losers aren't going to just go away, are they? Maybe they'll want to lay their despair off on somebody. Maybe they'll want to hurt somebody by way of getting even with the universe. So who are they going to look for?"

While I rambled, the good saint had his eyes closed,

either enduring my diatribe or communing with his associates.

He opened his eyes. "You will be protected. You have been troubled excessively already. They were supposed to win your support, not take it by intimidation. We will issue some addenda to the ground rules."

Divine figures moved toward and away from me in some rhythm known only to the gods themselves. I felt some poke around inside my head, picking my mental pockets as habit rather than policy. They were bored and wished those creatures from down where celestial glamour turned to celestial slum would take a powder and save their betters all this ugly, finger-dirtying *work*.

"Was there some point to my being dragged here?"

"The Shayir and the Godoroth collided not far off. They were out of control. It seemed possible the key might be at risk at an insalubrious juncture. You must remain alive for a while longer."

Had I been anything but disembodied vision I would have sniffed the air and checked my soles for accretions.

"Gracious of you. Can we work it so I can hang in here, the age I am now, for a couple thousand more years? Say until the last one of you Commission characters goes?"

"I could tell you what you want to hear, but you would realize its worthlessness as soon as the air blew past you." Saint Man had him a sense of humor after all. "If we made an exception for you, every man, woman, and child out there would petition us with unique circumstances."

Grumble grumble whine whine. Gods forfend anybody actually has to do their job.

"You were made the key because it was our hope that you, being mortal, could distinguish the superiority of one pantheon over another and thus resolve the question of which should remain on the Street of the Gods."

Boy, did they pick the wrong man. So much for omniscience. "I haven't fallen in love with any of the contenders. How about you hide me out till after the deadline and let them all suck the death pipe?"

"That is not an option. Persevere, Mr. Garrett. And work on your decision. Which temple should remain with us?"

He had rejected my suggestion already.

He began to shrink away from me. "Few mortals ever stand in judgment upon the gods."

Other Commission members fluttered about. Some swooped toward me, apparently curious. I got the distinct feeling that the gods from the uptown pantheons were way out of touch. They were like factory owners who never entered their factories for fear they would, somehow, sully themselves by associating with the people whose labor made it possible for them to live the high life. It was blatantly plain that for many, the notion that they had a responsibility to their followers was entirely alien. Many of these gods were what human teenagers would turn into, given unlimited resources and time. They watched me like I was a bug under glass.

"Good-bye for now, Mr. Garrett." His voice was a fading whisper.

Then I wasn't in a place where remote shimmers became curious gods and goddesses. I was where darkness was as thick as treacle. I swam hard. I was going to get out of town for real, let these crazies finish their incomprehensible game without me.

A genie in a bottle would have been a nice find. I could use her to straighten things out. But instead of something gorgeous and eager, I got another wave of darkness, of an altogether different kind. This invaded me, penetrated right down to the core of me. I began to feel better. Aches and pains vanished. My headache went away. Bruises and scratches healed. I felt the stitches in my scalp fall out. Suddenly I felt so good I almost turned positive. I almost wished I was bald so I could grow new hair. I felt younger, bouncier, eager to get into action—and more likely to do something stupid because I was regaining youth's impatience.

Then yet another darkness engulfed me. In a moment I felt nothing at all.

43

I awakened in an alley. Surprise. Surprise, I did it with a face nose to nose with mine. I was going in circles. At least it was a different face each time. "This is getting old." I tried to grab a throat again, but this scroat was no ratman. He was strong. He lifted me one-handed and shook me till my teeth wobbled. "Mom?" I asked. She used to shake me if I did something especially irritating. When I was still small enough to shake.

"Huh?"

Oh-oh. Another mental marvel.

He held me at arm's length so he could check me out. Turnabout is fair play. I checked him out right back.

He had long, wavy blonde hair. He had blue eyes to kill for. One blue eye, anyway. The other was covered by a black leather patch. He was nine feet tall. He was gorgeous. He had muscles on top of his muscles. Obviously, he didn't have much to do but work on his physique and study himself in a mirror.

I'd never seen his like running loose in TunFaire, so I assumed he was another pesky pewter god, though neither Godoroth nor Shayir.

"Now what?" I muttered. "Who the hell are you?"

My body still felt young and tough enough to whip its weight in wildcats.

Pretty boy shook me again.

Whip its weight in gerbils?

"You will speak when spoken to."

"Yeah. Right." Thought I was supposed to get protection?

Shake shake.

"Rhogiro! Trog!" I needed somebody big enough to get this guy's attention.

What I got was the Goddamn Parrot, who plummeted into the gloom from the afternoon sunlight above. "Where have you been?"

"Trying to deal with a whole parade of these characters." I got shaken again.

The bird said, "An apparent retard."

"You see him?"

The huge guy took a swipe at Mr. Big. He missed. The bird stayed over on his blind side, obviously seeing him.

"Be quiet, Garrett."

"Hard to do."

Pretty boy looked baffled. He wasn't used to having his orders ignored. He took a stab at Mr. Big. Maybe he was prejudiced against talking birds. The Goddamn Parrot evaded the blow.

"You try to talk to him?" the bird asked.

"Yeah. He told me to shut up. Then he started playing ragdoll with me. Got any idea who or what he is?"

The big guy pulled me right up close, eye to eye.

"There any divine dentists? He's got teeth all over his mouth, and most of them are rotten. He's got breath like a battlefield three days after . . ."

Bingo.

The Dead Man got it at the same time. "A war god."

Baffled, the war god set me on my feet and squatted. "You do not fear me?"

"I spent five years at your birthday party. You got nothing left to scare me with." I hoped he didn't have a big talent for bullshit detection. "Who are you? What do you want?"

"I am Shinrise the Destroyer." Roll of drums, please. Thunder of trumpets.

"I know your sister Maggie."

He frowned. He didn't get it. Maybe the world wreckers didn't get together and talk shop.

Where did I get the idea that gods were smarter than people?

"Garrett?" The Goddamn Parrot fluttered to my shoulder. "I don't know the name. Do you?"

"Actually, it seems I should. Maybe from somebody in the Corps."

Shinrise the Destroyer swung a fist in a mighty roundhouse. It tore a few hundred bricks out of the nearest wall. On the far side a couple in the throes of lovemaking took a moment to react. They gaped. The woman screamed. She had no trouble seeing Shinrise, either.

He stomped a foot. Bricks fell out of the wall. I said, "I'd better get out of here before he knocks everything down."

As suddenly as the rage took Shinrise it passed. He grabbed me again. "Have you found the key?"

"No."

"Don't even look."

Far, far off I sensed an echo of *Nog is inescapable.*

"Why not? What do you care? You're not Godoroth or Shayir."

"I have cause to wish misfortune upon both houses. You will refrain from . . ."

"Sure, big guy. Like your wishes are going to override theirs."

He started to shake me but frowned, tilted his head to one side. Maybe an idea was trying to get in.

The bird told me, "Others are coming." He fluttered upward.

"I know."

Shinrise completed his thought. He grinned. His teeth definitely were his weakness. "I will protect you." He sounded proud of himself.

"Of course you will. And here's where you start. Nog the Inescapable is coming here to snatch me. Discourage him while I find someplace to hide."

I jumped through the broken wall into the room just vacated by the lovers, then used the only door. I glanced back. Shinrise looked like he was beginning to wonder if he had been hornswoggled. Behind him, but close, came *Nog is inescapable!* strong and tinged with triumph. Nog had the scent.

What did Strait tell me? The Commission was going to caution the players about being so rough? Must not have gotten the word out yet. And Shinrise sure wasn't working for the Board. What he wanted was directly opposed to their desires.

Why didn't I find out what his interest was?

Oh, yeah. Nog.

Nog arrived.

Bricks flew. Thunder boomed. Lightning walked. I clamped my hands over my ears and kept moving. Shinrise the Destroyer lived up to his name by using Nog to finish off the damaged tenement and several of its neighbors.

People screamed.

These petty pewter gods were very much into our world now. Maybe whole platoons of minor gods would come out as the deadline got closer. Maybe . . .

But gods had moved up and down the Street before without the town getting torn up.

Nog is inescapable. Nog seemed amazed that he could be thwarted.

I wished I knew where the hell I was so I could get to where the hell I ought to be. Which, I had a notion, might be right in front of the main altar at Chattaree.

I was about to step into the street when I saw a blur coming. Jorken was earning his pay today. He streaked past, headed for the divine ass-kicking contest.

The excitement began to draw a crowd. I saw Shayir and Godoroth alike heading for the turmoil. I moved out, a man in shadow, employing all the caution I had learned during the big dance with the Venageti.

The racket got louder. Chimneys fell. Chunks of roof flew around. Members of the Guard arrived. Residents lost interest and fled the area. I went with them.

44

The Goddamn Parrot located me, dropped onto my shoulder, grabbed hold hard, then faded out on me. He would not answer questions. Apparently the Dead Man had no minds to spare for him. But he did not revert to his naturally obnoxious birdbrain style.

Unseasonal clouds were gathering. Lightning flickered within them. The wind suddenly seemed possessed of a hard, dark edge of desperate anger. The people in the street shivered, cursed, acted more bewildered than frightened. This was something new to everyone.

This was something that was getting out of hand. The Commission had to be napping. This couldn't do any religion any good. I wished I could stop it ... I knew how, yes. But I had no viable excuse to pick one god gang over another.

I got my bearings and wished I had not. The Board had done me no favor. I was miles from the Dream Quarter, or any sanctuary. Unless I wanted to duck into Ogre Town. No self-respecting human god would go in there.

No human who wanted to survive the gathering night would go there, either.

I was tired and hungry and thirsty and pissed off about being used and abused. Time was the only weapon I could turn against the gods. I was, definitely, inclined to let as many as possible drift off into oblivion.

It grew dark fast. The breeze became a chill wind. No stars came out. In the distance, lights continued to flicker and flash and reflect off the churning bellies of low clouds. Fires burned and smoke rose and emergency alarms beat at the cooling evening air. Drops of moisture hit my cheek. The last one came in chunk form and really stung.

The air was getting colder fast.

I trotted southward, making good time. Boy, was I getting my exercise today. I reached a familiar neighborhood. It was dark there, and unnaturally quiet. The strangeness was spreading throughout the city. I ducked into a place where I knew I would get served a decent pint and a sausage that wouldn't come with worries about the inclusion of rat, bat, dog, or cat.

"Yo, Beetle."

The proprietor glanced up from his mug polishing. "Garrett! You son of a bitch, where the hell you been? You ain't been in here in three months."

"Been working too hard. Don't get time to get over here the way I used to."

"I've heard some stories. I never believed them."

"The truth is worse than anything you've heard."

I took a pint, sucked down a long swallow, started telling him what had happened the past day and a half.

"Hope you brought a pitchfork, Garrett."

"Huh?"

He pretended to examine the soles of his shoes. "If you don't have a pitchfork, I'm going to make you clean that bullshit out of here with your bare hands."

He didn't believe me.

"I have a hard time believing it myself, Beetle. I wish I could introduce you to those owl sisters."

"My wife would never understand."

"Where the hell is everybody? I haven't seen the place this dead since Tommy Mack's wake."

"Weather."

Something was bothering him. "That all?"

He leaned closer. "Big part of it is, The Call won't put me on their approved list. Account of I let nonhumans drink here."

Only dwarves and ratmen do much drinking. And the dwarves tend to keep it at home.

I don't like ratmen much. I had to work to find the

charity to say, "Their money is no different color than anyone else's."

"There's scary stuff getting ready to happen, Garrett."

I touched my cheek where the sleet had bitten me. "How right you are, without knowing the half. What's ready to eat?"

He had drawn me another mug of the dark. I dropped a groat onto the counter. That would serve us both for a while.

"Specialty of the house. Sausage and kraut. Or sausage and black beans. Or, the missus made a kidney pie nobody's touched but old Skidrow yonder." He indicated the least respectable of his few customers.

"Where's Blowmetal?" Skidrow was half of the only pair of identical twin winos I'd ever seen.

Beetle shrugged. When his shoulders came up like that, you could see why the nickname. Back when he was a lot heavier it had fit much better. "Heard they had a fight. Over a woman."

"Shit. The guy is a hundred and twelve."

"That's in street years, Garrett. He's only a little older than you are."

I finished my mug, pushed it over for a refill. "Give me the sausage and kraut. And remind me not to get so far down on my luck that I've got to live like a ratman."

Beetle chuckled as he started digging around in a pot. He gave me an extra sausage. Both looked a little long in the tooth. They had been in the water a long time.

"Hey, Garrett. Don't get down on your luck. And try to turn the beer-drinking back into a hobby. Or you might get there."

"What's this about The Call? They trying to work the protection racket on you?"

"They don't call it that, but that's what it amounts to." He plopped a couple of boiled potatos on the plate on top of the kraut.

"I know somebody who might get them off your back."

That was just the kind of thing Relway and his secret police liked to bust up, and I had no love for The Call.

"Appreciate it." Beetle turned to hand me my plate. His gaze went over my shoulder. His face turned pale.

45

I turned.

A cascade of black paper was fluttering through the doorway, buoyed by no obvious wind. Through that came a huge dog, tongue dangling a foot, eyes burning red. A second dog followed, then Black Mona herself, bearing up well under the weight of all those weapons.

"What did you do now?" Beetle croaked.

He could see them?

"Who, me?"

"They ain't after me, Garrett."

"Yeah. You're right."

The doorframe behind Quilraq began to glow golden.

Shadows crept in. Good old Torbit was here, too. Maybe it was a Shayir family reunion.

Had they whipped the Godoroth?

I started wolfing kraut and sausage. The Shayir glared at me.

Beetle filled my mug. "What are those things?"

"You really don't want to know." He was a religious man. He would not want to think ill of the gods.

Cold air blasted through the doorway.

Blur. Black Mona staggered. Her hounds yipped. Quilraq rustled. Jorken materialized in front of me. He was not in a good mood. What a day he must have been having. He grabbed me by the shirt and tossed me over his shoulder.

The side wall of Beetle's place exploded inward. Daiged, Rhogiro, and Ringo charged through. I thought that now Beetle would have to believe my story.

Imar himself followed the flying wedge of double uglies, baby lightnings prancing in his hair. His eyes were not pleasant when they touched me, but his immediate attention belonged to the Shayir.

"Run for it, Beetle." As Jorken turned, though, I discovered that Beetle was prescient. He had taken my advice before I offered it.

Jorken sprinted through the hole opened by the ugly boys. Egad, we could have used a few like them down in the islands. The war wouldn't have lasted nearly so long.

The air ripped past so fast I could hardly snatch bites out of it. Light sleet was falling steadily. That dark coach loomed out of the night. Abyss, that darkness in darkness, stared down as Jorken tossed me inside without bothering to open the door. I picked up fresh scrapes on the window edges. I got a pat on the cheek from Magodor before she dismounted from the far side. Her tenderness was false. She was in full Destroyer avatar. She hurried off to do whatever she did. Jorken went with her.

I was alone. With Star. Who had what it would take to make a statue stand up and listen.

The coach started moving. So did Star.

That gal knew her business.

This insanity certainly did have its moments. The bad part was putting up with what went on in between.

Star relented after I begged for mercy. She settled opposite me, gloriously disheveled. She giggled like the last thing you could expect to find in her head was a thought. Every boy's dream.

I was tying my shoes when the horses screamed and something ripped the top off the coach.

"Damn!" I said. "Now for more of that stuff in between."

I flung myself out a door, into the cold. I rolled in sleet half an inch deep. A stray thought: What had become of the Goddamn Parrot?

Not far away, Abyss was pulling himself back out of the hole in a wall through which he had been thrown.

He was not pleased. The darkness within his hood was deeper than ever. Maybe the madder he got the more fathomless the nothingness there grew.

The right rear wheel of the coach collapsed. The nearest side door flopped open. In a sort of ghost glow I saw Star still sitting there jaybird, grinning, totally pleased with herself.

Time for Garrett to get in some more exercise.

Abyss moved to intercept me. Something whooshed through the night, slammed him through the air. He smashed into another wall. Business would be great for the brickyards tomorrow.

Abyss slid down, did not bounce back up. So. Even a god can go down for the count.

I heard the approach of heavy wings. Lila and Dimna dropped out of the night, became their charming girl selves. "It worked!" one piped. She started toward me like she had that old wickedness in mind. The other one clambered into the coach and planted a distinctly unsisterly kiss upon Star's lips. Star snuggled right up.

Golden light rippled through the night. Shadows pranced. Faun guy Torbit coalesced. He seemed baffled. "Stop that! All of you. Trog. Grab him and get out of here." Torbit and Star looked at one another. I had a feeling they would not stick to business long. Make love, not war.

The humongous guy with the club and divinely potent body odor came close enough to be seen. Chunks of coach still stuck to his weapon. He grabbed me up like a little girl grabs a doll. It took me only a moment to discover that struggling was futile.

I was not real happy. It had been one damned thing after another. And now sleet was getting down the back of my neck.

46

It didn't do any good to get mad. I wasn't going to kick any divine butts. The one weapon I had in this scrap lay between my ears, and it hadn't been real deadly so far.

I don't like whiners and excuse-makers, but ... it's hard to think when you're getting lugged around in one humongous hand, hardly gently. With hailstones hitting you in the face and sliding inside your clothing.

The bizarre weather had to be connected with the solid materializations of all these divinities. Maybe that required pulling the warmth right out of the mortal plane.

If only we could get the effect under control and harness it for use during high summer, I could make my fortune. How could I work a partnership deal with a god?

The big guy stopped walking. He began turning in place. *Zoom!* I saw why. Old Jorken was on the job, circling us. Poor Jorken. He'd had a rough day. If I was him I would demand a raise. *Boom!* Down came that tree of a club. It bashed a hole in the street. Jorken missed getting splattered by barely half a step.

I had an idea. I decided to put it to work before it got lonely. The Godoroth knew where I was, anyway.

I worked Magodor's cord loose from my waist. That was a real adventure, what with the big guy prancing around trying to get a solid whack at Jorken. I stretched an inch of rope out to four feet, tied a bowline, made the loop for getting invisible with the stretched section and got my feet worked through it all while being flailed around by the dancing giant. I saw scores of faces at windows, being entertained. I hoped nobody out there recognized me.

Trog's club flailed. A water trough exploded. A porch collapsed. Jorken stayed a step ahead. It was plain he was keeping the big guy in one place till slower Godoroth could catch up.

I wiggled until I got the invisibility loop over my top end, too, then continued to work the loop around so I could tighten it around the big guy's wrist. Then I stroked the cord the way Maggie had shown me, so it would shrink back to normal.

Old Trog froze, looked startled, then produced an all-time bellow of amazement and pain. And I splashed into the inch of melting sleet and hail masking some of TunFaire's more rugged cobblestones. The big guy's severed hand scrambled around inside the sack of invisibility with me.

That hand would not stop, I guess because it had been nipped off an immortal. I slithered to the side of the street, hoping my trail would not be too obvious. But nobody had much attention left over for me. Trog was in a real fury now. Jorken had a full-time job staying out of his way. Trog's club swished close enough to make him dizzy.

I wormed into a shadow and started sliding out of that sack. No need to tell anybody which way I was headed.

Jorken noticed me as I kicked Trog's hand away from me. He lost his concentration for an instant as he turned my way.

Wham! Trog gave new meaning to the expression "pound him into the ground." He was winding up for another swing when last I saw him.

I got the hell out of there fast.

Daiged and Rhogiro arrived just as I did my fade. Then the masonry really started to fly.

Something flapped past. I dodged, afraid I had an owl girl after me. "Awk!" The flyer smacked into a brick wall. "This thing cannot see in the dark." *Flap-flap.* "Garrett?"

"Where the hell have you been?" I felt around till I found the bird. It was really dark out now.

"You lost me when you stopped to eat. I had to tend to business elsewhere. I returned to a situation fraught with anticipation. As I flew up to reconnoiter it, the excitement began in earnest. I managed to trace you by staying close to the ugly one."

I muttered something about pots and kettles, got the critter installed on my shoulder, and resumed moving.

"Gotten real exciting, hasn't it?"

"They have begun to indulge in brutal destruction, like petulant children. Make for the park. And do move faster if you wish to get away."

"I can't go any faster." I was slipping and sliding all over, barely keeping my footing. The water under the sleet had frozen into a treacherous glaze.

And then it started to snow.

Snow leaves great tracks—unless it comes down real heavy. It began to look like this was just the night for that.

Another big blockbluster of a battle shaped up behind us. The gods shrieked and squawked like divine fishwives.

"I need warmer clothes," I said. "I'm going to freeze my butt off."

"You can afford to lose some of it. Head for the park. Miss Cat should meet us there. She will take us to safety." The bird was shaking too.

The snowfall lessened as we distanced ourselves from the battle, where thunder and lightning had begun to lark about. In fact, for a while that got so enthusiastic I figured Imar and Lang must be working it out god to god.

Them dancing gave us a chance to grab a new lead.

"I don't got much go-power left," I whimpered at the Goddamn Parrot as I stumbled into the park. The snow there was ankle deep and rising fast, but there was no ice or sleet underneath. It had to be real nasty back where it all started.

A breeze was rising, speeding toward the center of conflict. It slammed snowflakes into my face. They were big wet ones. I muttered and cursed. The Goddamn Parrot, just to be difficult, cursed and muttered. I trudged in what I guessed to be the general direction of the place where Cat had landed before. I couldn't tell anything for sure. It was darker than the inside of a shylock's heart.

47

"Garrett! Over here!"

Cat. I turned my head right and left to get a sense of her direction. I caught a toe on something, tumbled into a low place where snow had gathered eight inches deep. The Goddamn Parrot cussed me for being clumsy.

Cat appeared out of the milky shower. "Here." She offered me a blanket. I noticed that she was dressed for the weather. Which suggested she had an idea what was going on. But I didn't get a chance to ask. "Get up!" she barked. "We have to hurry. Come on! Some of them are on your trail again."

Her name was apt. She could see in the dark. She seemed to have trouble hearing in the dark, though. My "What the hell is going on?" fell into the snow without so much as a muted thump.

Cat led me about a hundred yards at right angles to my previous course. And there stood all her winged sidekicks, muttering seditiously amongst themselves. The weather didn't seem to bother Fourteen. The horses awarded me equine looks more laden than usual with the semi-intelligent malice of their tribe. But we did have something in common at last. They weren't happy about being out here, either.

"Shake your tail, Sugar Hips. Ya got bottom feeders headed your way."

I got a look at Cat's crew because way up in the snow clouds a pinpoint of light brighter than any noonday sun had popped and had taken a dozen seconds to fade away.

Cat helped me mount one of her beasts. It seemed to be the same one as before. And, behold! For the second time running I managed to get on top facing the same direction he was. It was an age of great wonders.

The Goddamn Parrot wanted to say something but couldn't squeeze it out. He couldn't control his shivering. Parrots are not meant for cold weather. I tucked him inside my blanket. He slithered around till he found a way inside my shirt. Then he settled down to shiver and mutter to himself.

"Cat, will you please tell me . . ."

Somewhere a wolf howled. Somewhere something named Nog polished its only thought. I didn't catch Cat's shout, but it was no answer.

The horses started to run. My blanket flapped in the wind. I held on with my legs while I tried to get myself wrapped again. I was shaking beyond all hope of control. It couldn't be long before the cold caused irreversible damage.

Fourteen zoomed past, bumblebee wings humming. "Grab your ass, Slick." He giggled. The bottom fell out.

My mount had run off the end of something again. Its huge wings extended, beat the flake-filled air. The cold breeze roared past, not quite as chilly now. I started to worry about frostbite but soon had trouble keeping a sharp edge on my thoughts.

Fourteen buzzed around running his mouth till even my ride got fed up and tried to take a bite out of him as he zipped past. A couple of cherub feathers whipped past me. Fourteen squealed and headed for Cat, plopping down into her lap.

Another one of those incredibly bright points of light popped over the north side of TunFaire. There was too much snow to tell anything else about it. I was trapped in a cold bubble in a sea of milk.

That flash made the flying horses whinny in dismay. They redoubled their efforts to gain altitude. Fourteen started cussing. Cat asked him what was going on. The horses turned directly away from the flash. Cat's mount drifted away from mine.

Curious. But I didn't have much hope of finding out what was going on. Everybody was giving me the mushroom treatment, keeping me in the dark and feeding me horse manure.

It all had to do with the feud going on back there, of course.

Something came down from the north and passed between my mount and Cat's. It went by too fast to see, arriving with a hiss, then leaving a baby thunderclap to mark its passing.

The horses yelped and tried desperately to get going faster.

Did my honey shout an explanation across, just in case it would help me stay alive? Sure she did. Right after she told me the guaranteed-to-win numbers I ought to bet in the Imperial Games.

I discovered that our course was southward because we arose above thinning clouds. I made out what had to be the Haiden Light at Great Cape, downriver thirty miles, south of town. We were way up high now, moving fast—and finding warmer air quickly, thanks to no gods. A little thumbnail clipping of a moon lay upon the eastern horizon, smiling or smirking.

I looked over my shoulder. TunFaire lay under an inverted bowl of clouds that flickered and glowed. Serpents of mist writhed upon the surface of the bowl and gradually sank toward the epicenter beneath.

The Goddamn Parrot got active suddenly. He wriggled till he got his ugly little head out into the wind. "Garrett. A dram of information. Shinrise the Destroyer turns out to be . . ."

"A Lambar Coast war god? Hangs around with cherubs and winged horses?"

"How did you know?" Next thing to a whine there, Old Bones.

"I remembered." Under stress some guys just can't shut up. Back when I was in the Corps we had had us one of those for a while, a kid from the Lambar Coast.

He had called on Shinrise whenever the going got tough.

One of those awful pinpoint flashes occurred on the far side of the city again. Ectoplasmic light expanded around it. For just an instant a point of darkness existed within that globe. Then cloud serpents began to spill down and twist into the lightning-laced mass below.

Lightning popped to our right front, *close* and overpoweringly intense. Cat and the horses screamed. Fourteen went on a cussing jag. Because I was still looking back to the north, I didn't suffer the blinding worst of it, but a brick wall of wind did smack me and almost bust me loose for one long and thrilling downward walk in the chill night air. I clutched mane hair and turned to see what had happened.

As I turned I thought I saw something cross the fragment of a moon. If I had not known that such things were mythical, the imaginings of men who hadn't ever seen an actual flying thunder lizard, I might have believed it was a dragon.

I faced front as that insane light's intensity dwindled to where it did not hurt the eye anymore. It was the same phenomenon again, only this time so close we got hit by the expanding ectoplasmic sphere. It smashed past me. My mount staggered. Blinded by the flash, he tried desperately to stay level while he recovered.

There was a hole in the night where the pop had taken place. It was a darkness deeper than that inside a coffin buried in an underground tomb on the dark side of a world without a sun. Then, just for an instant, something reached through that hole, something that was darker still, something so dark that it glistened in the light. Rainbows slithered over it like an oil film on water. It came my way, but I don't think it was after me.

The Goddamn Parrot went berserk inside my shirt. Either he wanted to get away bad or he had decided to snack on my guts.

Fourteen squealed like somebody had set his toes on fire.

Suddenly it was colder than any cold I had endured

yet. The reaching something popped back through its window of darkness. For an instant, before the hole shrank to invisibility, a dark alien eye glared through, filled with a malice that was almost crushing in its weight.

All that didn't last more than a couple of seconds. My horse barely had time to beat his wings a full stroke.

The cold penetrated right down to the core of me. I knew, whether I wanted to believe it or not, that I had looked right into the realm of the gods. Maybe the eye belonged to something so unpleasant that the gods would willingly destroy my world rather than be forced to go back where that waited.

Hmm. That didn't feel quite right, though I had a suspicion that I had just seen something a lot nastier than any of the gods who were complicating my life now.

Damn! I couldn't see Cat anywhere. And my mount seemed to be having a seizure. Not to mention the fact that the ground looked like it was about eleven miles down.

I don't like heights very much. They give me the jim-jams in a big way.

48

"Worse things waiting." When I was a kid, that was the inevitable response of the old folks if you complained about anything. "You got it easy, young man. They's worse things waiting."

They knew what they were talking about, too.

I hung on. I kept my eyes closed tight while we fell. My mount banged the air feebly with spasming wings. It screamed a horsey scream, only about fifteen times as loud as a normal ground-bound beast might have.

Just the way I always wanted to go, at the age of four hundred and eight. Riding a waking nightmare.

"They finally got me," I muttered. I took even tighter hold of the creature's mane. This one damned horse was going with me.

Another horse shrieked from far above. Sounded like it was coming closer fast. I cracked one eye to see how far we had fallen. "Oh, shit!"

I should have known better.

My mount didn't like the prognosis either. He got serious about the flapping and flopping and got his hooves right side down and his wings floundering around in the right direction.

The cherub came whirring out of the night, hummed around and around, just hanging out like he enjoyed watching things fall. He chuckled a lot. Then he held up suddenly, staring, aghast. "Oh, no! That blows everything."

I looked around, spied a half-dozen tower-tall, transparent, and obviously pissed-off figures striding toward TunFaire. None of them were Shayir or Godoroth.

Neither did I think they belonged to the Board, whose controls had failed so abominably. It looked like some of the really big guys had decided to forgo normal business—making guys sacrifice their firstborn or sneaking up on virgins disguised as critters—while they attended to some emergency heavenly housekeeping.

Fourteen shot toward me, grabbed hold, scrambled up under my blanket. I grumbled, "It's getting a little crowded in here." That distracted me from the screaming I wanted to do.

The damned horse got it all together. It beat hell out of the air with its monster wings. To no avail. We had too much downward momentum. *Whamboney!* We hit. We shot on down through about half a mile of tree branches. Lucky us, they slowed us down. Lucky us, none of them were big enough to stop us cold. Lucky us, when we hit water I only went in up to my ears.

We surfaced. The horse whooped and hooted and gasped after its lost breath. The Goddamn Parrot wriggled its head out of my clothes again, began a wet and lonely soliloquy filled with every cussword the Dead Man could recall from about fifty languages.

Old Chuckles has been around a long time.

The cherub came out and hovered. He agreed with the bird.

It was all my fault.

Same as it ever was.

Personally, I was too busy being glad I was still in one piece to give either one of them a hard time. But good ideas for later did occur to me.

"Where the hell are we?"

Fourteen snapped, "In a freaking swamp, moron."

That wasn't exactly hard to miss. There were mosquitoes out there big enough to carry off small pets. Otherwise, though, it was your typically wimpy Karentine swamp. If you overlooked a few poisonous bugs and snakes, it would be completely safe. Nothing like the swamps we endured down in the islands, where we faced snakes as long as anchor chains *and* the alligators who survived by eating them.

I found myself not feeling at all awful—for a guy who had just missed falling to his death and had missed drowning only by inches.

That horse had one ounce of brains. He didn't try to fly out of there. As soon as he got his breath back, he let out a couple of forlorn neighs. He seemed surprised when they were answered from above. Fourteen buzzed upward, rattling and clattering and cussing his way through the branches. In minutes he was back, a fresh, competition-class banger in his mouth. "This way." My mount headed out. He was not inclined to hear suggestions or commentary from me.

The beast pulled in his wings completely. He proceeded as straight horse and regained his strength quickly. The cherub led us to solid ground fast. Minutes later, we left the trees. The horse broke into a trot that graduated to a canter and then a vigorous gallop. This continued for a while, the horse not growing winded but not getting off the ground either. We went over hill and dale and farm while Cat and her mount cruised overhead. Our course tended southwest. Time seemed to take the night off. Before long we left the farmlands.

I checked the moon. For sure, it hadn't traveled nearly as far as it should have. We were on elf hill time. And covering a *lot* of ground. Already we were in territory that remained unsettled because people were too superstitious to live there.

A sudden vague glow limned some hills up ahead. It made them look like they were standing in a circle, looking down at something they had surrounded. "Oh boy." It just got worse. I poked the Goddamn Parrot.

That gaudy chicken did not respond—except to bite my finger. Evidently we were beyond the Dead Man's range. At last. With the Goddamn Parrot, mercifully, left with little command of his vocal apparatus.

Great. Once again I was getting a lesson in watching out what I wished for because my wishes might come true.

Those hills had to be the Bohdan Zhibak. That name translates into modern Karentine as "The Haunted Circle." Over the ages a lot of really awful things are sup-posed to have happened there. And tonight, it seemed, the fabled Fires of Doom were ablaze inside the Circle.

Fourteen didn't want to get any closer. He was not shy about telling everyone about it.

49

Cat landed. We dismounted. She told Fourteen to shut up or go away. I hung on to a stirrup in order to maintain my defiance of the seductions of gravity. I felt like I had been living in that saddle for days. I glared at Cat. "You saved me from those lunatics back in town so you could sacrifice me out here?"

"Calm down. Fourteen, you shut up. You can be put back away with your brothers and sisters."

That worked on the cherub but not on me, though I protested, "I am calm. If I wasn't a veteran of all that screwiness in TunFaire I might not be calm. I might have a case of the rattlemouth like my buddy Fourteen. But, I mean, what's to get excited about, just because I find myself alongside the Haunted Hills? Just because there's all that doom light burning up out of the ground over there without, I bet, there being a real fire anywhere around? None of that ought to frighten a mouse."

I saw something move across the valley ahead of us, little more than a shadow hurrying, late for work. I didn't want to be on its list of chores.

"Plans change, Garrett. Originally Mom just wanted to get you out of there. But that was before the disaster."

"Which disaster? They come in strings lately." I dug the Goddamn Parrot out of my shirt, looked around in there to see what damage he had done. I wasn't going to die, but I was sore enough that I would have strangled the ridiculous little feather duster if he had not been too dull-witted to appreciate what I was doing. I

parked him on my shoulder. He had just enough wit to
hang on. Fourteen had a notion to take up residence
opposite him. I did not feel guilty when I swatted him
away.

"Which disaster? The breakdown of discipline. The
squabbling. When they use their powers that way they
weaken the walls of reality. What *is* that thing?" She
meant the Goddamn Parrot.

"A really bad practical joke."

"Excuse me?"

"It's a parrot. Argh! Shiver me timbers! Like that."

"I'm so pleased that you can maintain your sense of
humor." But she didn't sound pleased.

"It's all I've got that's all mine. What the hell are we
doing out here?" Not even Winger would have the
numskull nerve to go wandering around the Bohdan
Zhibak.

"Because of the holes in the fabric. You saw what was
happening. One blew out right in your face. If the walls
really break down . . ."

I knew enough mythology to guess. Cold beyond
imaginable cold. Eternal darkness beyond imaginable
darkness. The end of the world. But just the unspeakable beginning for the unnamable eldritch horrors from
beyond the beginning of time. Never mind it all sprang
from the imagination in the first place. "Come on! This
is some game between two gangs of petty half-wit gods
who needed me to sort them out to see who gets to stay
respectable. All of a sudden I've got to save the world?"
I'm not big on world-saving. Way too much traveling
and not nearly enough reward in the end. Not to mention you don't get much sleep.

"No! Of course not. Don't be absurd! You think too
much of yourself. If you keep your mouth shut except
when somebody asks you a question and you don't
smart off when they do, you may survive long enough
to see the world get saved."

Put me in my place, she did. "What's going on here?"
We were sneaking between a couple of hills, crunching
dry grass and bare stone, in weather that was appropri-

ate for the season. Fourteen buzzed hither and yon, ahead, but very tentatively and very low to the ground. He wanted to be there less than I did. There was an astonishing shawl of stars flung across the shoulders of a cloudless sky. The moon was in no hurry yet, though it had climbed higher.

The light up ahead wavered, waxed, waned. Sounds came down the valley, inarticulate but angry. "I don't like this, Cat. Last time I came home from the Cantard I swore I'd never leave TunFaire again. Till now I've stuck to that." More or less. But no lapse of mine had brought me this far afield.

Damn! This could turn *real* nasty. I might have to walk home.

"The gods have a secret, Garrett." She allowed the cherub to settle into her arms for a moment of rest. She held and patted him as if he were a baby. He seemed to like that.

"Just one? Then a lot of paper has gone to waste turning out holy books that claim to explain the ten million mysteries . . ."

"There you go again. Can't you ever just listen?"

Maybe when I run my yap I feel like I'm in control. I needed some control here. Desperately.

"Go ahead."

The cherub lit up a fresh banger that he pulled out of his diaper. He got fire by snapping his fingers.

Cat took the smoke. "Not now. Not here. Garrett, all gods, whatever their pantheon, whatever dogma has accreted around them, came from the same place and started out much the same. You looked into that place a while ago. The gods fled it because it's so terrible. But over here they can't stay functional, can't hang on, without belief to sustain them. Or without drawing power from the other side, which risks opening new gateways. If they have no sustenance at all, eventually they fall back to the other side. Naturally, they don't want to go home."

"You mean they're all related?"

"No. Is everyone in TunFaire related? Of course not.

They're not even all of the same race. Say this is like some of the humans going off somewhere together, in search of a better life. If they found it they might not want to come back."

"You telling me they're refugees?" The gods are refugees from somewhere else? Wouldn't that stir some excitement in the Dream Quarter? Wouldn't that be dangerous knowledge for some non-god to be lugging around?

This was no place for me. I had a notion I was one of the non-gods.

"Cat, you're a doll and I love you, but this isn't my idea of the perfect date. I've got a sneaking suspicion my prospects would be a lot better if I headed some other direction." Like any damned direction but this one.

Cat grabbed my hand. She was strong. My course remained steady, straight ahead. She told me, "You have a tool."

"Huh?"

"You can make yourself invisible."

"Yeah. But when I do, the Godoroth always know where I'm at."

"And you think they'd try something here?"

"Why the hell not? They've already proved they're bonkers. But you know them. I don't."

"We should remain unnoticed. For now."

"That's what I had in mind when I said let's go." I started to head for the horses. Just this once they looked like the lesser evil.

Cat still had my hand and she hadn't gotten any weaker. I got nowhere.

We were near the edge of the light and had attracted no attention yet. Shapes and shadows haunted the hillsides. Wouldn't you know a place called the Haunted Circle would be like that? I didn't recognize any of them. Few were in anthropomorphic form.

More arrived by the moment, flopping, flying, slithering, jogging in on two hundred legs. "Sooner or later something is going to trip over us." I tried beating feet again.

Have I mentioned Cat's unusual strength? I didn't go anywhere this time either.

I took out Magodor's cord, stretched it, knotted it, created a loop big enough for two. We hopped inside. "This may get real friendly," I warned.

Cat smiled a wicked smile that told me the deviltry was in her but she wasn't feeling flirtatious right now. She could stick to business where her mother could not.

It seemed my sack of invisibility could be made as big as whatever loop I started with, plus however high I could raise that loop before I closed it up. By holding hands and staying in step, Cat and I were able to move the sack with little trouble. She insisted on heading right out into the middle of the lighted ground. Once we were there we could see all the hillsides. Our presence didn't attract any attention.

Still I saw nothing I recognized.

The mob fell silent. The result was spooky. All that many humans in one place would have created a racket like hurricanes raising hell amongst the boughs of tropical forests. I turned slowly, examining every hill. I was scared, but I was not out of control. Not like Fourteen, who was down between our feet trying to vanish into our footprints, unable, apparently, to believe we were truly invisible.

I whispered, "I take it little ones like him don't get treated real well by the big guys."

"Cruelty is in their nature."

I didn't stop turning, studying. Few of these gods clung to any shape I had seen in the Dream Quarter. Maybe out here the belief of their worshippers was attenuated enough to let them relax. Scary to think things as ugly as Ringo and as attractive as Star might be identical blobs on one of those hillsides.

Pity, that.

I whispered, "You know any of those things?" I noticed a few taking imaginable shapes for flickering instants. Maybe their worshippers were thinking of them.

"No. My mother worked hard to keep me a secret from them. If Imar found out about me ..."

Of course. It was just ducky being a half god if a god was your pop and your mom was human. A divine tradition. The great heroes of antiquity all had some heavenly blood. But goddesses aren't supposed to boff the suckers, apparently.

The old double standard was alive and well amongst the sons of heaven. Or whatever you called that over there. Always nice to know that some things are the same in heaven as they are on earth. Lets everybody know where they stand.

The shadows continued to gather like buzzards to a freshly fallen thunder lizard. The great towering ones began to arrive, their eyes like cities burning, their hair the ugliest thunderheads. I whispered, "What's happening here, anyway?" I was sure no such assembly had taken place before, ever.

"When they came here the gods left weak places in the fabric of the barriers between. When they want to show off or perform miracles, they use power they pull through those weak places. When they do they create a momentary opening. There are worse things still back there. They would like to come here, too. The fighting between the Godoroth and Shayir would have opened a lot of holes. Some of those things over there found them before they closed up again. They tried to break through. That's what caused those flashes. The stupid fighting went on so long and the fabric of the barrier grew so weak that those horrors might actually bust their own hole through. This assembly is going to decide how to handle that. It's also going to discuss the Shayir and Godoroth. They aren't so stupid they didn't know better. A universal terror of the evils left behind has underlain all divine law for ten thousand years."

"How the hell do you all of a sudden know all this?" I knew she couldn't have known much of it when we arrived.

"I can catch snatches of their debate." She tapped her temple. "It's really hot."

On that level where the Dead Man communicates with me, inside my head, I was aware of a continuous dull buzz, like I was catching just the remotest edge of mindspeech going on in a somewhat similar manner. That buzz was extremely stressful. Before long I was going to have one ferocious headache.

Then I spotted somebody I knew.

50

Magodor stalked along the foot of a hill about a hundred feet away. She was no shadow. She was set solidly in her nastiest avatar. She looked right at me. She knew I was there. Good old Driver of the Spoil. She didn't look pleased but seemed unlikely to try making my life less pleasant than it was already.

I recalled that people in TunFaire had been unable to see the divine clowns lurking around me. "Cat, you can see these things, can't you?"

"I see Magodor. She sees us, too."

"No. But she knows I'm here. She gave me the cord. She can tell where it is."

"Uhm!" She seemed to have lost interest. Aha! Her mother had arrived. Imara seemed quite regal and totally indifferent to the censure of fellow gods.

The rest of the Shayir and Godoroth arrived, all frozen into their city forms. The anger around us grew palpable. My headache began worsening fast. Among the stragglers I spotted interesting faces. "Cat. Do you know that character there?" I indicated a huge, handsome, one-eyed guy who was neither Godoroth nor Shayir.

"That's Bogge. He's Mom's lover."

"Bogge? You sure?" He looked a lot like Shinrise the Destroyer. "Gets around, don't she?" I wondered if a god would lie to a mortal about his identity. Or if a mother would lie to her daughter.

My thoughtless remark earned me a dirty look.

I asked, "How about the redhead there? The one who looks like an ordinary mortal." Ordinary, hell. All women ought to look so ordinary. She looked like Star might if she decided to conform to my peculiar prejudices.

"Not in that form." There was a small catch in her voice.

"She got me into this. She was watching my house. I decided to follow her."

"She isn't Godoroth or Shayir."

Indeed. But you do have some ideas . . .

Nog is inescapable.

Well, of course he was. He kept coming back like an unemployed cousin, Nog did.

I recalled a little old lady at the mouth of an alley and reflected that goddesses were not required to keep one look. "The name Adeth mean anything? Magodor said an Adeth was trying to trap me. I thought she meant that woman."

Nervously, Cat said, "One of the Krone Gods is called Adeth . . ." and cut herself off.

"What? Give, darling. Look around. We don't need to play games."

"Adeth is one of a bunch of tribal deities from way down south. The people are fur traders and rock hunters. They've never had enough people here to win a place on the Street of the Gods."

Now that rolled off her tongue so smooth it must have been distilled twice.

She said, "I don't see why some primitives like that would get involved. Though her name does mean Treachery, I think."

"There's a lot of that going on these days." That redhead was just too polished to be the wishful thinking of fur trappers still using stone tools. Those guys go for malicious rocks and trees and such. And storm gods. They love gods who stomp around and bellow and smash things up a lot.

Be right at home around here.

Nog is inescapable.

"That boy needs a hobby," I muttered. The thing itself oozed out of a valley, stopped, turned in place slowly for half a minute, then began to shuffle our way.

"Oh, damn," Cat murmured.

A spear blade twelve feet tall slammed into the earth in front of Nog, nearly shaving his nose off. It was slightly transparent but did have a definite impact when it hit. Clods flew a hundred feet. Lightning slithered down the spear shaft. Sparks played tag along the edges of the blade.

One of the very tall, very big-time gods had admonished Nog.

Fourteen was whimpering out loud now. He was down flat on his pudgy belly with his chubby, too short arms trying to cover his head.

I said, "I'm beginning to wonder, Cat."

She grimaced but didn't answer.

Nog considered his situation, decided that since he was inescapable he could afford to wait. He resumed moving along a new course. He joined the rest of the Godoroth gang. Those swinging party guys had gathered at the foot of a slope opposite the Shayir. Both crews looked troubled. And angry, though no actual lightning bolts flew.

The last stragglers must have arrived because all of a sudden most all the gods tried to assume their worldly avatars. About a third were not successful. Maybe there wasn't enough power to go around.

I had an idea. This happens on occasion. "Are the walls between the worlds thinner in the Dream Quarter?"

"Will you stop blubbering?" Cat stuck a toe into the cherub's ribs. Then she looked at me almost suspiciously. She seemed reluctant to answer my questions now.

I said, "It seems reasonable to assume that they would cluster where it would be easiest to tap their sources of power." Which, of course, added meaning to the struggle of the Shayir and Godoroth to remain on the Street.

Cat grunted.

There was a change in the painful background racket gurgling down in the bottom of my mind. It faded. I caught the edge of what had to be one big guy really booming. There was no motion at all on the surrounding slopes.

The meeting had been called to order.

I thought about gods and points of power. Seemed likely that in addition to collecting where power was most accessible they would develop caste systems based on ability to grab and manipulate that power. Somebody like my little ankle-biting buddy Fourteen would be way down at the bottom of the pile.

If I have the innate ability to seize sixty percent of the power available and you can grab only thirty percent, guess who is in charge? Assuming we subscribe to the sociopathic attitudes generally ascribed to the gods.

Sudden anger surged along the thought stream I sensed so marginally. With the pure cold voice I had felt no pain, but this anger was a powerful blow, however glancing. It sent me to my knees. I ground the heels of my fists into my temples. I managed not to scream.

Imar came out from the Godoroth team. Lang moved forward, too. They raced to see who could grow big the fastest. Each surrounded himself with all the noisy, dramatic effects demanded by mortal worshippers.

Since I was down already, I settled against a not entirely uncomfortable rock. I patted Fourteen's bottom like he really was a baby and reflected, "I should have brought a lunch. This punch-out is going to take a while."

I saw representatives of the Board called on the carpet while the mirror-image boss gods looked one another over. The mind stream had a blistery touch. The supreme busybodies seemed to want to give everybody a yellow card for unnecessary roughness.

Me, I thought they all deserved big penalties for unnecessary stupidity.

I kept one eye on Imara and another on her boyfriend, whatever name he was using. I kept one on the incipient ruckus out front and another on the redhead Cat was determined to keep mysterious. That didn't really leave a lot of eyes for anything else.

51

Boy. Talk about a big bunch of nothing! There I was, all bent over and scrunched up expecting the Midnight of the Gods, or at least the little ones getting their pants pulled down and their holy heinies spanked, and all I got was a headache that left me nostalgic for my hangover.

"Nobody is doing anything," I whined.

"There's plenty going on. You don't see it because you can't listen in. The Shayir and the Godoroth are really upset."

I did note a certain restlessness on the sidelines, reflected by the squared-off boss gods, who, I now suspected, were supposed to shake hands and make up. And I noted that Imara sort of drifted slowly throughout the midfield confrontation. She got smaller as she moved. And she assumed a whole new look.

Interesting. *Very* interesting.

"Cat. You keeping an eye on your mom?"

"Huh? Why?"

I pointed. "That's her there. Sliding over to her boyfriend. She's been changing her looks as she goes." I assumed she was disguising herself on levels seen only by gods, too.

"Oh. She looks a lot younger."

"She sure does. She's turning herself into a dead ringer for you." I kicked the cherub. I wanted him to stop whining long enough to get a good look at this transformation, too. "You got any thoughts about this, Cat?"

My suspicion was that Cat might not be as big a secret as she thought. I had a hunch she might be just another angle in a carefully managed escape maneuver.

Cat's eyes narrowed. She glared at her mother. She glared at me. She didn't have to be told that I suspected the worst. We both knew that gods and goddesses don't cling to any wordly code of conduct.

Cat said, "Maybe we ought to leave."

"That might have been a good idea a while ago. Before anybody knew we were here. But now? How far could we run? Could we run fast enough?"

"Nothing is settled here. The deadline still hasn't come." But she climbed to her feet and grabbed up her little buddy, plainly interested in quick relocation.

I got up myself. The whole situation had me thinking, which, according to some, doesn't happen all that often.

And according to the Dead Man, not often enough.

"Cat. The world was here before the coming of the gods. Right?"

"Yes. Of course it was. Why?"

Because, then, these were not really gods in the way I had been taught to think of gods. Even the gods I had been told were the one and only real and they're-gonna-send-all-them-infidels-to-burn-in-hell gods just belonged to the same bunch of transdimensional refugees. Or fugitives?

"Cat, did these gods come here by choice?"

"What?"

"It occurs to me they might be exiles. Thrown out of the old home for bad behavior or just excessive stupidity."

"No. None of them want to go back. That's what the fighting is all about."

"Maybe." I had some thoughts that included suspicions of setups. I surveyed the audience. More gods had settled into their earthly forms. I saw some really big names. Out here, though, they just looked luckier than bunches like the Godoroth and Shayir. Probably had better publicity wazoos.

What I didn't see anymore was a goddess named

Imara. What I didn't see was a redhead maybe called Adeth hanging out with raggedy-ass jungle gods. I did see Shinrise the Destroyer—or maybe Bogge the Sucker—standing around stupidly now, looking like he had just lost something.

The ranks of the Godoroth and Shayir seemed short handed on females.

I checked some of the more successful gangs but couldn't tell if they had gone shorthanded, too. They just looked more prosperous. A supply of believers surely helped, but maybe also a knack for drawing power from beyond this reality.

Maybe gods are like sausages and politics and should not be examined closely.

I always expect the worst. That means I can be pleasantly surprised sometimes. This didn't seem to be one of those times. Circumstances appeared to support my most cynical suspicions.

There were thousands of gods there, though most were hangers-on, many even smaller than Fourteen.

The cherub seemed to have settled down. Maybe he realized that nobody was paying him any attention. I *knew* I was invisible but still felt naked to every divine eye.

There was some subtle movement out there, and tension rising. The hair on my arms tingled.

52

There was big anger in the air again, much worse than before. Fourteen whimpered. Something had happened. The crowd around Lang and Imar were all in a rage.

"We need to leave now," Cat said. Her voice squeaked. "A ruling was handed down. The Shayir and Godoroth refuse to accept it."

Holding hands, in step, each laboring under the weight of a garbage-mouthed curse, we headed for our horses. "Explain," I squeaked. My throat was tight, too. I noticed Magodor drifting through the mob. She seemed intent on tracking us. I wondered why.

"Because of their behavior in town, the senior gods have banished the Godoroth and the Shayir from the Street of the Gods *and* TunFaire."

"And our boys won't go quietly?"

"Imar and Lang pretty much said, 'Stick it in your ear!' "

"Can they do that?" Of course they could. Anybody can tell anybody anything, anytime. The tricky part is surviving the aftermath.

"There may be a confrontation."

Oh. "Uh-oh."

"And this is definitely the wrong place for that. This is where the gods originally arrived. It takes a lot longer than ten thousand years for wounds like that to heal. The walls here are tissue."

Which might explain why the little guys thought they could thumb their noses, except that I didn't credit them with sense enough to consider that subtle an angle.

"Keep hiking, girl. Runt, you stop sniveling or I'll kick you out of here."

Fourteen sneered. He wasn't afraid of any mortal. I was too busy staying in step with Cat to follow up.

I glanced back. I didn't see Magodor anymore. I did see a whirlwind of black paper chips and a mist of golden light around Lang, who raised his left fist and pumped his thumb in and out of his clenched fingers in a classic obscene gesture directed at the big boys. Then he struck suddenly right-handed, swinging a sword of lightning at Imar's throat. Just as suddenly, you had Jorken streaking around, the ugly guys looking for throats to crush, Imar flailing around with his own lightning. Trog went berserk with his hammer. Torbit, Quilraq, and others went wild. Black Mona galloped in with her hounds, her weapons flying everywhere.

"Hang on, Cat. Just a second." I watched as the fray disappeared inside a cloud of dust, then a light storm as those incredibly brilliant pops began ripping the fabric of reality. In seconds it began to snow. And Cat and I were moving again, faster than ever.

"Why did you stop?"

"Wanted to make sure I'd seen something right."

"What?"

"None of the females are in that mess, except Black Mona. And she's got more hair on her ass than anybody but Trog." Not even Magodor was involved. Maybe especially not even Magodor. What's an end of the world dustup without a Destroyer?

The temperature plummeted. My headache worsened till Cat had to help me stay on my feet. Numerous top god types tried to break up the fight. The Godoroth and Shayir went on like fools with nothing to lose and a complete willingness to take everybody with them. And they seemed to get support from some odds and ends of petty pewter types from other pantheons, mainly of the strike-from-behind, score-settling sort.

We made good time despite being inside the bag. We were behind the knee of a hill when the Bohdan Zhibak lit up with the grandaddy of all light pops.

I went down. "Bet they saw that back in town." My headache grew so intense I blacked out.

I recovered in seconds. "What are you doing?"

"Trying to get us out of this."

Trying to take a powder, actually. Hell. Give her the benefit. Say she was trying to scram because I was out and she couldn't move the sack with all that dead weight in it.

My head didn't hurt nearly so much now. I found the knot, got us out in seconds. Fourteen went catatonic with terror. I restored my cord to normal, wrapped it around my waist again.

There was a lot of noise from the other side of the hill. Cat told me, "We've got to keep going."

"In a minute." I wanted a peek. Just one little look. I was pretty sure my Midnight of the Gods was cooking now. Be a shame not to witness some of the action.

53

I kept a tight grip on Cat. Just in case. Much as I hate horses and heights, I hated the prospect of walking home more. Especially walking home while suffering a headache and a psychotic parrot.

She had the strength to break away. She just didn't try.

Ever seen a sea anemone? Thing like a little flower a couple inches across, pale tentacles that just drift around? Maybe not. I had the advantage of an all-but-the-pain expenses-paid trip to remote islands. Anyway, these little guys just sit there with their arms up and when something drifts by they snag it.

A black version thirty feet in diameter with two hundred tentacles fifty feet long was stuck in a hole in the air where Lang and Imar had been banging on each other. It was twenty feet off the ground, tilted forty degrees and wiggling like crazy. "No wonder the gods wanted to come over here."

The thing plugged the hole so tight no cold could come through. The snow had begun to melt.

The gods were active. Frantically. Some tried to deal with the interloper. Some tried to get loose from it. The really big guys were feeding it. I saw Ringo get flung into the middle of the tentacle forest. Many of the visible victims, in fact, seemed to be of Shayir or Godoroth extraction. Guess this will settle that question.

Other old scores were being recalculated as well. A general trimming of the divine population was under way.

There seemed to be enough gods actually taking care of business to push that thing back. While I watched, the hole shrank several feet.

Nog is inescapable. Oh my. Somebody fell through the cracks.

"Time to go."

Cat had gotten it, too. She outran me, though not by much. Wonder of wonders, her flying pals had not left us twisting in the wind. Considering Fourteen's timidity, I'd figured to find them long gone.

Nog is inescapable.

Maybe so. He was closing in fast.

He was so close, in fact, that he leaped and landed a raking blow on my mount's left flank as we went airborne. Which naturally irritated the horse. It gained some altitude, turned, dove, did a fine job of thunking all four hooves off Nog's noggin. Nog said, *Ow Stop! That hurts!*

The retard had double the vocabulary I had thought. But I didn't dwell on that. I was too busy screaming at the horse to get the hell out of there before I fell off or Nog showed us what other divine talents he possessed—or Magodor caught up or the other gods got bored with feeding each other to their new pet.

The winged horse took my advice.

As we gained altitude again my headache diminished. I was soaked with sweat from gutting it out.

The moon had climbed only slightly higher. At this rate, if we hustled, we could get back to town before we left. Or at least met ourselves on the way. I could warn me not to go.

I looked down. The Haunted Circle crawled like the proverbial anthill. There had been a lot of breakthroughs. The one I had seen was just the biggest. In numerous places one or two tentacles reached through and tried to find something to grab. But the gods had covered themselves. There wasn't so much as a bush out there. When a tentacle grabbed a boulder somebody zapped that into pea gravel. The home gods were winning. Rah! The wannabes were being driven back. Rah!

Rah! But at terrible cost. Boo! This insanity would decimate every pantheon in the Dream Quarter. Wait! Would that be so awful?

None of this was likely to touch the man on the street. I could not see, for example, the New Concord Managerial Recidivist gods informing their faithful that good old Gerona the Tallykeeper was no more, so they needn't trouble themselves with bringing in those tithes. More likely they would hear about several new diocesan appeals, maybe aimed at fixing up the mother temple in TimsNoroë or financing another mission to the heathen Venageti. And one sceat out of every silver mark really would go toward carrying out the fund's dedicated purpose.

Not that the gods would themselves be much concerned about money or precious metals.

Well! Look at this. Not every god is woven of the stuff of heroes. I was too far up there to recognize individuals, but quite a few had run from the bad place. Was it all cowardice, though? One group of several dozen was headed north in a purposeful manner. I had a notion that if I dared swoop down there, I would find some very familiar folks.

In fact . . .

54

In fact, a pair of familiar shapes hurtled past, *zip! zap!* to my right front from my left rear, angling down from above, too swift to see but trailing giggles that gave them away. One looped back and took a seat right in front of me, where she changed into a half-naked girl. The other one circled and complained.

"I got here first, slowpoke. Hi, Garrett! Surprised? Can we talk? We're lots smarter than we always acted."

"I'm real uncomfortable up here. That first step down is a killer. No offense, but do you think you could maybe keep your hands to yourself till we get a little closer to the ground? I don't have your advantages over gravity. If I get distracted I just fall."

The circling owl girl giggled. The other answered peevishly, "He is not! He's just behaving like a mortal." She did not take her hands off me. "Wouldn't it be exciting way up here, Garrett? I've never played with mortals anywhere but down on the ground."

Does a bimbo become any less a bimbo because she is smarter than everybody thinks?

"For about as long as it takes for me to lose track and let go here." I tried to get a hint of the color of her rags. "Look, Dimna, darling, you're just about the greatest thing that ever happened to me." Wow! I got it right first try! "But now just isn't the time to show you just how much I mean that. I hate horses. I'm terrified of heights. I have a murderous headache from all the power in that mess back there, and I haven't eaten or slept since this insanity began."

So I exaggerated. We all do that to save somebody's

feelings. Or to avoid getting tossed off a two-thousand-foot drop for our thoughtlessness.

She sure did look good, though.

I am a pig, I know. I have been told. But I can't help it. Maybe if I didn't run into this kind of woman all the time? Maybe if I got into a more boring line of work?

Maybe I could just drop over the side right now, die happy making Dimna squeal all the way down.

She rubbed her firm little puffies up against me, let a hand drop familiarly, told me, "I don't think you're that incapacitated."

"Darling, I promise you, if I give in now I'll be incapacitated forever. Because I'll fall off here for sure. And I can't turn into anything else but a tired old ex-Marine."

The owl girl actually seemed flattered that I considered a dalliance with her potentially suicidal.

Who am I to argue?

"Awk?" said the Goddamn Parrot, making a sound for the first time since the latter stage of the journey outward.

"You aren't going to believe this, Old Bones." I didn't know if he was listening, but anticipating his nags about paying attention to business, I turned Dimna's temptations back upon her, a tickle here and a pinch there that she seemed happy to accept. She sneered at Lila, closed her eyes and relaxed. Her twin flapped off in a huff.

I kept talking, mostly just making noise with a little content in case the Dead Man could hear but occasionally asking a question and leaving a silence for Dimna to fill.

She might claim to be smarter than she let on, but she was no genius. Too bad that was recognized by others. She had been let in on very little of substance. But she definitely enjoyed being interrogated.

I felt so used.

Right.

"Talk to me," the Goddamn Parrot squawked.

You get distracted.

"You know I have company."

"Not, I suspect, another No-Neck."

Did he hear in monotones? Couldn't he see through Mr. Big's eyes? Interesting. "The sweetest company a growing boy could imagine, Chuckles. Every boy ought to meet Dimna on his sixteenth birthday." I gave Dimna a strained smile and a kiss. If she wanted anything more out of life she sure didn't tell me.

In pain still, sweaty, tired, and hungry, all I really wanted was to get home. I felt safe enough now.

I could not tell what Cat thought about the owl girls. She was too far away and staying slightly ahead, navigating.

55

Cat landed in Brookside Park. The snow there had not yet all melted. I told her, "Cat, I've had all the fun I can stand with you and your mom and your friends. Suppose you all carry on without me? The Shayir and Godoroth shouldn't be a problem anymore."

She dismissed the horses. They trotted into the darkness. Fourteen stayed with Cat. He was about as active as a twelve-pound brick. Cat stuck with me. So did Lila and Dimna. Maybe they just didn't know where else to go now that the Shayir pantheon was defunct. I can't say I was thrilled, though it would be fun to walk into Morley's joint with an owl girl on each arm.

At first Cat wouldn't talk in front of them, but finally she grumbled, "If you add everything up, you have to believe my mother and her cronies engineered what happened."

"That bothers you?"

"Because it looks like they didn't think about the consequences. They wanted rid of some deadwood, so they put Imar and Lang in a spot where they would betray themselves for the duds they were. I don't think Mom realized that could damage the barriers between the worlds."

I reserved my opinion, naturally, but that told me Mom was as much a dud as her husband. She just hadn't had as much chance to show it.

"Cat, you glance over history, you'll see that females, on average, aren't brighter or better than males. They can be stupid or wise, foolish or crafty, too. They can be petty or magnanimous, and blind to the blazingly obvious. One thing some religions push that I agree with is that people ought to be trying to improve themselves as a whole. But I'm a cynic. I see no evidence that it's ever going to happen."

"You may be a realist, not a cynic. I've been closer to more gods and goddesses than anyone who ever lived."

She did not seem inclined to expand upon her remarks.

I didn't get to bed. I didn't even get to eat right away. In fact, if it hadn't been for the Dead Man pushing Dean, I wouldn't have gotten in until morning. The old man had all the chains on and was sound asleep.

I gave it to him good.

An hour later I was in the Dead Man's room. Cat and Fourteen were with us. The owl girls were in the small front room with the Goddamn Parrot. I was barely awake. Dean was sulking in the kitchen, fixing something to eat. I think he was waiting for it to grow up so he could butcher it. I thought about siccing the twins on him. He needed an attitude boost. Unfortunately, only the Dead Man, Cat, and I could see them or Fourteen.

His Nibs issued an opinion. *Imara and several other goddesses engineered this thing. I imagine they just intended to rid themselves of stupid males who . . .*

"Cat already told me that."

. . . gave no thought to consequences.

"And didn't listen, no doubt."

He ignored me, began spinning out a storm of dreamlike images and speculations. My weary brain tried to translate them, but his thinking was alien because he experienced the world in so different a way. Once my mind processed his thoughts I drifted through a fairy-tale realm where all lies and surface posturings were illusions to be ignored because truths and real motives could not be hidden behind them.

"Can you get anything from the girls?"

They are exactly what they appear to be. They do not have the depth to be anything else. They could if they so desire, but they are perfectly happy with themselves just as they are. This should thrill you. For you they are a dream come true, saddled by no more inhibitions than alley cats in heat.

"That is wonderful, isn't it? But, to paraphrase the immoral philosopher Morley Dotes, what do I do with them the other twenty-three hours a day?"

Not to fear. You will not remain amusing long. Some insects have longer attention spans.

Not exactly an ego bash, that. I figured that out moments after meeting those dolls.

My own attention began to slip its moorings. Nothing would keep me awake much longer.

The Dead Man continued to spin confusions off all his minds at once.

"You tossing a mental salad, Old Bones?"

My apologies, Garrett. I was not aware that I was drawing you in. I am trying to identify the missing ingredient. I am reviewing events as reported while sorting the clutter in your head. There must be something you know, although you are unaware that you know it. You would be unaware, in fact, that there is knowledge of which to be aware.

"You're zigging before I even get the chance to zag, sidekick."

There has to be something more to this.

"You've been inside my head. You know I didn't want to hear that. You say nothing is ever what it seems?"

It never is when I get involved.

Actually, I fear that, in this particular case it did indeed start out being what it seems. However, as is often the case with both human and divine endeavors, powerful outside forces and normal social dynamics will force what ought to be simple to become complex and devious.

I leaned back and swilled me a long, long draft. Dean had bent that much. I had been so ragged when I turned up I hadn't considered arguing over a few beers. Possibly he received some encouragement from the Dead Man. The Dead Man has no interest in whether or not food or drink is good for you.

"At least the original problem is solved."

Is it?

"There's no need for anybody to choose between the Shayir and Godoroth. They don't exist anymore."

Nog is inescapable.

"Oh, shit!" I gulped air. I had forgotten Nog. Couldn't he wait until I'd gotten some sleep? Then I I caught on. "You had me going for a second."

Amused. *I see. I do not indulge in practical jokes, do I?*

"Not too often."

Consider it a dramatized warning.

"It *was* you?"

Reminding you that at least one survivor of the Haunted Circle massacre likely carries a grudge.

"Wish I could figure out a way to make this all your fault. But all I can think of is I didn't have problems like this before I moved in with you."

Life was simpler in the old days. Not more pleasant, but definitely simpler. Life in the islands had been simpler still, if pure hell.

The Dead Man made a mental noise that sort of implied intense festering disgust. *If the anomaly is there, even I am blind to it. Maybe there is nothing after all. Possibly no one had any real, long-term plans. Self-proclaimed masters of the universe, yet they do everything by improvisation.*

"Tell you the truth, I've never seen any gods whose depth was more than a few pages."

Clever boy.

"Yeah. So clever I go out chasing redheads because they look interesting. I'm dead. I can't stay awake another twenty seconds."

Wait.

"Come on. It can keep for a few hours."

The redhead. The shapechanger. Adeth? There is no place for her in the central events.

"I told you that already. She led me into it but hasn't been around much since. She visited me once—I think it was her—when the Godoroth had me. She didn't make much sense. I saw her once in the Haunted Circle. Maybe one or two other glimpses round and about. Talk to Cat about Adeth. She knows something she won't tell me." I didn't bother to glance at Cat. "I'm gone upstairs. Tell Dean to do whatever he wants with these people."

The beer, while just about the most wonderful liquid I had ever swallowed, had sapped my ability to stay awake.

I met Dean in the hall, headed toward the Dead Man's room. I grabbed a greasy sausage off the platter he carried. I gave him a quick review of what I had told Himself.

I was asleep before my head hit the goosedown.

56

I plunged down the well of sleep faster than ever I had without the aid of somebody whapping me on the gourd. Only the well became a tunnel. At its far end an incredible woman waited, radiant in her dark beauty. She extended a taloned hand in welcome, offered green lips for my kiss. A snake winked at me from her hair.

"Not yet, Maggie."

She smiled. The tip of a fang sparkled, though there was no light. Still smiling, she touched my cheek with a forefinger—then raked me with its nail. I felt hot blood on cold skin. It was chilly there, though I had been unaware of that until that moment. Soon it was cold beyond any imagining.

Magodor tugged at my hand. She didn't speak. Words wouldn't carry there. She led me to the tunnel's end, high on the face of an immense black cliff, on a constructed balcony overlooking a vast black lake, facing a city on the far shore, that made TunFaire seem like a pig farmers' village. Some towers had fallen. No light showed. There were no lights anywhere. The sun in the sky shed no light either. Neither did three black moons.

Things swam in that lake and crawled across that landscape and flew in that sky so cold it held no air. They were things like nothing of our world, cold things that ate only the strange rays that wander between the stars, things for whom hope and despair and all other emotions were notions without meaning, utterly beyond comprehension. They were all ancient things, half as old as time, and for an eon they had been trying to es-

cape that cold prison. They were not evil as we con-
ceive of evil. There was no more malice in them than in
a flood or earthquake or killing storm. No more than
in the man who plows a field and turns up the nests of
voles and rabbits and crushes the tunnels of moles.

Yet they were imprisoned. Something had felt obliged
to isolate them from the rest of existence. Eternally.

Out in the lake something broke the surface of liquid
as thick as warm tar. The light of remote and feeble
stars was too weak to provide me a good look. Maybe
that was just as well. I did not want a good look at
something like that, ever.

I think somebody, possibly in drug dreams, must have
seen that place before me. That would explain all those
tales of eldritch horrors and unnameable names and unspeakable spooks—though I expect a lot is exaggeration
for the sake of extra impact.

I wouldn't want to live in that place either, though.

A glimmering, pale, drowned man's sort of hand
reached up from the darkness and grabbed the edge of
the balcony. A corpse with pools of shadow for eyes
pulled itself up until its empty mouth was level with the
platform. It took me a moment to recognize the face, it
was so filled with despair. Imar. The All-Father. The
Harvester of Souls. Lord of the Hanged Men. Ass-
Kicker Supreme.

He extended his other quaking hand toward
Magodor, the Destroyer, the Driver of the Spoil, and all
that stuff, his Executive Officer and First Assistant Supreme Kicker of Butts.

Magodor stomped his fingers. She put a foot in his
face and shoved. So much for company loyalty. Without
a sound, Imar twisted and fell into the gulf below.

I started walking back up the tunnel. Magodor stayed
beside me a while, smiling up like we were headed
home after a perfect date. She was excited. She could
not stop shifting shape—although she never drifted far
from human.

Maybe we had grown on them over the millennia,
too.

Might be worth some speculation. Might have something to do with why they weren't as all-powerful as they wanted us to believe.

I faded out of the tunnel into normal sleep. Normal sleep did not last nearly as long as I would have liked.

Surprise, surprise.

57

When first I awakened I was confused. My head hurt. But I hadn't been drinking. There was noise outside in the street. But it was way too early for any reasonable being to be up and about.

Didn't I do this already? Had I been dreaming, and been dreaming dreams within dreams?

It was the same damned racket out there. The same damned bigoted morons trying to start the same damned brickbat party.

I groaned as I tried to get up. My imagination was so good I had bruises and sore muscles.

I just had to try to destroy my eyeballs. I pulled a corner of a curtain back . . . Whoops! They had thrown extra logs onto the fires of the sun this morning, then done away with any clouds that might temper its brilliance. I backed off until my eyes stopped watering and aching. Then I eased into it.

Yep! Same old bunches of fools with too much time on their hands. Same old mischief looking for a place to happen.

Across the street there . . . rooted in exactly the same spot. Exactly the same redhead. Looking right at me, just like before. But this time I knew what she was. Trouble. This time I knew better. This time I wouldn't chase her and let her make a fool of me. I can manage that fine all by myself, thank you.

I felt a slight tingle way back in my mind. The Dead Man was there. I realized he must have been there all night. Meaning maybe he had had a thread connected during my nocturnal adventure. Which suggested that he was very concerned indeed. I tried to give him a good look at the redhead.

As though she realized she was under special scrutiny she sort of stepped sideways and backward and evaporated into a mob surrounding two women glaring at one another nose to nose. One was a very short, fat, ugly human woman. The other was a tall, skinny, beautiful dwarf. They looked like sisters.

Somebody had noticed and made mention of that fact. Somebody had been stirring with a big, big spoon.

A woman left the knot. There was a ghost of a hint of furtiveness about her. "That her?"

Indeed. I am able to follow her by sensing her as a sort of absence of presence in motion.

I didn't ask him to explain. I didn't care. I was watching the wonder of the latter half of our century. Mrs. Cardonlos and her broom were breaking up the all-female confrontation. She found the assistance of a public-spirited giantess invaluable.

"Damn me, the old harridan ain't all bad after all. What'll I do for somebody to hate?"

The Goddamn Parrot squawked on cue.

"Of course. Thanks, Morley."

Mr. Dotes himself was coming up Macunado, his sartorial elegance causing a stir all the way. Or maybe that stir was caused by the grolls accompanying him, a pair of ugly green guys fifteen feet tall. They had snaggly fangs in their mouths and knobbly clubs in their hands and raggedy sacks on their shoulders. They were smiling, but a smiling groll looks twice as fierce as a frowning groll.

Grolls are the result of careless dalliances between giants and trolls. These two came from a single lapse in judgment. They were brothers. Doris and Marsha by name.

Nobody alive in TunFaire would rag those two about their names. They are slow of wit and slower to anger, but once they get started you really don't want to be in the same county.

They were related to Morley in some obscure fashion.

Why was he leading them to my house?

"You still tracking Adeth, Old Bones?" Looking at Doris and Marsha left me wondering how The Call could take itself seriously. Boys like these could be more trouble than any fool wanted.

I am. Her movements seem haphazard. Perhaps even aimless.

"Think she knows you're onto her?"

Improbable.

I considered reminding him that *he* was highly improbable, but now Morley was just fifty feet from my stoop. The grolls were not his only companions. Several of his old crew, including Sarge, Puddle, and Dojango Roze, pint-size brother of the grolls, were with him. All were armed as heavily as the law allowed. All in all, that crowd had barely enough candlepower to light up the inside of a one-hole outhouse, but they had muscle enough to toss the toilet half a mile.

The Dead Man warned Dean. As Morley reached the foot of my steps the Goddamn Parrot went flapping into the morning, turning to follow Adeth. The shiny little buzzard was entirely under the Dead Man's control. He let fall a gift that would have spoiled Morley's splendor in a grand way, but Dotes was far too alert and quick. He eased out of the way.

Chuckling, I dropped the curtain, got myself dressed in something presentable, stumbled downstairs. I had aches and pains everywhere. And my head hurt, too. For nothing. Damn! You get up feeling awful, you ought to at least have had some drinks and fun.

58

At the foot of the stair I turned right into the kitchen. Dean wasn't back yet. I snagged a couple of fresh biscuits, broke them open and pasted them with butter, then smeared on great gobs of honey. Then I poured me a mug of tea and put some honey into that. Then I dug out an old teapot and put some water on to heat so I could follow the regular tea with an infusion of willow bark.

Dean returned to the kitchen shaking his head. "I hope he knows what he's doing."

"That pot is for willow bark tea."

"Don't talk with your mouth full. You didn't drink anything last night."

"Just one long one. This pain is from the job."

He frowned suspiciously. "What *is* this job? Nothing honest would pay so much."

He always worries about us getting paid at all. I've never heard him carp about us getting overpaid. "Huh?"

"Mr. Dotes just brought in what looks like a pirates' treasure."

"Argh! And she be a huge un, aye, matey?"

"Too huge."

"Great. I won't have to work for a while."

"Wrong. Mr. Weider requires your help as soon as you clean up this mess."

I sighed, buttered another biscuit. "It's a conspiracy. Everybody thinks I should work. You ever see a cat do anything more than he has to to get by? The world would be a better place if we all took a lesson from the cat."

"Cats don't leave anything for their children."

"Dean, take a quick head count here. How many kids? How many can even have kids? We don't need to give a damn about posterity because we don't have no posterity."

Dean sighed. "Perhaps not. You can't even learn not to talk with your mouth full."

He should have been somebody's mother. He was a worse nag than my mom ever was. He was more determined, too.

"I'll be in there with the rest." I left him.

I visited the front door first and used the peephole to check the stoop. Sure enough, the grolls and Dojango were seated out there, gossiping in grollish. Dojango Roze was Morley's size but claimed he and the grolls were triplets born of different mothers. Morley backed him up. I'd always considered that a bad joke, but after having wallowed in the mythological for a few days I had no trouble imagining one of our religions boasting some dire prophecy about the coming of triplets born of different mothers.

I took one cautious peek into the small front room. No owl girls. Maybe they left with the Goddamn Parrot. I wasn't surprised to see them gone.

I headed for the Dead Man's room. "You put out the Cat?"

Upstairs asleep.

The cherub, I noted, remained immobile. And visible. Sarge and Puddle were looking it over. Curious. "And the owls?"

Gone. Bored. But they will return. I fear they may be so simple they will think of nowhere else to go.

"That could make life interesting."

Pshaw!

"Thought you didn't like cats?" Morley said.

"You know me. Big soft spot for strays."

"Two-legged strays. Of the under twenty-five and female sort."

I turned. "How you hanging, Puddle? Sarge? The new business going all right?"

"Fugginay, Garrett. Only problem is da kind a people ya got ta put up wit'. All dem highfalutin, nose-in-da-air types, dey can be a real pain in da ass."

"Hell, people are the big problem in any line of work."

"Fugginay. 'Specially dem Call guys. Dey's gonna find some a dem cut up inta stew meat . . ."

Morley cleared his throat.

"Fugginay. Boss, you really need us here?" Puddle, doing all the talking, had been keeping one nervous eye on the Dead Man. The Dead Man can be salt on the raw nerves of folks without clear consciences.

"Wait out front with the Rozes. Try to keep them from getting into another brawl." Dotes shrugged my way. "Every time I turn around some damned human rights fool is starting something with Doris or Marsha."

"Sounds like a problem that will cure itself, given time. Good for the human race, too. Eliminate the stupid blood from the breeding stock."

"There aren't enough grolls and trolls and giants in the world to accomplish that, working full time. I dug up your treasure." He indicated the sacks scattered around us.

It wasn't likely that he'd done any digging with his own hands. These days he was acutely conscious of the line between management and labor.

Just for grins I remarked, "I see you've gotten your share already."

He gave me exactly the look I expected. Little boy caught with hand in cookie jar. Only, "I took some to pay the guys to dig and carry and guard. They don't work for free, Garrett."

Not when they were exhuming a treasure. I was surprised that any of it had made it to my house.

I poked around like I knew what I was doing. Morley couldn't know that I had no real idea of the size of the treasure, or of its makeup.

He said, "Instead of playing games you could ask your partner."

I could. But where was the fun in that? "He's a tenant here, not a partner. Tell you what. Since you've been such a big help I'll see that you get something unique in all TunFaire. Maybe in the whole world."

"I'm not taking the parrot back."

Damn! Everybody is a mind reader anymore.

When he wants to bother, the Dead Man can move stuff with his thoughts. The treasure sacks tinkled and stirred. "Big mice around here." What was he doing?

Morley asked, "What's this all about, anyway? How did you find a treasure right here in town?"

"Eyewitness to the burial told me all about it. It was her way of paying me to do a job." Which, I had to remember, had not been completed to her satisfaction.

Morley didn't believe me. "Those coins are ancient, Garrett."

There are artifacts here which we dare not market as they are.

"Huh?"

There are crowns and scepters and other royal insignia that today's Crown would demand if its agents became aware that they have been recovered.

"What? Karenta didn't even exist then. Even the Empire was still up the road. It would take some really bizarre legal reasoning to . . ."

Nevertheless.

"Of course." Silly me. Logic, right, and justice had nothing to do with it. Royal claims are founded rock solid upon the inarguable fact that the Crown has more swords than anybody else. "You didn't give your guys anything unusual when you paid them?"

Morley shook his head. "I've handled treasures before, Garrett. You need somebody to break that stuff down and move it, I know somebody who'll make you a deal."

No doubt. And he would get a couple points back for steering the fence.

That's the way it works.

I said, "I know people who might be interested in the coinage for its collectible value. How about we just bid out the rest as a lot?"

Not a good idea. That might put us at risk, as we would be identifiable as the source of the whole. Also, many of these items have value well beyond the intrinsic.

"But this stuff has been out of sight for ages. Nobody ought to even remember it."

Put the material under my chair and elsewhere out of sight. Give Mr. Dotes his fee.

"No need to get testy. I was just ribbing him."

I am aware of that, as is Mr. Dotes. The cleanup is necessary, as we are about to receive guests who may ask embarrassing questions should those bags be lying about, dribbling coins and bracelets.

"Huh?" I started slinging sacks. Morley helped, paying himself off as he went. He was not unreasonable about how much he hurt me. "What kind of guests, Chuckles?" Off the top of my head I couldn't think of anybody with nerve enough to push through the group on my stoop just so they could aggravate me by pounding on my door.

But somebody started hammering away.

Priests, the Dead Man sent.

Help!

59

Not just priests. A whole gang of priests, some of them quite well armed. I looked them over as I let a few come inside, a courtesy they obtained only at the Dead Man's insistence. None of them looked like they were used to the streets. Maybe that explained the numbers and the weapons.

"Who's minding the store, guys? Thieves are going to be carrying off everything but the roof tiles."

A guy so old they must have carried him over squinted. He grunted. He dug inside his cassock till he located a pair of TenHagen cheaters thicker than window glass. He readied them with shaking, liver-spotted hands. Once he got them on, he pushed them way out to the end of his pointy nose, then leaned his head back so he could examine me through them. He grunted again. "You must be Garrett."

His voice was a surprise. It was not an old man's voice. And it belonged to somebody used to telling others what to do. But I didn't recognize him. I had thought I knew the faces of the key people at Chattaree.

"I fear you have me at a disadvantage, Father."

The old man tilted his head farther. "They did say that you are lapsed. Perhaps even apostate."

No argument there. *They* were right. But who were *they*? I had had a brush with the powers at Chattaree, but I'd thought that was forgotten. Maybe not. Maybe all those saints have nothing better to do than to keep track of me and to report me to the priests.

"I am Melton Carnifan." Pause. Grown pregnant before, "Secretary to His Holiness."

"Gotcha, Mel." Yep. A real heavyweight in his own mind. Bishop Melton Carnifan was a power-behind-the-throne kind of guy capable of putting a bug in his boss's ear. They were scared of him inside the Church. Only the Grand Inquisitor and his merry henchmen frightened them more.

Any good religion has to have a really sound foundation of personal terror.

As Brother Melton suggested, I wasn't inside anymore. And today way less than ever before.

I said, "I suppose I should be honored. A whole platoon of you guys just to win me back? No?"

Carnifan smiled. The old man did have a sense of humor, though it was in the same class as silk flowers. No doubt it showed best when he and the Inquisitors were showing heretics the incredible extent of their errors.

"I am entirely indifferent to the welfare of your soul, Mr. Garrett. Your record suggests that the Church would get nothing but grief out of you even if you did reach out for salvation."

No doubt. "I didn't figure you were here to refund my dear mother's tithes." I swallowed any further comment. These guys might not be the big deals they pretended to be or wished they were, but they could still make life miserable. Religion is always a good excuse for unpleasant behavior.

"No, Mr. Garrett. Not at all. No. Actually, His Holiness had a dream. Or a vision, if you will, because he was awake at the time that it actually happened."

"Don't tell me. Saint Strait showed up, slung an arm around the old boy's shoulders, told him he ought to get together with me for a game of backgammon."

The old man's jaw dropped again. I had him going. He huffed and puffed for a couple of seconds. The two younger priests I had let in with him moved closer, maybe to catch him if he collapsed from apoplexy. Neither one actually dared to touch him.

Bring them in here, Garrett.

Good idea. "Come with me. We can get off our feet." They came. Ha.

The Dead Man is impressive first time you see him, even if you know about him. Even if you think you're hot shit yourself. The old man paused a couple of steps inside the doorway, stared. Just to tweek him I said, "Yep. Every single thought. Especially everything you want to hide because you can't help thinking about it now."

Garrett!

I ignored the Dead Man, said, "Get to the point, Bishop. I've had a rough few days lately because of the gods. I'm not in a real hospitable mood."

You have him, Garrett. He is quite rattled. He is very much the sort of creature your cynical side believes all priests to be. However, his disbelief in his own religion's dogma has been seriously rattled. It seems many of the Church's senior people shared the vision of Saint Strait.

I won the intelligence award with my response. "Wha?"

Although Bishop Carnifan was sent here, he came principally to satisfy himself that his own disbelief is justified.

Ah! He has decided to be straightforward and forthcoming, having realized that it is impossible for humans to lie to the Loghyr.

Bullhooley. You can lie to a Loghyr any time you want. You just have to know how. And have to be willing to practice on a daily basis.

Bishop Carnifan hobbled to the chair I usually used, lowered himself gingerly. He folded his hands in his lap. He looked the absolute picture of the perfect holy man and he knew it. It was the sort of image cynical priests have cultivated for generations. He intoned, "Kamow. Bondurant. Would you step into the hallway for a moment, please?"

"Sir?"

"I want to consult Mr. Garrett privately."

He is about to exercise his curiosity.

I caught the edge of his message to Dean cautioning him that brothers Bondurant and Kamow would be leaving the room and ought not to be allowed to exercise their own curiosity about our domicile.

The door closed behind the last young priest. I told Carnifan, "They're all real. Every last one of them, from the least sprite to the biggest thunderbasher, no matter how ridiculous we've imagined them. But they sure aren't what you priests have been telling the rest of us."

The Bishop's jaw sagged again. He glared at the Dead Man. "Of course." He considered Morley, who leaned against a bookcase and said nothing, just looked like a stylish mannequin. I had, quite intentionally, not introduced him, nor had I explained his presence.

The Dead Man nudged me.

I said, "You want to know what happened last night, eh? You want to hedge some bets by getting the straight skinny from a guy who really has talked to gods? You want to know if there's an angle for you or the Church anywhere in this? I don't blame you. If I was a priest I'd be feeling *real* uncomfortable about now."

The Dead Man decided to have fun with the situation, too. Suddenly I was reliving the the highs and lows of recent days as His Nibs sucked them out of me and pounded them right into the Bishop's brain.

He didn't leave out one damned thing. He rooted through my head for every glimpse and nuance, exactly as I had suffered it all, and he put good buddy Bishop Melton Carnifan through it exactly as though he was living it all himself. This time around it lasted only half an hour—and didn't hurt near so bad because I knew I would get through it—but that old boy came out exactly familiar with what it was like to deal direct with TunFaire's swarms of gods.

What a cruel thing to do, even to a man who had been an atheist on the inside.

Morley stood with fingers pinching chin, puzzled, as Carnifan displayed a catalog of changes. The Dead Man had given him nothing.

Give the Bishop time to get his bearings, Garrett.

I did so.

Carnifan recovered quickly. His eyes focused. He demanded, "That's really true?"

"Would I make up something that absurd? That's exactly the way it happened."

"I can't go back with that."

"Make something up." He didn't get it. He just looked at me strangely. I asked, "Who's going to believe you?"

Carnifan actually smiled. "Point taken. Nobody is going to want to."

"What did you really want here?"

"Not what you've given me. I didn't believe all that was anything but extremely weird weather. I thought we were just jumping on it to market our product. But now you've convinced me that the gods *do* exist. *All* of them, probably including a lot I've never heard of. But you've also convinced me that that is worse than having no gods at all."

I agreed, privately. "But the belief in what they could be ... That's a comfort to a lot of people."

"And just the opposite to me. This has been a cruel day, Mr. Garrett." His eyes glazed momentarily. He asked, "It's not over yet, is it? This shakeout. There are loose ends. There are traces of several conspiracies, some of which may not have run their course."

I rubbed my forehead. I had enjoyed life much more back when my worst worry was how unhappy I had made some crime kingpin. The Bohdan Zhibak returned to mind. Ten thousand shadows had infested those hills. Every single one of those absurdities had to know my name now. I never liked catching the eyes of the lords on the Hill. How much more dangerous would catching the interest of the gods be?

And I had, for certain. Else this sleazeball bishop would not have come visiting. Saint Strait, eh? Spokesman for the Board. Probably as straight as his servant Brother Carnifan. I wondered if every church and temple in the Dream Quarter was bulging with priests experiencing bizarre visions featuring me in some role.

Worse, were they all going to turn up here to hear words of wisdom, like I was some kind of prophet?

"Damn! What an opportunity," I mused aloud. "I could . . ."

Morley and Bishop Carnifan eyed me curiously. The Dead Man sent a mental chuckle. *A pity you do not have an appropriate mind-set. It might be amusing to play the prophet game—particularly if we could arrange continued contacts with these deities.*

I said, "Weider's difficulties are starting to look attractive." I turned to the bishop. "Brother. Father. Bishop. Whatever. I don't want to be rude, but I've had a real rough couple of days and you're not helping anything."

The Dead Man continued to speculate. *Perhaps Mr. Playmate could join us as front man. He has wanted to assume the religious mantle for some time.* My partner was as cynical as I about some things. It seemed that even concrete proof of the existence of gods didn't soften his religious skepticism.

I told Carnifan, "Unless there is something specific I can still do, I really wish you would go away." I softened that with a conspiratorial smile. "And please spread the word in the Dream Quarter. I can't do anything for anybody else, either. Far as I'm concerned, my part in this insanity is over."

Nog is inescapable.

I jumped a yard. But the Dead Man couldn't keep a mental straight face.

60

Carnifan departed. His gang looked like a small, dark army slithering up Macunado Street. Using the peephole, I watched the redhead watch them go.

"Hey, Old Bones. What was that really all about?"

The Bishop—and, presumably, many other shakers in the Dream Quarter—erroneously assumed a greater and more favored role for you than was the case. If you examine their position and way of thinking, it should be no surprise that many priests will set new records for conclusion jumping.

"What?"

You have been driven into an untenable position. You are dealing with men who, in most institutions, have taken their gods entirely on faith for dozens of generations. Now they are learning that one man's genuine contacts have proven the whole process trivial. The gods, of all stripes, turned out to be small-minded, petty creatures with no more vision or aspiration than most mortals.

"I never did worry much about being popular."

Life could get difficult.

"Hey, I'm a famous cynic. Remember? I can talk, but I can't produce concrete proof. Even if I got some great god like Hano to step up and confess, most true believers wouldn't buy it. You ask me, the great wonder that makes religion work is the fact that otherwise rational beings actually accept the irrational and implausible dogmas underlying them."

Believers are not a problem. However, those who live off the believers could be—particularly if their continued existence and prosperity depend upon the good will of their believers.

Morley asked, "What's going on, Garrett?"

We ignored him.

I entered one of my more intellectual remarks. "Huh?"

The man in the street will be no problem. He has other troubles. Economics and riots are more threatening today. Priests, feeling their livelihoods imperiled, might represent short-term threats, till they understand that we are indifferent . . .

"Speak for yourself, Chuckles." I'd as soon put them all out of business. The sanctimonious emotional gangsters. I reminded, "Adeth is back across the street."

Indeed. And the one great tool we need has not yet been invented.

"Huh?" That was fast becoming my favorite word.

A godtrap!

"Ha ha. What did Cat have hidden inside?"

He avoided a direct answer. *That child can be very opaque.*

Morley headed for the door. "I'm not big on being talked around and over. Obviously, I'm not needed here anymore."

Not entirely true, Mr. Dotes. Exercise patience, if you will, while Garrett and I discuss threats more immediate than any you yourself can help us avert.

That was sufficiently obscure. Morley donned an air of put-upon patience.

I told him, "You want to break away from The Palms and meet me someplace in keeping with my station, I'll tell you about the whole mess. After we figure out how to keep from getting gobbled up by the loose ends."

Dotes eyed me briefly, some secret smile stirring the corners of his mouth. "It's always the loose ends that get you, Garrett. You particularly because you refuse to take the pragmatic step when you can. You love this grand pretense of cynicism, but whenever you face what you consider a moral choice you inevitably opt for belief in the essential goodness of humanity—however often humanity grinds your nose in the fact that it is garbage on the hoof."

"We all need a moral polestar, Morley. That's how we convince ourselves that we're the good guys. Garbage on the hoof is garbage because somewhere somebody told it it's garbage on the hoof."

"Which, of course, absolves those guys of all responsibility for their own behavior. They don't have to stop and decide before they do something."

Wait a minute. How come the professional bad guy was dishing up the law-and-order arguments? "What's this devil's advocate stuff?"

"Because you try to complicate everything with peripheral issues."

"I can't help that. It's my mother's fault. She could bitch for an hour about anybody, but she found the good in everybody, too. No matter how bad somebody screwed up, she could find an excuse for them."

This discussion, in one form or another, has been going on for years. Neither of you has done more than entertain the other with it. I suggest we not waste time on it. Mr. Dotes. Unless you would like to assist Mr. Tharpe and Miss Winger . . .

I lost him there, except for an echo that included Glory Mooncalled's name. I wished he would forget Glory Mooncalled, the Cantard war, and all his other hobbies. I wished he would stick to business, just for a while. Maybe a couple of weeks. Maybe till we got everything squared away and he could snooze to his heart's desire while I loafed and experimented with new strains of beer. Till Dean could spend his days just being inventive in the kitchen, with no need to distress himself answering the door.

Idly, I wondered how expensive it would be to have a spell cast so people couldn't find any particular address when they came looking.

Nog is inescapable, the Dead Man reminded me.

"I know. I know. Morley, take your ill-gotten gains and scoot. Go con the rich johns so they'll pay big money to suck down carrot juice cocktails while gobbling turnip steaks."

Dotes took that opportunity to explain to me, at

some length, how my health and disposition would improve dramatically if I would just let him set up a dietary plan customized to my peculiar lifestyle.

"But I like being just plain old crabby Garrett who gorges on bloody steaks and leaves the rabbit food for rabbits so they get nice and plump before we roast them."

" 'Crabby' is the key word here, Garrett. You take most of your vegetable input in liquid form. I'm sorry, beer just doesn't contain enough essential fiber, which you have to have to . . ."

"Yeah. I know you get plenty of fiber because you're full of it up to your ears."

He offered a mock two-finger salute and a thin smile. "Like I said. Crabby." He asked the Dead Man, "Did you have something for me? Or not?"

Old Chuckles did, in fact, have a lot to talk over with Morley, but it had no bearing on the problem at hand. I would not have stayed around at all if it hadn't had to do with my future, too.

61

Morley was gone. After five thoughtful minutes I asked, "You really think the troubles might get that bad?"

They are barely into their infancy now and people are dying every day. Glory Mooncalled appears to be contributing by neglect, if not by plan.

"You're determined to have him here in town, aren't you?"

There is no doubt whatsoever that he is either in the city or somewhere close by. You came close to him last week.

"Why?"

He could see my thoughts. He understood the question.

Glory Mooncalled has betrayed no lack of confidence in his own abilities. About that all respondents always agree. Nor do they disagree that he has only disdain and contempt for the various persons who manage the Karentine state. He knows only those he encountered in the Cantard. And in the Cantard he did learn to respect the overwhelming force that lords and wizards could bring to bear—by direct experience. He believes it will be an entirely different game in TunFaire.

"I got a feeling maybe friend Mooncalled is gonna run into a couple of surprises here." Here at home not all our functionaries are people who inherited their jobs, nor are all of them so enchanted with their own importance that they do nothing but polish their images.

Exactly. The Dead Man was still tapped into my mind. *And there is every possibility that someone like Relway may be the real best hope for averting complete chaos.*

"You think Glory Mooncalled might *want* to precipitate such a state?"

Perhaps. As I observed, he suffers from no lack of confidence. And he is aware that he has been something of a folk hero here, in the past. He might believe that ordinary Karentines will proclaim him their savior if things turn bad enough.

Which is really what happened in the Cantard during the war. The native tribes, tired of generations of being caught between two vicious, corrupt, inept empires, had fallen in behind Glory Mooncalled.

Hell, Glory had been a hero of mine because he had bucked the ruling classes and had shown no tolerance for corruption or incompetence. Without Mooncalled there would have been no victory in the Cantard. No one, from the King to the least trooper, would deny that—though different interpretations can be placed upon the exact nature of his role in the triumph. He has no friends on high. And guess who pays the salaries of the guys who are going to write the histories of the great war?

"I wouldn't like to think that he would be that cold-bloodedly, blatantly manipulative."

He has little more love for the Karentine aristocracy than he did for the Venageti.

Coldly and systematically, practically from the moment he had come over to our side, Glory Mooncalled had embarrassed, humiliated, and eliminated a parade of Venageti generals, wizards, and lords who had abused his dignity.

"Could it be that this man who never guesses wrong has, just marginally, misinterpreted the Karentine character?"

He has, without a doubt. Karentines are inordinately fond of their Royals and aristocrats—although you murder them with alarming frequency.

Actually, they murder one another. We have some outrageously bizarre revolutionaries on the streets these days, but I have never heard even the most deranged suggest that we dispense with the monarchy.

I *have* heard the suggestion, though. Only from non-humans. And guess who is the one big lump really sticking in the craw of the mob already?

Miss Winger and Mr. Tharpe are due here soon, should you be interested in an update on Glory Mooncalled's latest efforts.

"Tell you the truth, I'm a whole lot more interested in the activities of certain gods and goddesses who may save us the trouble of having to survive your coming troubles."

Reluctantly, the Dead Man admitted that that might be a more immediate concern.

"Can you read Adeth at all?"

Only her presence and general location.

"If I get her in here, can you do anything with her?"

He didn't answer for a while. I was about to nudge him when he offered, *What good is nerve if you do not employ it?*

62

I peeked through the peephole. Adeth continued her vigil. My estimation of the gods continued its decline. This one did not seem omniscient enough to know when she was being observed by a mortal.

Maybe she didn't believe that that could be done. Conviction leaves us all with huge blind spots.

"What are you doing?"

I jumped. "Don't sneak up like that."

Dean glowered. Somehow, he was a lot less diffident than he had been before he had discovered that he could get a niece married without me—either as victim or as co-conspirator. And he was just a tad too confident of his employment here.

"I've been thinking, Dean. It might just be worth doing my own cooking to be able to get into my house whenever I want."

"Excuse me?"

"I've been thinking. And one worry that came up was, what do I do if the Dead Man decides to take a nap right before you have one of your paranoid seizures and go berserk with all your locks and chains? Here I come, dead on my feet, looking forward to ten hours in the sack. But he's snoring, you're off to bed, and there's enough iron holding the door to drag a groll to the bottom of the river. Wahoo! I get to spend the rest of the night on the stoop because I can't get into my own house. Seems to me it would be worth doing my own cooking to avoid that inconvenience."

I peeked again, while Dean struggled to invent a new line of excuses. The redhead hadn't moved. I didn't see the Goddamn Parrot. I crossed my fingers. Two good omens. Maybe my luck was turning.

Slip out the back. See if she can be approached unexpectedly. I will keep watch and inform you of any changes while you maneuver.

"Right." I peeked once more, while Dean still sputtered. The Dead Man had allowed him to listen in because his help would be critical if I were to depart via the back. We undertake that means of egress in extreme circumstances only, it ordinarily being our intent to have the bad boys think there is just one way to get in or out. "Oh my. Here comes your company, Old Bones."

Saucerhead and Winger were coming up the street. Some strange half-breed, all white bony knees and elbows, skipped along between them. He grinned like somebody had promised him a hundred marks. He wore tan leather shorts and a vile green shirt. I'd never seen the look before.

I wondered what had become of their earlier accomplice, Morley's man Agonistes.

There is no end to the demands of the living once you allow them the slightest opening. Like them coming here wasn't his idea. *Dean, please get Garrett out of here. Garrett, sneak up on her, see if she can be surprised, then bring her to me.*

"Suppose she don't want to come?"

Then you will have to resort to your usual charm. Let confidence and a boyish smile be your tools just this one more time.

Well, I did come up with the idea originally, but ... He was possessed of the misapprehension that anytime I want I can grin and hoist an eyebrow and great ladies and maybe even goddesses will melt. At least he pretends to believe it, maybe because he thinks that forces me to live up to his expectations.

I could sense him chuckling to himself as he nudged Dean to rush me off so he could be at the front door when Saucerhead and his companions arrived. But there is no hurrying when it comes to getting out the back. If it was easy, folks from the street would come in to do their shopping. Winger and Saucerhead would be thoroughly peeved before Dean got to them. And Winger isn't big on coddling people's feelings. I hit the alley smiling, even greeted a couple of self-employed ratmen with pleasant greetings. They responded suspiciously, not because they knew me but because of the current social climate.

I jogged down to Wizard's Reach, cut across to Macunado, looked uphill toward the house. I couldn't see the redhead. I crossed Macunado and found myself a slice of shade miraculously free of tenants. It was early still, but it was warm. It promised to be a blistering day.

Chatter on the street was all about the night's bizarre weather, the devastation, the strange things seen prowling and brawling. There was still plenty of snow in areas where the scrap had turned bitterest. There were witnesses who thought we faced the end of the world. Others were sure TunFaire was about to be punished for its wickedness. And, of course, a variety of entrepreneurs were taking advantage of the windfall.

Just goes to prove no wind is an ill wind for everyone.

I had my breath back. I rose on tiptoe, tried to spot Adeth. I had no luck, but that might have been just because the crowd was so thick.

The Goddamn Parrot dropped in out of nowhere, smacked down on my shoulder, staggered me. Several people nearby jumped. He startled them even more when he squawked, "Why are you just standing here?"

"I don't see her."

"She has not moved an inch. Get on with it. I need to free up another mind to deal with Miss Winger."

A long, lean, ratty character with the look of the born hustler eyed the bird. "How much ya want for dat crow?"

"Ha! Walk with me, my man. Let us negotiate." As I stared I glimpsed a wild spray of red hair tossing in the breeze. "Start by making me an offer." Try any number greater than zero. I'll lie to Morley. Poor Mr. Big. A hero! He flew into a burning building to waken sleeping babies.

I guess I was too eager. The mark grew suspicious. "I get it. You're one a dem ventrical twisters and dat's yer con. Sellin' talkin' birds."

"He has your number, Garrett. Whawk!" There is nothing quite like the sound of a parrot snickering.

"I'd drink a beer to show him it's really you who does all the talking for both of us, but then you wouldn't say a word just to spite me."

I caught another glimpse of red hair. She was exactly where I had seen her last, but obscured by windrows of taller people.

My new friend told me, "Be worth somethin' ta me ta learn dat trick. How you get it ta move its beak like dat?"

"You take a strand of spider silk and tie it around his little bird balls. You run it down your sleeve. You tie it to your pinky, which you wiggle whenever you want him to move his mouth."

"Hey! Slick." Then he realized that he was being put on. He suggested I engage in an act of self-admiration physically impossible for most of my species and then flung himself into the crowd. He was so irritated he lost his concentration and moments later became involved in a scuffle when he tugged a purse a tad too hard and numerous dwarves began to admonish him with cudgels.

"Please move faster, Garrett. That could be the seed of another riot."

He was right. Already some humans were wanting to know why dwarves were abusing their brother. If they were the sort who believed dwarves deserved to be robbed just for being dwarves, the fur would fly.

63

I scrambled up a stoop on the south side of Macunado, opposite my own, trying for a better look at Adeth. At that moment a very large fellow, who had some nonhuman in him from several generations back, broke up the developing melee. He asked what happened to start it. People shut up when he said he wanted to hear the dwarves' story first. Something about him suggested secret police. Nobody argued with Relway's men. By the time I'd gotten a look at Adeth and plotted my course, the big guy had allowed the dwarves to go back to pummeling the cutpurse. Everyone else just stood around watching justice take its course.

As I descended the steps a wiseass neighbor asked, "What you supposed to be now, Garrett? Some kind a pirate?"

"Argh! Shiver me timbers. Keelhaul the blighter."

I slipped into the press before further distraction could develop.

Being taller than most people and now closer, I found it easier to keep Adeth's position fixed. Of course, she didn't move. And there seemed to be an island of stillness around her. Nobody saw her, but nobody tried to walk through her. Everybody gave her a foot and a half of clearance.

I stayed as far to the side of the street as I could. Stoops and stairwells down to low-level apartments got in my way. Beggars and homeless people had mats and blankets spread in odd shady corners, as did small businessmen who dealt in trinkets of dubious provenance. How much worse would it be on the commercial streets? Macunado is just a meandering trafficway passing through an area that is mostly residential.

Something stirred in a shadow beside me, suddenly. Something stung my left cheek. A woman in front of me, headed my way, flung a hand to her mouth and shrieked. I touched my cheek.

It was bloody.

Magodor occupied the shadow. She smiled as she tasted a razor-sharp fingernail. "Tokens of love," I muttered. I shook out a grubby handkerchief. I might end up with a scar. I could claim it was a saber wound. I could make up a story about a duel in defense of a virgin princess's honor . . . Nobody would believe that. All the women I know are neither.

The Goddamn Parrot squawked, "I'm blind. Talk to me."

"Magodor just ambushed me," I said. "You read me?"

"Only the bird." The Goddamn Parrot took off, putting distance between himself and risk before Magodor understood that he was more than decoration. Seconds later Winger and Saucerhead burst out my front door, descended the steps part way, paused in a stance that meant they were harking back to the Dead Man. Dean stepped out behind them, holding the door open.

The cavalry was on the scene, but there wasn't much it could do.

Magodor laughed, though not cruelly. She was amused.

I slowed but kept moving. Only steps away now. Adeth looked like she was in a trance. Or on weed. Which reminded me. We still had a banger-loving cherub in the Dead Man's room, solid as an ugly hunk of rock, visible to anyone who looked.

I felt a vague brush. His Nibs was trying to reach me. His touch was being turned away.

Maggie laughed again.

I took Adeth's hand. She did not respond. I slipped an arm around her waist. Had I been snookered again?

People passing tried not to stare at the goofball dancing with air.

"Is that some kind of mime, Momma?"

Adeth started. "Easy," I pleaded, before she did anything I would regret. "I just want you to come over to the house for a minute."

People gaped.

"Momma, mimes aren't 'sposed to talk."

Could you make a goddess visible by tossing paint on her? I wondered.

Adeth didn't speak. She flickered, though. People jerked their heads, having caught something from the corners of their eyes. A ripple spread, the old TunFairen sixth sense for the strange or dangerous. Open space expanded around me.

Maggie laughed yet again, softly, behind me. She was having fun. I told her, "Come on, darling. You're invited, too."

"Momma, who is the mime man talking to?"

Momma didn't want to know. Momma just wanted to get on down the street. Not that that was likely to position her more securely in regard to TunFaire's weirdnesses. Things were strange everywhere, and bound to get stranger.

"Wonderful. I've wanted to see your place," Maggie said, accepting my invitation. That both astonished and frightened me. What the hell? What was I in for now?

She came up and slipped under my free arm. She flickered, too. I got the impression some people caught glimpses from straight on. The open area expanded rapidly.

And, of course, Mrs. Cardonlos was out on her stoop to observe everything.

Winger and Saucerhead sort of oozed down to street level and out of the way. I think Dean really wanted to slam and bolt the door. As he was about to surrender to temptation, a pair of owls swooped down and changed over right there, without bothering not to be seen. He went catatonic in mid-motion.

Magodor went angry.

Saucerhead and Winger went away, as fast as their heels and toes would shuffle. I have no idea what became of their funny-looking friend.

64

"Maggie. Maggie! Darling! Nobody, not even the love-liest goddess, ever learned anything with her mouth open."

"You are insolent beyond all tolerance, Garrett."

"Yeah. Show me where I've got a lot to lose. I'm not on anybody's side. Never have been. But I can't make any of you gods accept that. I don't care any more about your survival than you do about mine. Since everything I do offends somebody, why should I worry about it? Come on and join the Garrett zoo."

Dean forced the door open wider as we mounted the steps, but he did not look at us. His whole attention was on the shadows in the hallway. I told him, "You want to drool, you ought to see Star."

Magodor spat, "She's a moron."

"It isn't her mind that precipitates salivation."

"I am aware of how males see these things."

On my other hand, Adeth seemed to regain the lost spark of life. Suddenly Dean could see her.

He did not lose interest in the owl girls, but he was distracted. A redhead will do that to the most stout-hearted of men.

I said, "Sometimes daydreams come true." He would recognize Adeth as a close approximation of my perfect fantasy woman. "And some nightmares do, too." Because Magodor suddenly chose to materialize in one of her more unpleasant forms.

Dean said, "I'll make tea," and headed for the kitchen.

I returned to the door long enough to get the Goddamn Parrot inside. He was perched on the railing out there, reciting poetry. I have trouble enough with the neighbors.

Magodor eyed Adeth warily but behaved herself. I guided them into the Dead Man's room, though I had no idea what good this would do.

Cat was there already, a recovered Fourteen in her lap, shaking. Magodor seemed surprised. "Who is she?" The cherub she recognized, at least by tribe.

The Dead Man touched me weakly. *Bring the Shayir girls, Garrett. Ladies, if you please, a little less intense.*

Like the Loghyr said, what good is nerve if you don't use it?

I went to the small front room. The owl girls cowered in a corner, too frightened to try a getaway. Maggie must be a real smouldering bitch.

Guess you don't pick up a nickname like The Destroyer because you fudge at marbles.

"Come with me, girls. Calmly. No need to be scared. We're just going to talk."

One—Dimna, I think—tried to run. I caught her, held on, patted her back. She settled right down. I opened an arm, and the other came for a hug. They really were simple.

The followers of the Shayir pantheon must have been pretty simple themselves.

Hell, I think No-Neck said they were lowest common denominator back when we were field-testing the Weider product. Or was that the Dead Man? Did it matter?

"It'll be all right," I promised the girls. I didn't mind seeing Imar and Lang plop back into the Black Lake of Whatsis, but to condemn similarly these two would be too cruel. The world could use more happy gods and goddesses.

I yelled, "Dean! Bring beer for me."

Dean came from the kitchen as I held the Dead Man's door for the girls. He had a big pot of tea, several mugs, and all the side stuff. The water must have been on. My beer was there. With backup. He told me, "I thought you *might* need fortification." He could not keep his eyes off the girls. His tray started to shake.

"That's an understatement."

Dean started to ask something but then saw Magodor trying to intimidate everyone with one of her nastier looks.

"Maggie, knock it off!" I snapped before I thought. "No wonder you guys worked your way down to the strong end of the Street. You had a stupid boss, yeah, but I haven't seen much to recommend the rest of you, either. Cat! Stop shaking. That cup belonged to my mother. It's about the last thing of hers I have left."

The Dead Man managed to slide in, *What are you doing?*

65

I was trying to break everybody's mental stride. If they were off balance they might think instead of just reacting.

It worked. Sort of.

Everybody stopped to gawk at me.

I said, "We came close to disaster last night. Because of stupidity and thoughtlessness. Imar and Lang nearly cost us the wall between this world and the darkness. The goddesses who set them up didn't show any forethought, either. It shouldn't have taken any genius to anticipate their behavior. Magodor, you never seemed stupid. When you maneuvered the ladies so they would manipulate the males . . ."

Garrett.

I was on a roll. I didn't want to hear from anybody yet.

"No," Magodor snapped.

Garrett, I fear it may be less simple than you think, complex as that is.

"Huh?"

Cat, Fourteen, and the owl girls contributed silence. I expected nothing more. Adeth, though, was turning out to be an unexpected zero.

The Adeth creature is no goddess, Garrett. I can read nothing there. And this is for the very good reason that there is nothing there.

"What?" It was me off balance now.

This Adeth is a construct. A golem or dibbuk, if you will, here specifically to catch your eye. We should get it out of the house. Its ultimate purpose may be more sinister.

I slipped my arm around the redhead's waist. I tried to lead her away.

Nope. Nothing doing. All of a sudden that little bit had the inertia of a pyramid.

"Cat. You know something about Adeth. You'd better let us know." I watched Magodor. Near as I could tell, she was unaware of what the Dead Man had sent me.

She cannot read me at all. I cannot get through to her. Presumably the dibbuk is blocking me.

Cat did not respond immediately.

I relayed the Dead Man's observations. The owl girls developed cases of the sniffles. Magodor considered Adeth. "Interesting. You were trying to get rid of her?"

"Yeah."

Magodor seemed to vibrate. A baby thunderclap announced Adeth's departure. "She is in the street again."

"Do you know anything about Adeth?"

"She was someone Imara knew. I never heard of her before Imara organized the plot to rid us of Imar and Lang and the others. She had no trouble making herself visible to mortals and could change her appearance quickly. Her only direct part was supposed to be to bring you to us, making Abyss, Daiged, and those think she might be one of the Shayir."

Cat said, "Mother got the whole plot idea from Adeth."

Did that make Maggie sit up? You betcha. Me, too.

"How long ago?" I asked. "Cat, I don't think you were any accident. You were created deliberately so your mother could assume . . ."

"Stop."

"I'm sorry. But . . ."

"Just stop."

"Plausible," Magodor observed. "Very plausible. Assuming she feared someone very powerful, a mortal identity would be a good place to hide."

"Please stop."

Adeth.

"Who or what is Adeth? It's very important."

"She was my mother's friend. I don't know. Maybe

even her lover. She had a lot. When Imar wasn't looking. Adeth was just always around, ever since I was little. She never even noticed me."

Magodor snapped, "Where is your mother now?
Where is the real Adeth?"

"I don't know. I've been here."

I heard Dean scoot along the hallway. The front door
opened, then slammed. "What the hell?"

The bird. I had him put out.

"Good. Find him a cat to play with." I asked
Magodor, "What do you know about Adeth?"

"Nothing. The name was new to me when Imara said
we would use her to manage you. Her plot had many
friends."

"How many of you are there? You really don't know
everyone in your racket?"

"No, I don't. No one has any idea how many thousands or what kinds of us came across in the great mi-
gration. There's never been any reason to know. Do you
know everyone in this great sump of a city?"

No. Of course not. I don't even know everybody on
my block. People come and go. But that was different.
Wasn't it? I wasn't in the Three-O racket. Nobody expected omniscience, omnipotence, or omnipresence
from me.

Petty pewter, No-Neck. Petty pewter. All of them.

The more I had contact with them, the smaller the
gods seemed. Maybe the poet was right about familiar-
ity breeding contempt.

*Gurrett. The dibbuk has decided to return. Or has been
instructed to do so.*

Whichever, a tremendous crash came from the front
of the house. A moment later Dean and the Goddamn
Parrot both started exercising their voices in protest.

I told Magodor, "It came back."

66

Magodor tossed the goddess-golem back into the street. "I'm not strong enough to push it any farther." She was surprised.

The dibbuk headed for the house again.

People were aware that something weird was happening. The street was clearing fast.

I whimpered about the damage to my door until I saw smug Mrs. Cardonlos staring, grinning because she'd just found fresh ammunition to use in her campaign to condemn me.

"What do you think, Old Bones?"

Wholly on an intuitional level, I suspect we would find no Adeth—not this Adeth—on any roll of gods.

Intuition, for him, is filling gaps in already chancy information webs by applying his several minds. He is very good at filling gaps with plausible and possible gossamers. But he won't betray his thinking until he has everything nailed down, beyond dispute. He hates being wrong way more than he hates being dead.

"You're that sure? That you'll tell me now?"

No. There is a matter of probabilities and risks and their comparative magnitude. If I am correct, time wasted filling the remaining gaps is time we can ill afford to waste. Particularly now that the villains must face the possibility that I suspect the truth.

Only the Dead Man would think enough of himself to fancy himself a threat to the gods.

"Better come out with it, then."

Relay this. I cannot reach the others all at once.

"Listen up, folks. His Nibs has a big story coming out."

The Adeth dibbuk was created specifically as an instrument by which you could be manipulated, Garrett. You were chosen because you were certain to become a focus for conflict. You were intended and expected to become a continuous provocation.

"Little old me? Broke their hearts, didn't I?"

Enough, Garrett. Listen. You can do your tongue exercises later.

The reprimand seemed to get through to everyone else.

Behind the contest for the last place on the Street of the Gods, behind the feminist schemes of Imara and her allies in several pantheons, beyond even Magodor's secret ambition to anoint herself the senior power of a grim new all-female religion, there has been a manipulator whose sole mission has been to provoke clashes like those at the Haunted Circle.

Wait! he snapped as Magodor started to snarl something in reply.

The ultimate cause behind the conflict is not that animating Imara and her sisters, Garrett. You told me that numerous gods not of Godoroth or Shayir provenance joined the fighting. But there is no reason they should have favored one cause above another. Revenge amidst confusion, of course, makes sense. But they would have needed to be primed and ready for sudden opportunity. Having followed the road this far, the questions I come up against are Who? and Why? And the why comes easier than the who.

"I'll bite," I told him. Magodor and the owl girls, even Cat and Fourteen, were intrigued, too.

Your dream, in which Magodor showed you the home of the gods, indicates that at some level it is possible to communicate between this world and that. I am going to strut out onto a limb now. I am going to postulate that the Great Old Ones over there have seduced someone here into opening the way. He or she has failed a few times. Another effort will be imminent. Even the dullest conspirator would have to be concerned that enough random evidence is loose to suggest the truth to anyone interested enough to put the pieces together.

Add the fact that I am known to be involved, and desperate measures are sure to follow.

The Dead Man lacks nothing in his confidence in his own significance.

I thought maybe he was reaching a little, but I couldn't think of any reason to reject his big picture. It did not contradict any known facts, nor did I notice any left over. That wasn't the case with any of my theories.

"Maggie?"

"Garrett, I weary of your familiarities. But I will restrain my ire. There may be substance to what you say. It illuminates many strangenesses of recent times." She became introspective. Her appearance deteriorated. She developed a bad case of too many arms and fangs. Body odor began to be a problem, too.

I started to say something. She raised a hand. "Wait." She thought some more. "I cannot guess who is at the center. But I am sure that someone knows or soon will know whatever the Adeth thing learned here. There will be an effort to silence us."

Oh boy. What a promotion. I always wanted to be the dot at the center of a really big target. "Ah . . ."

"Word must be spread, even if it isn't believed. Fast. Everywhere, like a tree spreading a million seeds. So that one takes root somewhere. You. You. You." She seized the owl girls and Fourteen. She glared into their eyes. They shuddered, whimpered, disappeared. For an instant I feared Magodor herself might be the mole of darkness.

"I scattered them, Garrett. Sent them to deities I know well, armed with tokens guaranteeing that I sent the message. I asked for help, too. I will stay here. Adeth will come here."

"I applaud your confidence."

"I am Magodor the Destroyer. I deal in violent confrontation."

"I know, but . . ."

"Reinforcements will be welcome."

"Witnesses, too."

I looked at the Dead Man. He sent, *I am trying to*

fathom the identity of the traitor. There is insufficient evidence.

I relayed that to Magodor, said, "There isn't any evidence. But at this point I don't think it much matters. We just don't turn our backs on anybody who might be a holy shapeshifter."

In a tiny voice Cat suggested, "It must be my mother."

I hadn't seen a lot of Imara, but I felt comfortable saying, "No. She isn't smart enough."

The Dead Man offered his own opinion. *Not impossible, Garrett. If the genuine Imara has been displaced. You said it yourself. Adeth is a shapechanger.*

I saw something then. "The plan wouldn't have been for Imara to replace Cat. It would've been for Adeth to. Cat has a real history, even if it's been secret. And a mortal is easier to do away with and dispose of. Cat's demigoddess nature would cover a lot of questions about her replacement being odd. And the whole imposture would only have to last till the breakthrough came."

My guesses meant it had to be an old, old plot, reaching back for decades, always pointed toward the moment when pantheons like the Godoroth and Shayir could be brought into conflict. But the gods have time to unwind protracted schemes.

Cat was in a bad spot emotionally. I was willing to bet that she'd entertained similar suspicions for quite a while. Like everyone dealt a cruel hand, she had trouble facing the truth squarely.

The tears started. I held her. She shook violently with the hurt, with the grief.

67

We do not know that Imara was lost.

"Doesn't matter, though. If we've guessed right."

No.

"You feel Magodor?" Old sweet and deadly had vanished while I was getting Cat settled.

She is all around us. I have a better sense of her inner being now that she is not incarnate.

"For some reason that don't sound good."

He avoided the implicit question about the nature of the soul of a goddess. Such a goddess! *She is troubled. There has been no response to her messages. She fears they were intercepted.*

It could not have been more then ten minutes, but, "Shit!" I don't swear a lot, but I don't make last stands against hordes of male-bashing goddesses very often, either. And that is what I expected. All Imara's pals would turn up to put the last seal on their triumph. "It was nice knowing you, Old Bones. Once in a while. We'd better get Dean out of here." I didn't see any reason for them to be after him. He didn't know anything.

Make haste.

I went into the kitchen. Dean was boiling water for more tea. But it was just boiling. He was terrified, trying to cope by working to rote. "Go to one of your nieces' places, Dean. Now. Don't stop to pack. Don't stop to do anything. Just put the pot down and get out."

He looked at me, jaw frozen. He must have overheard and guessed enough.

Too bad. He'd been a religious man.

"Now, Dean. There's no time for anything else." I

gripped his shoulder, shook him gently. His eyes un-
glazed. He moved, but without much speed. "Hurry!"

There were people in the street when I let him out,
but only the most daring souls. There was a crackling
sense of expectancy out there. I saw no sign of the
Adeth golem.

Mrs. Cardonlos seemed positively orgiastic, so eager
was she for the gathering shitfall to head my way.
Someday I need to take time out to figure why she has
so much bile for me.

I waved, tossed her a kiss.

That will help.

"Nothing will help. Might as well have fun with her."
Considering what could be headed our way, Mrs.
Cardonlos' displeasure wasn't particularly worrisome.

The light began to take on a strange quality. It went
to a dark butter tone and on to butterscotch.

"What's happening, Old Bones?"

Magodor is forming herself into a protective dome.

Sweet, sweet Maggie. I never had a bad thought
about you, darling.

She was just in time. As Mrs. Cardonlos began to
glower nervously at whatever she saw from her vantage,
and as the handful of folks in the street hastened to correct their error, a lightning bolt struck from the cloudless sky. It ricocheted, crisped down the street scant
yards from my irksome neighbor, spent itself on the
lightning rod of a small apartment building.

Its sparkle had not yet died when a humping lump of
darkness appeared, coming down Macunado. *Nog is inescapable.* Just in case I had forgotten.

"Gods damn."

Easy.

"He's not alone." All the Shayir females except Black
Mona accompanied him, as did that flutter of black
leaves. Quilraq had not been lost at Bohdan Zhibak. I
chuckled. Today Mrs. Cardonlos could see them, too.

Lila and Dimna got through.

I glanced down Macunado's slight grade. Dean was

still visible, but he was wasting no time. I wished he
would turn into a side street and get out of sight.

He staggered as something flashed past. An instant
later, Jorken materialized in the middle of Macunado.
He trailed a mist that gathered itself to become Star.
She certainly bugged Mrs. Cardonlos' eyes.

The Godoroth and Shayir ignored one another. The
air crackled as Magodor communicated with everyone.
My head began to hurt.

"Old Bones, how come Star and the Shayir girls are
here? Weren't they part of Imara's plot?"

Another lightning bolt ricocheted and racketed
around.

*In Star's case, Imara probably was not willing to trust so
shallow a mind. With regard to the Shayir, the question deserves close scrutiny. Obviously, Lang was slated for disposal.
Black Mona remained loyal and shared his fate. Therefore
one or more of . . .*

Whatever he sent I repeated aloud. As I said "Therefore . . ." small hell broke loose. Paving geysered amidst
the Shayir. A frosty brick fell at my feet. One female
surrendered immediately. I got the feeling, on that level
where pain was gnawing its way into my head, that she
accepted Magodor's accusations and wanted to change
sides. She was a spring-type goddess, into renewal and
that sort of thing.

Another, darker sort ran for it. Nog whooped, *Nog is
inescapable* and took off after her. I sensed an old ani-
mosity.

Minutes of quiet followed. There was nobody in the
street but gods. Each time I glanced in a new direction, I
saw that more had appeared. I didn't recognize many, but
I was pleased. Somewhere, somehow, Lila, Dimna, Fourteen, and now Jorken were getting the message out. The
owl girls must really have been concentrating.

A fusilade of lightning ripped the neighborhood. Not
one bolt did any damage.

"Maggie, Maggie, I love you," I said. "Just keep going this way. Passive and controlled."

Apparently she did understand that this was no time

to let herself be provoked into drawing energy from the other side. And I could sense that she was trying to get that message across to the gathering crowd.

Gargoyles settled onto neighboring rooftops. Things with no name floated on the wind. Shapes almost human gathered in the street. Shapes not human moved among them, some bigger than mammoths.

Mrs. Cardonlos saw them all. Nothing was going to intimidate her into going inside.

A massive bombardment began. The temperature dropped swiftly. The wind rose. Clouds formed. Rain fell. Soon it became sleet.

And then it stopped, sharp and sudden as a knife slash.

The sun came out. Shadows scampered across the city.

Word had reached the big guys in the high end of the Dream Quarter. The air throbbed with their irritation. Their hands moved. Messages went out like puffy cloudlets, spinning off truths to Adeth's dupes. Wherever they fell, something happened. Each happening I sensed as a slight turning of the tide.

Those top guys were near Three-O.

A wobbling lump rolled into sight. Triumphantly, it announced, *Nog is inescapable.*

Good old Nog. I hoped he didn't think he still had a contract on me.

The pain.

Damned right, the pain. There was pain enough for seven hells.

Cat came outside. She stared in awe. Gods filled the street. They perched on rooftops and flew through the air and clung to balconies. They wore every size and shape ever conjured by the imagination of man. And they kept coming, most now females who seemed chagrined and eager to make amends.

There was one truly huge difference between here and the Haunted Circle, where they'd all been farther away. Here they smelled. Awful. Apparently not many ever bathed their physical avatars.

"All-smelling" isn't usually listed among the divine attributes, is it?

The pain began fading. The really big guys started going back to their cribbage games or whatever filled their time. The sense was that it was all over but the weeping. Only a handful of villains were unaccounted for. Hardly any of those would dare be so recidivist as to actually stick to a plot to bring the Great Old Ones across.

I even spotted Imara amidst the crowd, looking seriously sheepish as she came toward the house.

I nudged Cat, pointed. "All's well that ends well."

68

Cat started forward. I caught her arm. "There's still no reason to let those guys know about you." Many were the sort who didn't mind erasing mistakes.

In the back of my aching head I wondered if I had any chance to survive this thing.

Fourteen fluttered down to perch on a rail post. The Goddamn Parrot flapped around above the god mob. It looked like he was following Imara, but that made no sense till Cat, staring, said, "That's not my mother." She eased back behind me.

Get inside fast, Garrett.

I whirled and dove. Fourteen hit me in the back in his own sudden desire to be anywhere but out there. Cat and I rolled around in a tangle of limbs. Thunder barked, drowned out imaginative remarks by the Goddamn Parrot. Lightning struck the remains of hinges and locks in and around the remnants of my door. Splinters flew. Wood smoke filled the entryway. I separated myself from Cat, cursing. Good doors are expensive. As Cat rose, I swatted her behind to get her moving. I could make no tracks with her in my way.

The very air reddened with rage as Magodor realized she had been caught flat-footed. I yelled, "No!" for whatever good it might do. Even as I tried to keep from drizzling down my leg in terror, one screwball part of my mind wondered if I could sue some Dream Quarter temple for damages. Your mind goes weird places under stress.

A blow hit like an earthquake, banged me off the wall, spun me around, dropped me to my knees. I clung to the bones of my doorframe with one hand. It felt like all the air was being sucked out of the house.

Uh . . . Well. Maybe all the air was being sucked out of TunFaire.

There was a hole in the air out there, halfway between my place and the Cardonlos homestead. The hole was fifteen feet across. It gave you a tourist's-eye view of that huge black city on the other side, along with a gang of characters distinguished mainly by festoons of tentacles. They galumphed in mad circles while what had to be a raging hot wind blasted across their treacle lake, blowing harder than any hurricane. All sorts of trash and loose whatever was whipping through that hole.

The big boys got busy doing a little trash duty. A few unfortunates suddenly found themselves deported to the old country. Despite the howl of the wind, I heard Mrs. Cardonlos' bellow of rage when part of her roof pulled away and ran off to visit another world. She was far too damned solid to go there herself.

She would become impossible now.

Look on the bright side, Garrett. The Goddamn Parrot was outside when the big guys opened that interdimensional oubliette. That damned talking chicken had to be over there where they deserved him.

Gah! He might take over and do a better job breaking through next time.

"Gather up all the ratmen," I muttered to the wind. "Get all the human rights nutcases. Sweep this burg clean while you're at it."

A nice sentiment, perhaps, but all the gods were involved in this. That meant everybody's gods, including the gods of the ratmen and the nuts. Nobody's prayers were going to get answered today.

The hole to the other realm shrank. In moments it was a point, then it ceased to be.

The street was now almost the same as before my dive. Every god and goddess and weird supernatural critter was right where it was before, excepting Imara who was Adeth, nearly the most perfect redhead of all time.

I could shed a tear.

Almost.

All of a sudden one fine-looking woman was standing in my doorway, right shoulder leaning against the frame. She looked like she had done a lot of research on arc and proportion. Definitely legs that went all the way to the ground and ample amplitude in the curves and softnesses departments. Somebody must have been peeking over Star's shoulder when she was doing her design layouts.

"It over?" I gasped.

"Wrapped, Garrett. It's time."

"Uh . . ." I said. "Like . . ." She was for sure no Destroyer now. "I'm not feeling real suicidal right now, Maggie."

Her smile was deadly. My spine turned to gelatin. "No risk, Garrett. Except you might not want to come up for air." Her eyes were as hypnotic as those of the snake that supposedly entrances a rat.

Help! Eleanor! Save me! But I didn't want to be saved. Not really.

One divine arm went around my neck. Then another. Then a hand trailed down each of my sides, toward my belt buckle. Interesting, those extra . . .

69

"Excuse me."

The voice came from behind the new, improved, impossibly sensual Magodor. She glanced back, displeased. Can't honestly say I was thrilled, either.

I said, "Go away."

I could see parts of the street. There were no gods out there now. There was no strangeness at all. Just silence. My part of TunFaire was five minutes short of being back to the way things always had been.

"I cannot. I remain the Board agent assigned to you. And you remain the key to the untenanted temple on the Street of the Gods."

"You sonofabitch. Godsdamned bureaucrat. Where the hell were you when my ass was in a sling?"

I caught a whiff of weed. Fourteen drifted up in a cloud, an all-time smouldering banger in his mouth. His eyelids drooped. He was happy. "You tell 'im, Chief."

I guess my complaint was the last straw. Strait went off on all the grief I had caused him. I was amazed. You don't often hear that much whining outside Royal offices, where some functionary always represents being asked to do his job.

"Go away, Strait."

Open the temple, Garrett. It is the last act necessary in this divine comedy.

Maggie, snarling, leaned forward. Her lips touched my left ear. "Later, Garrett," she whispered. Sudden pain. Blood trickled down my neck. A needle tooth had pierced my earlobe.

Then Magodor was gone.

Maybe Eleanor was on the job after all.

Magodor never came back. Thank you very much. Because I had a bone to pick with Miss Nastiness, and not the one you think.

All those clever hands at the last minute had made a certain very useful piece of cord vanish. A piece of cord I'd had in mind trimming some in the middle of a loop before I gave it up ... Damn my habit of vacillating.

Spilled milk, Garrett.

Maggie never came back. She left me with some powerful curiosities, but I never went over to the temple where she set up as boss yahoo of the combined and restructured and now intensely feminist Shayir/Godoroth cult. Whenever I was tempted, I had only to touch my scarred earlobe, my thumping carotid artery, and I had little trouble resisting. If I still felt the tug, somewhere in the back of my mind I heard *Nog is inescapable* and I recalled who all else might be there waiting for me.

No pack of earth mothers, that bunch.

I was too busy to commit suicide, anyway.

The very next time there was a shakeout in the Dream Quarter, Maggie's gang headed west ten places. They had managed to turn the near destruction of TunFaire into a public relations coup.

The really bad, horrible, awful part of the whole ordeal, more a cause for despair than any interdimensional hole with a starving tentacle factory stuck in it, came when a nasty little neighbor brat pounded on the drunken, leaning remains of my door and hollered, "Mr. Garrett?"

"What?" demanded the drunken, leaning remains of me.

"Mrs. Cardonlos told me bring this back to you." He handed me a bedraggled, frosty, half-drowned parrot. At the exact moment that Morley Dotes chose to arrive, having hustled over to see if I was all right.

I cursed some. I whined some. To no avail. Mrs.

Cardonlos tossed me a cheerful wave motivated by 190-proof malice. And the Dead Man sent, *I had to prevent his being pulled through, Garrett. He is far too valuable to let go.*

"Valuable to who?"

Morley stood there smiling wickedly.

As I carried the bird to his perch I wondered if I burned the house could I get him and the Dead Man both?

ABOUT THE AUTHOR

Glen Cook was born in 1944 in New York City. He has served in the United States Navy, and lived in Columbus, Indiana; Rocklin, California; and Columbia, Missouri, where he went to the state university. He attended the Clarion Writers Workshop in 1970, where he met his wife, Carol. "Unlike most writers, I have not had strange jobs like chicken plucking and swamping out health bars," he says. "Only full-time employer I've ever had is General Motors." He is now retired from GM. He's "still a stamp collector and book collector, but mostly, these days, I hang around the house and write." He has three sons—an Army officer, an architect, and a music major.

In addition to the Garrett, P.I., series, he is also the author of the ever-popular Black Company series.

SWEET SILVER BLUES
Book 1 in the Garrett, P.I. Series

by Glen Cook

It should have been a simple job.

But for Garrett, a human detective in a fantastical world, tracking down the woman to whom his dead pal Danny left a fortune in silver is no slight task. Even with the aid of Morley, the toughest half-elf around, Garrett isn't sure he'll make it through this case in a land where magic can be murder, the dead still talk, and vampires are always hungry for human blood.

Also Available:
Bitter Gold Hearts
Cold Copper Tears
Old Tin Sorrows
Dread Brass Shadows
Deadly Quicksilver Lies
Whispering Nickel Idols
Cruel Zinc Melodies